A DEMON'S WORK IS NEVER DONE

LATTER DAY DEMONS SERIES, BOOK TWO

CONNIE SUTTLE

Print Second Edition (2018)
Print ISBN: 1-63478-044-2
Print ISBN-13: 978-1-63478-044-5
eBook ISBN: 1-93975-937-4
eBook ISBN-13: 978-1-93975-937-5

Published by:
SubtleDemon Publishing, LLC
PO Box 95696
Oklahoma City, OK 73143

Cover art by Renée Barratt @ The Cover Counts

To Walter, Joe, Larry, Lee, Dianne, Sarah and Mark.
Thank you.

ACKNOWLEDGMENTS

As always, this book is the result of collaboration. If it weren't for the support of my editor, my cover artist and my beta readers, it would be less than it is. All mistakes, as usual, are mine and no other's.

About the Author:
Connie Suttle lives in Oklahoma with her husband and a conglomerate of cats. They have finally banded together to make their demands, which has proven disconcerting to all humans involved.

You may find Connie in the following ways:
Facebook: Connie Suttle Author
Twitter: @subtledemon
Website and Blog: subtledemon.com

High Demon Series:

Demon Lost

Demon Revealed

Demon's King

Demon's Quest

Demon's Revenge

Demon's Dream

God Wars Series:

Blood Double

Blood Trouble

Blood Revolution

Blood Love

Blood Finale

Saa Thalarr Series:

Hope and Vengeance

Wyvern and Company

Observe and Protect*

First Ordinance Series:

Finder

Keeper

BlackWing

SpellBreaker

WhiteWing

R-D Series:

Cloud Dust

Cloud Invasion

Cloud Rebel

Latter Day Demons Series:

Hot Demon in the City

A Demon's Work is Never Done

A Demon's Due

~

Seattle Elementals Series:

Your Money's Worth

Worth Your While*

~

BlackWing Pirates Series

MindSighted

MindMage

MindRogue

MindMaster*

~

Black Rose Sorceress Series

The Rose Mark

Rose and Thorn

Black Rose Queen

Queen of Thorns and Roses

~

Future Wars Series

Buffer Zone

Black Zone*

~

Other Titles from SubtleDemon Publishing:

Malefactor

Transgressor

Underhanded*

by Joe Scholes

*Forthcoming

CHAPTER 1

Lexsi

Kory lay beside me, a lock of wayward, dark hair falling across his forehead as he breathed evenly in his sleep. I knew he'd wake with a start if I touched his face to smooth the hair back, so I didn't. Shoving that urge aside, I slipped out of bed, grabbed a robe and skipped into the kitchen for coffee and food.

No, we hadn't done anything except sleep for twenty hours—we were too exhausted. The whole kiss-and-bite thing still lay between us, after all. I admit that it was nice to have his arms around me when I fell asleep. I felt comforted and safe, at least for a while.

I drank a third cup of coffee while the remnants of a plate of eggs and bacon lay on the island in front of me.

Anita shuffled into the kitchen. I turned to look at her.

She muffled a scream before hauling me into her arms and dancing around the kitchen, while I swayed in her embrace like a favorite rag doll.

When she finally accepted that I was alive, she set me down and frowned severely.

"Kory's asleep in my bed. No, we didn't do anything," I held up a hand.

"Watson's gone," she turned away.

"Oh, no," I whispered. "I am so sorry." I reached for her hand and squeezed it.

"I guess we'll never know how or when," Anita turned back to me, her eyes misty.

"Sit down; I'll fix you coffee and breakfast." I stood while Anita sat.

"Is that young guy really Jamie Rome?" Anita asked as I pulled eggs and bacon from the fridge and lit the fire under the skillet.

"Yeah. There's something you ought to know, too," I said while shoving a pan of bacon under the broiler, then cracking eggs.

"What's that?"

"Well, the guy posing as Jamie Rome—when I saw him at Hannah's party?"

"Yeah?"

"If that was a spell, I should have nullified it, right?"

"True," Anita nodded after considering my words for a moment.

"Well, same for the real Jamie Rome. If he only looked like that from a warlock's spell, I should have seen the real thing."

"Also true."

"Now, the people posing as real criminals in prisons—I don't doubt for a second that they're victims of a duplication spell. Jamie Rome, on the other hand, what was done to him is illegal in both Alliances and on most worlds that don't belong to an Alliance."

"A brain transfer."

"Yeah."

"So Laurel wasn't taking any chances, was she?"

"Not with him, no. I have no idea how long the real Jamie Rome was chained in her closet, either."

"I put him in Kory's room," Anita sighed. "So he could sleep and not be disturbed by the werewolves. Thomas and Davis left last night with three agents who survived; he said they had things to sort out and wanted to connect with spies in Colombia concerning the events in Peru. Something about seeing who was killed here and who got away."

"I hope we got the bastard warlock, but I'm not betting on it," I said. "My money's on the possibility that there's more than one. Maybe more than two."

"Not good for us," Anita grumped. "Whoever was in charge last night had Kory dancing in circles. Somebody planned that whole attack very, very well. What they weren't expecting in all this was you—and what you ended up doing."

"Yeah." I was still coming to grips with what I'd done, and still wondered how it was possible.

"A mix of your heritage, maybe?" Anita almost read my mind.

"It's possible." I slid eggs over easy onto a plate and pulled broiled bacon from the oven. "Want toast?"

"Sure."

"How's the cleanup going in the city?" I asked.

"Lots of businesses forced to close. Some buildings can't be saved—they're a total loss. Nearly sixty people dead—more than that injured. Rome Enterprises has been officially shut down by the Feds—they're being investigated by everybody, including the Securities and Exchange Commission. Authorities are trying to calm people down—a bunch of them are convinced it's the beginning of Armageddon."

"Armageddon. Right." I hesitated for a second. "So the SEC is investigating that whole investment thing the Romes had going?"

"Yeah. Davis was on the phone for an hour before he left last night. I think he was talking to his boss, the Secretary of Defense, and probably the President at the same time."

"So we're out of a job, even if we didn't formally resign or get fired," I mused.

"Looks that way."

"I'm not brokenhearted over it."

"Me, either."

"Ah, young one. I am most pleased to see you," Klancy glided into the kitchen.

"Hi, Klancy. I'm glad to see you, too." I moved to give him a hug.

"We are missing a werewolf," Klancy said, his face a mask.

"Anita told me. This sucks. What about Tibby?" I thought to ask.

"His cousin Martin was killed, but he and Diego survived."

"I wish you could have seen them attack Milton," I said.

"Perhaps that is a story you could tell us soon. Mason and I must go to bed—Dawn will be here shortly."

"Sure," I shrugged. "Whenever you want."

When the door to Klancy and Mason's bedroom closed, I blew out the breath I'd been holding.

"We have deaths to mourn," I sighed.

"And to avenge." Anita lifted her coffee cup and drank.

"Is there anything to eat?" James Rome Jr., in a much younger body, stepped tentatively into the kitchen. No doubt, the scent of food woke him. He had close-cropped dark hair, dark eyes with sleep still in them and a bit of stubble that only made him more handsome in his current incarnation.

"Have a seat," I said. "I'll fix something for you. Want coffee, milk or juice?"

"All three?"

"Yup. Have a seat."

"What happened to you?" Anita asked as Jamie gulped the glass of milk I'd set in front of him.

"Laurel," he muttered without bothering to hide his anger. "I don't know where she met Deris Arden or Berke Gillson, but I ended up getting screwed by both. It wasn't a pleasant experience."

"We know about Deris," I said. "Three eggs or four?"

"Four, please. Berke, well, you see what he looked like," Jamie tapped his chin. "Laurel and he were fucking like bunnies until I caught them. Before I could file for divorce, Deris placed a spell until the doctor showed up."

The word doctor was spit from his mouth, as if it left a bad taste there. "Now, somebody else who looks like me is destroying Rome Enterprises, while fucking my ex."

"Oh, they're doing more than that," Anita said. "I'm sorry to be the bearer of bad news, but Rome Enterprises is shut down while being investigated by every government agency in the country. Probably a few foreign ones, too. Know anything about an investment thing in Peru?"

"Nothing," Jamie shook his head. "I've been in that fucking closet for months."

"I'm surprised they didn't lay an obsession," Anita snorted.

"They tried. It didn't work because of my brother," he began.

"Your brother did what? Who is he?"

"He doesn't live on Earth anymore. I know that sounds crazy," he held up a hand.

"No it doesn't. Lexsi and I aren't from here," Anita explained. "We know about Alliances and other worlds."

"My brother made sure I wasn't susceptible to obsession or compulsion. Said it was a gift from him to me. When Laurel and her new buddies tried it, it didn't work. They only kept me alive because I had information about the company that they needed and nobody else knew. They'd trade food for knowledge."

"And starved you the rest of the time." I set a plate of eggs and bacon in front of him, then pulled jam and butter from the fridge to put on his toast.

"Uh-hmm," he mumbled around a mouthful of food.

"We're pretty sure Laurel had Abe and Donna Raven killed, because they didn't want to invest in whatever Laurel has going," I said.

Jamie stopped chewing for a moment and closed his eyes. I understood then that he'd been close friends with them.

"Eat your breakfast; the rest of this can wait," I said, motioning for him to go back to his food. With a nod, he piled more scrambled eggs on his fork and shoveled them into his mouth.

Looked like Jamie had deaths to avenge, just as Anita and I did.

~

Kordevik

I woke alone. That wasn't part of my plan. Instead of Lexsi pressed against me, I had a pillow.

Huge difference.

Yeah, I had morning wood.

Big morning wood.

I considered that a sign that my Thifilathi was healed of its wounds. Thifilathis tended to heal quickly, but a wing hole was dangerous if I chose to fly before it healed.

Baby, where are you? I sent.

In the kitchen, talking to Anita and Jamie Rome.

I'll be there in a few.

I was planning a shower and a date with my hand, first.

Lexsi

Barry called before Kory was out of the shower.

"I guess you heard," he said. I could tell he was depressed about his job.

"Yeah. Say, has anyone heard from George?"

"Yes, I called him earlier," Barry confirmed. I breathed a relieved sigh—I was concerned that Claudia's bunch would kill him outright. I worried about the obsessions and/or compulsions laid on both, however.

"All funds are frozen, so there won't be paychecks on Friday," Barry went on.

"That's all right; my Aunt left me some money to live on until I find another job," I said. "That means I'm turning in my notice."

"Then you got lucky. There's no word from the Romes, so I have to lay everybody off until further notice."

"I understand. Good luck, Barry."

"Thanks."

"You'll get a call, too," I blinked at Anita after ending the call. She'd listened to my side of the conversation from her seat at the island.

"No word from the Romes," Jamie mimicked sarcastically. He'd heard that part, at least.

"I can't wait to explain this to Davis and Thomas," I said. "That we have James Rome, Jr., right here in my aunt's house, while his wife does who knows what in Peru."

"Ex-wife," Jamie corrected me. "That idiot she's with is married to her, now."

"You let him do that, you give up your stake in the company," Anita pointed out.

"Yeah. There's that," he jerked his head in a nod.

"I think we can feed you and scrounge up clothes in the meantime," I changed the subject. Jamie looked as if he'd like his hands on Laurel's neck right then. The truth was, I wanted my hands on her neck, too, and there was no telling what Kory, Klancy or some of the others might do to her.

Anita, on the other hand—she intended to avenge Watson's death. "We should give Laurel to Anita," I said aloud.

"Huh?" Jamie's head swiveled in my direction.

"Because she will exact revenge," I shrugged.

"Oh, yeah." Anita nodded.

Kordevik

My cell phone rang the moment I stepped out of the shower. Tucking a towel around my waist, I lifted the phone to see who was calling.

Davis.

"Hello?" I said.

"We need to see you and Lexsi," he said. "Anita, too."

"Where and when?"

"We'll drop by the house. We'll have two others with us. Any chance of getting lunch?"

"I can check with Lexsi," I said.

"Anything will do—we're on a tight schedule."

"All right. I'll call back if lunch is a problem."

"Thanks."

Davis ended the call. Tossing the phone on Lexsi's bed, I went in search of clothing.

~

Lexsi

"Baby?" Kory's greeting was a question.

"Oh. Hey," I said, suddenly self-conscious. "Want breakfast?" I turned toward the stove.

"Yeah." He was behind me, wrapping his arms about me. He'd had a shower and smelled fresh. Good.

Amazing.

"Just eggs and bacon," he breathed on my nape. I froze in his arms.

It's okay—I'm backing off, he reassured me and let me go. "Davis and Thomas are on their way with two guests, and are asking for lunch," he said aloud.

"Oh. I can make flatbread pizzas," I said.

"They'd probably love that." Kory grinned, silently telling me everything was all right.

Ten minutes later, the flatbread pizzas were ready for the oven when the doorbell rang. "That'll be Davis," Kory said and loped toward the front door.

It wasn't Davis.

Anita almost shrieked when a woman walked in, holding an injured Watson up. He was bloody and limping. The woman was covered in his blood and some of her own.

"You're Anita?" the woman lifted her eyes to Anita's face.

Yes, I was terrified that she and Anita would fight one another for Watson, who needed medical treatment instead of a catfight.

"Yes," Anita nodded slowly.

"I'm Watson's sister," she said. "Can you help me get him to bed? He challenged Claudia and killed her. That's when my bastard husband attacked him, so we both killed him. It's all legal, according to Pack law."

"Let me," Kory offered. Watson hadn't lifted his head—that's how bad off he was. I could hear his labored breathing from several feet away. I watched as Kory lifted Watson in his arms and carried him easily down the hall, while Anita and Watson's sister followed.

It wasn't time to ask questions—Watson needed help and fast.

Kordevik

"I hope one of you has medical training," I said when I answered the door and found Davis, Thomas and two others on the porch.

Thomas and one of the strangers nodded. "I have an injured werewolf," I said as I led the way toward Watson's bedroom. "Got beat up pretty bad. I think he has a broken leg, too."

"I'm Opal Tadewi," the only woman in the group introduced herself to Watson. She was American Indian, with lovely, dark eyes and long, black hair she'd braided down her back. Her last name—*Tadewi*—meant wind woman.

Watson blinked at her; he was in pain—that was easy enough to see. Anita and Watson's sister, Sandra, were still cleaning away the blood and assessing the damage. Sandra moved aside when Opal stepped toward the bed.

"I hope you can set a broken leg," Watson hissed as Anita cleaned out a deep bite on his shoulder.

"I can, with some help," Opal said. "I'm the Director of the Joint NSA and Homeland Security Department," she added.

"Shifter," Watson grimaced as Anita cleaned debris from the bite.

"Yes. What do you have in the way of pain relief?" Opal turned her dark eyes on Lexsi, who stood nearby.

"I have ibuprofen, but that's it."

"Davis, get on the phone and get Mel over here. Quick. With his med kit and supplies."

"I can pick somebody up," I volunteered.

"I have the address," Davis said.

"Good. Let's go."

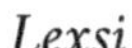

Lexsi

Mel turned out to be a physician who worked for the paranormal division of the Joint NSA/Homeland Security Department. He was a shapeshifter, but didn't elaborate past that as he went to work on Watson's broken leg.

Opal, who'd identified herself as the Director of the Joint NSA/Homeland Security Department, helped the physician set the leg, after giving Watson something to dull the pain.

"He'll heal fast." Sandra, Watson's sister sighed as she, Anita and I watched Opal and Mel pull on Watson's leg to get the bone back in place. Watson's eyes rolled in relief when the bone was finally positioned properly.

"Felicia was the one who broke his leg," Sandra snorted.

"Felicia?" Anita turned toward Sandra.

"His so-called girlfriend. He tried to get her away; she didn't want to go. She and that dickhead she married tried to kill my brother, then took off toward the vineyards. My guess is they got fried when everybody else did. Still don't know what caused the explosion, but good riddance to that pack of dog shit."

"She caused the explosion," Anita jerked her head in my direction. "You're lucky you got Watson away."

"I didn't," Sandra shrugged. "Somehow, we were standing on a small island on the eastern edge of the crater. Other than the wounds we took in the fight, we were untouched by the blast. When it was over, I hauled him away as best I could—found a car parked on a nearby road. Belonged to a werewolf. Keys were in the ignition, so I got Watson inside and drove where he told me to drive. Went to my house first, but I knew I couldn't set his leg and he needed help. That's why we're here."

Aunt Bree, I sent to Anita. *She came to him when he was in that wreck. She wouldn't just let him die after that, I don't think. Still, we shouldn't press our luck.*

Agreed, Anita replied. *I'm just glad he's still in one piece. Sort of.*

He'll be okay, and you can baby him after they get the splint on his leg.

Hmmph, she replied, but I saw the edge of her mouth curl into an almost-smile.

"So you're really James Rome," Opal studied Jamie. Her unblinking, dark eyes assessed him as she drank a cup of coffee at the kitchen island. I'd put the flatbread pizzas in the oven to bake while Kory and I explained about the Rome house in the LA area and how we'd found Jamie in the closet there, half starved.

"Yeah." Jamie wasn't happy to be placed under such scrutiny. Opal didn't appear surprised that he was a victim of an unwilling brain transfer, and listened closely as he described Laurel and Berke's questioning during his confinement.

"Do they have access to all your accounts?" Opal asked after a moment.

"They don't have information about one of my Swiss accounts," Jamie said, letting his shoulders droop while attempting to hide his shame.

"Good," Opal said. "I'd hate for you to be penniless while we have everything else that belongs to you tied up." She smiled at him, then. "Don't worry, I've met your brother," she said and reached out to pat his shoulder. "You can probably figure out how and why."

"You worked with him, didn't you?" Jamie's eyes lit up.

"Yes. We didn't always agree, but he did a creditable job when he held the Director's position."

"Thank goodness," Jamie released a sigh. "I thought I would have to jump through hoops just to prove who I really am."

"I'll see to it that you have a new identity," Opal said. "One you can live with while we're tracking down your wife and her lover. I have a feeling they're in deep with a crowd of undesirables, and we want all of them arrested and brought to justice."

"Thank you. That means a lot," Jamie said. "At least I'm alive—if Kory and Lexsi hadn't found me, I would have starved to death in that closet."

"You're not going to starve if we have anything to say about it," I declared, setting an entire flatbread pizza in front of him before cutting up three more for the others. "I can make more if this isn't enough, but I'll have to go to the store, first."

"Do you have a name you'd like to use?" Opal asked Jamie, whose mouth was full of pizza. He shrugged an answer.

"I say keep the first name and change the last name," Kory suggested. "That way he won't be confused when somebody yells at him."

"Why would they yell at him?" I frowned at Kory.

"Not like that—like if he's across the room or something." Kory wrinkled his nose at me. At least he felt like teasing.

"Food?" Farin wandered into the kitchen, yawning.

"Flatbread pizza," I said, setting out a plate for her. "Where's Tibby?"

"He's on his way," Farin said, pulling a piece of pizza off the pan and setting it on her plate. "He has a fight scheduled in two weeks in Vegas, so he went to the gym."

"Are you kidding?" I gaped at Farin. "He almost gets killed and he's worried about a fight in Vegas?"

"Who?" Jamie Rome perked up.

"His fighting name is Snark Demonio," Farin sounded proud.

"I have a bet on him," Jamie grinned. "He's coming here?"

"She said that," I pointed out.

"I'd love to meet him," Jamie said.

"Watson's asleep," I told Farin. "His sister brought him in—he's pretty banged up."

"He's alive?" Farin's eyes grew round and she stopped eating for a moment.

"Yeah. I really need to go to the store—they'll be hungry, too," I said.

"I'll have somebody pick up what you need," Opal lifted her cell phone off the island.

The Director of the Joint NSA/Homeland Security Department was going to help run my errands? I stared at her for seconds in shock.

"You make good pizza," she grinned at me. I couldn't help but grin back.

~

Kordevik

Opal explained why she'd come after conveying Lexsi's grocery list to a nameless agent on the other end of a cell-phone conversation.

"I want to hire both of you," she said. I wasn't surprised by the request, but Lexsi was. If I were honest, I wasn't sure I wanted Lexsi involved in this any further than she was already, but I realized soon enough that it was my Thifilathi expressing the desire to keep her safe.

That's why I chose to ignore it—Lexsi had saved all of us two nights earlier, and Opal understood that as well as anyone.

"We have no idea what or who was firing at us the other night," Opal explained, her dark eyes unblinking and sincere. "We really need to investigate this, as you can imagine. We can use your unique talents, I believe, if we expect to have any success at it. Besides, we pay well and I hear you're out of a job at the moment."

Her last statement was spoken in a teasing manner—she probably knew that Lexsi could get a job as a field reporter with any news station in the city.

"I'm willing," I said. "I won't mind working with Davis, Thomas and the others."

"What about you, Lexsi?" Opal turned to her. I watched as Lexsi worried her lower lip with her teeth—this was new to her, and she felt uncomfortable and out of her depth.

"Whatever you want to do, baby," I reached out to cover her hand with mine.

"I don't know what to do—not really," she said.

"We'll get you through it," Opal reassured her. "I think you have more than enough natural talent, and you'll have good people around you if you have questions."

"Are you sure?" She asked me.

At that moment, my Thifilathi wanted to skip her away and make sure she was protected. I fought it back; she'd protected us two nights ago with no qualms as to what it could cost her. I nodded and gave her a smile.

"All right." She still didn't sound sure of herself or her decision.

I'll be with you, baby, I sent. *We'll get through it together.*

"Good. I'll get IDs for you. Do you think Anita will be interested in a job, too? We could use her and her werewolf friend, when he's back on his feet." Opal slapped the island, as if that finalized everything.

"Ask Anita if she wants the job," I said. "She needs work, too, and Watson just killed his boss, or so I hear."

"It's Pack law," Opal shrugged. "He's the rightful Packmaster of San Francisco, now, but there's not much of a Pack left for him to govern. He'll have to rebuild."

"The money will be nice," Anita walked in on our conversation. "If you want us, I think we'd both be interested. Sandra, too, if you want."

"Watson will have to make that decision—Sandra and a few others are the only pack members he has at the moment," Opal nodded. "I'll get the paperwork put in, but I'll need information from all of you. Davis and Thomas can give you the necessary questionnaires to fill out. We'll have you onboard by tomorrow, although Watson will have to stay off his feet for at least three days."

"Hear that?" Anita swatted Lexsi's shoulder. "We'll be special-friggin'-agents."

"I don't feel so special," Lexsi sighed. "I feel sick."

"Baby?" I was on my feet immediately.

"I'm not going to barf on your shoes," she held up a hand. "I just feel unsure of myself. That's all."

"I'm meeting with someone this afternoon who has been sent here to help," Opal stood and nodded to us. "If he fits in, he may be working directly with you. If what I've heard is correct, he has extensive experience in this sort of thing."

"Shapeshifter?" Anita asked.

"Vampire," Opal shrugged. "Somebody I haven't worked with before. We'll see how good he is."

"What's his name?" Anita asked. "Will he fit in with Klancy and Mason?"

"His name is Kell, and I have no idea."

CHAPTER 2

*L*exsi

"Farin, I think you can get hired by any station you want,"
I said.

"Chica, you don't have to look for a job," Tibby said. "At least not
right away. I know how much you love your work," he held up a hand.
"Abuela says she likes your weather reports online, too. It's up to you
if you want to wait awhile; I want to take you to Vegas with me."

"Your gran watches weather online?" I blinked at Tibby.

"My abuela is very knowledgeable. She has to be—she is the
Packmaster of our kind in San Diego. She will also come to watch me
fight in Vegas."

"I never imagined you'd be a shapeshifter," Jamie said, lifting an
open bottle of beer to salute Tibby.

"I never imagined you would be so accepting," Tibby nodded. "I am
grateful."

"I'm all for it," Jamie said. "I've been following your career since you
started."

"Who knew one of the richest men in California would like
boxing," Anita said. "Or even know that there are shapeshifters and
vampires."

"Someday, I'd like to introduce you to my brother," he grumped and lowered his eyes. "We just don't look like brothers anymore."

"Look at it this way," Kory observed. "You get a chance at youth again. Not many do, or so I hear."

"I'm still trying to figure out what you are," Jamie lifted an eyebrow at Kory. "I hear the house in L.A. is burned to the ground and the fire department couldn't make a dent in the flames."

"I think of them as the good devils," Tibby grinned. "Set against the bad ones, who tried to kill us the other night. I wouldn't argue—they saved your culo."

"I know they saved my culo," Jamie grinned for the first time. "I'm not hungry anymore because that woman can cook like nobody I've ever met," he nodded to me. "I'm grateful."

"You're welcome. Just be glad somebody sent the message that you were trapped in that closet," I said. "I knew I had to get you out after that. Sorry for burning your place down, but I got one look at all of Laurel's expensive clothes and jewelry and lost it."

"Don't worry," Jamie said. "That's exactly what I wanted to do, too —burn all her things because I've been faithful to her all these years, and she does this."

"I'll do worse than burn her things," Anita grumbled. "Sorry if that offends you, but she may not survive—she's caused too many innocents to die."

"I get that," Jamie said and pushed his beer bottle toward me, silently asking for another. "Is it terrible to say I don't have a problem with it?"

Kory's phone dinged while I grabbed a fresh beer from the fridge for Jamie.

"Davis and Thomas are on their way back—they want to talk about prisoners in jail that may not be the originals," Kory's dark eyes held mine.

I knew what that meant. He and I—we'd nullify any spells placed on those people while I could tell whether they were lying.

"How many prisons?" I asked.

"A lot," Kory frowned.

Kordevik

Lexsi busied herself in the kitchen—I understood she was occupying herself with something she felt confident doing. Being thrust into a job with the Joint NSA/Homeland Security Department had made her temporarily uncomfortable.

I wanted to wrap my arms around her and tell her that every new job or assignment came with that same uncertainty—until you went to work and built up confidence in your abilities all over again.

I wanted to tell her that she was young and hadn't dealt with this— but that could be taken the wrong way, so I kept that thought to myself.

I was fighting a battle with my Thifilathi, too—one it was determined to win. It demanded that I make her mine.

Immediately.

Fuck off, I informed it sternly. *You'll have to wait.*

"What are you making?" I rubbed Lexsi's back while she worked at the island.

"Salmon croquettes," she said. "Sandra says they're one of Watson's favorites, so I'm hoping to feed him when he wakes."

"He's still asleep?" I turned her toward me and pulled her into an embrace.

"Yeah," she muffled against my shoulder. "That doctor gave him plenty of pain medication so he'd sleep while his leg, the deep bites and cartilage tears heal. I'm grateful werewolves recover so fast. If he were human, it could take weeks or months for him to get over these injuries."

"I'm grateful werewolves are so damned hard to kill," I said softly. I wasn't ready to let go—Watson had been the first to befriend me on an unfamiliar planet. Mason, Klancy and the others—I was grateful for them, too.

Most of all, though, I was grateful for Lexsi. I kissed her forehead before she pulled away.

"He's waking up," Anita arrived in the kitchen. "How close are we to having food ready?"

"It'll take about five minutes, once I put them on to fry," Lexsi said, placing a skillet on the burner and turning it on.

"Great. What else do we have?"

"I still have some bacon—you can microwave that until these are done."

"Let me," I grinned and placed my Thifilathi's hand on the skillet, heating the oil before the flame underneath could do its job.

"Nice work, dude," Anita grinned at me and trotted toward the fridge for the bacon.

"Yeah, what she said," Lexsi laughed and placed the first of six salmon croquettes in the skillet.

~

Kell

I'd been asked—in such a way that I understood my refusal wouldn't be accepted. Earth would never have been my choice for a visit—it was constantly at war with itself, with so many countries and factions within countries it could make anyone wary.

The inhabitants often shrugged it off—they'd seen so much discord in their lives it became familiar. Commonplace. Any move to change was always met with opposition—money was king and all were its servants.

I had a meeting scheduled with the Director of one of several security agencies tasked with protecting the same country—unlike the ASD, which covered everything for many, many worlds combined.

In the country known as the United States, these agencies vied with one another—for funding, power and resources. Yes, I'd done research on Earth and its various countries after accepting this assignment. Frankly, it baffled me.

I was grateful I knew the languages now—Queen Lissa gave them to me before I left Le-Ath Veronis. Rigo smiled encouragement before I was transported to Earth by the Queen's Falchani mates.

I was left in a hotel room, which had been prepaid for two days. A car was scheduled to arrive momentarily, so I stood in the hotel lobby, waiting for someone to call for me.

The English language felt awkward on my tongue as I told a hotel employee that I waited for a ride and didn't need assistance. He nodded—he found me attractive and was more than willing to put forth an extra effort.

At least the clothing was comfortable, although a bit more casual than what I'd have worn on Hraede for a meeting.

Black jeans and boots, a pale yellow, long-sleeved button-down collar shirt and a belt that matched the boots. No need to explain my true feelings about carrying a wallet—in the Alliances, the chip beneath my wrist was the only ID and funding needed. On Earth, I realized quickly, things were very old-fashioned and mostly inconvenient.

"Kell Abenott?" A man strode into the lobby. He was tall, dark-haired and a werewolf; I could tell by his scent. I knew I'd be working with vampires and werewolves in a special division of the designated agency, but hadn't expected one to drive me to my destination.

"Yes," I nodded and held out my hand—it was proper protocol for the United States.

"Good to meet you. I'm Jorden Billings," he grinned. "Special agent and sometimes driver for the boss lady. Come on, I'll get you there in time for your meeting."

"Is your boss lady also werewolf?" I asked as we walked out of the hotel toward a dark-blue vehicle nearby. I'd softened my voice—the humanoid inhabitants of Earth were still very much in the dark as far as the supernatural community was concerned.

"Nah. She's a shifter, though. Won't tell any of us what kind."

"Where are you from, Jorden Billings?" I asked.

"California," he said. "That's where you'll be headed soon enough, if my guess is correct."

"I've researched the recent events in San Francisco, but have had to rely heavily on human news programs for the information," I said as Jorden opened the passenger side door for me.

"None of those programs will give you an accurate description," Jorden sighed as he slid onto the driver's seat of the vehicle. I shut my door with a nod. "I thought as much," I replied as he placed the vehicle in gear and drove away from the hotel. "What can you tell me about it?" I continued as he navigated his way through heavy traffic.

"I'll let the boss lady do that—she knows more than I do. If she sends you to the West Coast like I think she will, you'll get firsthand accounts from a few who survived the whole, nasty mess."

"That's good, I suppose," I said.

"Where are you from?" Jorden asked.

"Hraede," I said with a shrug and a smile.

Opal

All I heard from Bree was this vampire was some kind of super spy, who'd been so deep undercover for centuries on Hraede that even his vampire child thought him dead. I had no idea how he could help me with this problem. Every time I considered it, I broke out in hives. A velociraptor shapeshifter *never* broke out in hives about *anything*.

Laurel Rome had thrown her lot—and her husband's considerable fortune—in with those from other worlds. A drug—drakus seed—was probably their intended cash crop and they'd pretty much taken over the country of Peru to grow the stuff.

Laurel believed she was in charge.

I believed she was anything but.

Warlocks and witches tended to be in charge, because they held the power. If they worked for someone else, then that someone else might believe they held the power because they paid the witch and warlock.

"See previous statement," I mumbled to myself as I scooted a tablet to the side of my desk.

Kell Abenott was scheduled to arrive at any moment, and I wasn't sure how I felt about that. "See previous statement," I repeated. After all, *I* was supposed to be in charge. Kell Abenott was older than I, and I was ancient. Would he attempt to take over? I anticipated a struggle of some sort, and wasn't prepared for it to be with an old and powerful vampire.

"Ms. Tadewi?" my assistant knocked on the door before opening it.

I lifted an eyebrow at Chaya as she stood in the doorway.

"They're here—Jorden and Mr. Abenott."

"Send them in," I said, squelching a sigh.

Jorden grinned at me when he walked in first, followed by—*wow*.

Lexsi

"Honey, if you eat any more, it'll make you sick," Anita cautioned as Watson held up his plate for a refill.

"Woman, are you telling me no?" he turned a frown in her direction.

"When it's for your own good, I'll tell you no, twenty-four-seven," she said.

"I agree with Anita," Sandra said. "I've cleaned out your bites and cuts. I really don't want to clean up your barf, too."

"When's breakfast?" Watson handed his plate to Anita and settled back against his pillow. We'd fed him in bed—which he appreciated greatly.

"I think you can have a snack in an hour or two," I said. "Give your dinner time to settle, first."

"Fine."

"Dude, you're lucky to be alive," Kory pointed out. "Food takes a back seat to your life."

"Sandy," Watson turned to his sister, "Do we have anything on Claudia's bank accounts?"

"She emptied them," Sandra replied. "Sent everything, including the Pack funds, to a South American bank. There's no way to get to any of that back. Plus, I think Opal would order any accounts frozen due to Claudia's involvement in this entire fiasco with Laurel Rome."

"That's what I was afraid of," Watson let his head sink farther into his pillow and closed his eyes. "How can we rebuild the San Francisco Pack when there's nothing to rebuild it with? Which Pack members are still alive—besides us?" His eyes popped open again.

"Only a few—a couple of old ones and the few who'd pulled their membership out of the Pack because they didn't agree with Claudia's recent decisions."

"Damn." Watson's eyes closed again.

"I know you licked her shoes for me," Sandra said, taking his hand. "I appreciate that."

"I'd do worse than that to keep you out of Jack Pitt's hands," Watson mumbled. "This one was bad enough. Jack—a thousand times worse."

"Can we ask your agents to investigate Jack Pitt?" Sandra turned pleading eyes on Kory. "I have a feeling he's in this to his ear tips with Claudia."

"Where is he?" Kory asked.

"In Ohio. His whole family is big in martial arts. They claim to be the best fighters anywhere," Sandra said. "Jack likes to abuse women. Claudia tried to sell me to him." She turned her head away. It troubled her deeply—that Watson, in some way, had made a deal with Claudia to keep his sister away from a monster. It wasn't just Watson's girlfriend, as I'd imagined before.

I was beginning to have a much deeper respect for him.

"Opal wants to hire you, Anita and Sandra, too, if you want to work for her on all this," I said. "I don't know what the money is like, but it's better than nothing, right? Maybe you can get the Pack's funds back, if we can solve this," I added.

"You and Kory already signed on?" Watson's eyes opened. A glint shone in their depths—one that spoke of revenge against Claudia's new business partners, who had the Pack's money he needed to rebuild.

"Yeah," Kory replied.

"Then I'm in," Watson declared. "Sis, you and Anita decide for yourselves."

"Oh, I'm way ahead of you," Anita said. "I have a date with Laurel Rome, and she may not look so pretty when we're done."

"You know I'll stand beside you," Sandra said. "For what you've done for me."

"Ah, young werewolf," Klancy glided into the room, followed closely by Mason. "I cannot tell you how pleased I am to see you alive."

$\sim$

Kell

I hate space travel. Travel by Earth aircraft was so much worse. Narrow seats, talkative humans who hadn't bathed recently—I felt ill. If I hadn't had the memory of my meeting with Opal Tadewi to distract me, I might have complained to her about riding in coach.

Alas, it was the last seat on the plane, she'd said, after an attempt to procure a first-class ticket. I'd gazed into her dark, fathomless, beautiful eyes and said it was fine.

I would suffer much worse for her. The moment we'd met, I went breathless at her beauty. Since my heart began beating again, the drumming of it against my ribs had never been so evident.

I watched her every, graceful movement as she explained whom I'd be working with and what she wished to learn. Eventually, she'd told me, I could find myself in Peru. I'd studied Peru tentatively, and was resolved to study it in depth in my free time. Had I been allowed to use my comp-vid, I'd have done so on the plane.

A comp-vid was alien technology to those who sat around me; therefore, I refrained from pulling the device from my carry-on. Still, I hoped I'd find time to read and ask questions before traveling to that country.

Drakus seed I was familiar with already. What it looked and smelled like—even the scent of the leaves, roots and stems, were they nearby.

Clever of these to grow it on a non-Alliance world, where it could be transported by warlocks or witches to its final destination.

Clever, indeed.

Opal's—and my—worry was that the drakus seed would filter into the population here before we could stop it. A hunger existed for new and exciting drugs among Earth's populations, and drakus seed gave dreams beyond imaginings, if the reports were true.

The downside, of course, was that the seed had to be measured precisely to achieve the desired results. A grain too much could result in the user's death. The other downside was its immediate addiction. Taking too much too close together could also result in death, and that's exactly what would happen. The user craved it more and more —until they died.

Drakus seed was a dangerous, dangerous drug; one that commanded the highest of prices. Of the few who'd survived their addiction, it had taken a very long time for their cravings to subside. Other drugs didn't help, and the withdrawal symptoms were often worse than death.

It was outlawed in both Alliances as a result, with an automatic life sentence to the penal planet if one were found engaging in any activity that grew, sold or transported drakus seed.

"Are you married?" The woman sitting to my left asked.

"No Madam, but I am considering it," I said. "Look, I believe we are arriving."

We were. I was grateful—it kept her from asking more personal questions. As she gathered her things, I was left with the thought that I would be forced to navigate San Francisco Airport on my own, with only the sketchiest of maps on the back of a brochure to guide me.

Luggage first, I reminded myself. Then, to passenger pickup, where someone would find me. Afterward, a drive to San Rafael, where I would meet those with whom I'd be working.

I hoped a meal would be provided somewhere along the way—I found I was hungry.

~

Opal

You did this on purpose, didn't you? I sent mindspeech to Bree. *I don't need a distraction,* I added.

His name and title is Lord Kellik of Abenott, came the reply. *He created the Rith Naeri. I doubt he'll be too much of a distraction.* I heard her laugh before she cut it off.

Trust the Mighty Heart to know what your heart needs most, I fumed. The timing—well, that could have used improvement.

Kordevik

"Have room for one more?" Davis was at the door with someone new. "He's vampire, but he can walk in daylight," Davis held up a hand.

"Kell," the newcomer held out a hand.

"Kell, I think we can find a bedroom somewhere," I said. "This place is full of them."

"He's also starving," Davis announced as I stood aside to let them through the door.

"Lexsi may have some salmon left," I said. "She makes really good salmon croquettes."

"Anything would be welcome," Kell said.

"Then give me your bags and follow your nose to the kitchen," I told him. "Lexsi and Anita are in there, cleaning up after dinner."

"You are most kind," Kell nodded and walked toward the kitchen.

"What is it about old vampires?" Davis asked as we watched Kell disappear. "You never hear their footsteps. Like they're walking on air a millimeter above the floor."

"Could be," I shrugged. "Maybe I ought to give him my room and move in with Lexsi."

"I wouldn't—not without asking first," Davis grinned.

"Then he gets the mother-in-law suite behind the garage," I said and turned to go in that direction.

Lexsi

Kell enjoyed his food. I understood about modified vampires and wondered who'd given him blood. It took special blood to neutralize the part of vampirism that required darkness and a blood diet.

Kell still had his strength, his sense of smell and unless I missed my guess, other abilities he wasn't willing to talk about.

"This salmon is delicious," Kell nodded his appreciation. "Your skill in the preparation is extraordinary."

"Thank you," I said, taking the empty plate from him. "I'm glad you enjoyed it. It's one of the easier things I cook."

"I hear we have a journey ahead of us tomorrow—to a prison in Colorado," Kell said, placing his napkin on the island in front of him.

"I hadn't heard that yet, but it's not a surprise," I said. "There are several prisons we're expected to visit. We think quite a few prisoners were swapped with innocent victims of a duplication spell."

"Is there an underlying reason for duplication spells—other than money?" Kell asked.

"We think most of the prisoners involved were serving time for drug related offenses," Anita explained. "The ones we're after are probably growing drugs in Peru, so they wanted experienced help. At least one of the innocents was put to death in the guilty one's place, because the guilty one had money, and his family has even more money. They weren't willing to answer questions afterward, and we believe the real criminal killed again after he was set free—in Texas."

"How did you determine that an innocent died in his place?" Kell asked. "I'm familiar with the duplication spell—a high Third-level witch or warlock is capable of casting it—provided they have an eye for detail. It only affects the outside appearance, including fingerprints and such," he added. "It does nothing to change blood type or basic scents, but those are generally subtle enough that humanoids fail to notice. I once identified a duplication spell by the taste of the victim's blood. It did not compare to the original in many ways."

"Wicked," Anita whispered. "Lexsi, here," she turned toward me, "Can tell if what they say is truth or a lie. They didn't have time for the Sirenali to place obsession on that particular victim, and he said he wasn't Loftin Qualls when they were leading him to the execution chamber. Lexsi knew then he was telling the truth. Unfortunately, they killed him anyway, and then cremated his remains. We may never know who died that night."

"You are a Guli?" Kell asked. He was interested immediately.

"Well," I dropped my eyes. It embarrassed me for some reason. My mother was a Guli, and she was so much better than I at all of this.

"You are." Kell dipped his chin in a slight nod when I looked up at him. "A fortunate thing for us, I think. You and your High Demon mate will nullify any spells, and your Guli skills will know truth from lie—perhaps past a Sirenali's obsession, even?" He turned back to Anita.

"We hope so; we just don't know how strong the obsession is," Anita admitted. Already, Kell knew what she was. I wanted to ask him where he'd come across Sirenali before, but I didn't. I didn't want to pry. Not yet, anyway.

Davis and Kory walked into the kitchen while we were talking, Davis' eyes brightening with hope when he saw there was still salmon left to make more croquettes. "How many do you want?" I smiled at him.

"Six?" He grinned.

"I think I can do six," I said and went to work.

Kordevik

Lexsi hesitated outside her bedroom door. She was tired; we had an early start scheduled the following morning and there was no time for a discussion concerning what lay between us.

A kiss, a bite—immediate unconsciousness—and a lifetime mate.

"Baby, we'll find time to discuss this," I said. "When you're ready and not before. Okay?"

Her eyes, the blue of a fresh, spring day, blinked before she nodded. "Yeah." She dropped her gaze and reached for the doorknob.

I love you, I sent. *I—and my Thifilathi—will never harm you.* I turned then and walked into my bedroom across the hall. I had to, before I broke my promise and rushed to her, to crush her body and her mouth against mine.

~

Lexsi

Kell was satisfied that we had better transportation than a commercial flight the next morning, although a seven AM arrival at the airport wasn't on anybody's wish list.

The jet was supplied by the military, but it had more room than a commercial flight for long legs and wide shoulders.

Kell's approval shone in his eyes as he took a seat next to Davis. Thomas sat beside Anita, while Kory and I took the next set of seats. "Have you ever flown an aircraft?" Kory grinned at me as we buckled our seat belts.

"I flew a couple—nothing like this," I said. Nenzi had taken me many times to show me how to fly hoverchoppers and such. This plane didn't have the computers onboard that I was used to. I wouldn't attempt to fly this thing.

"I learned how to fly a few things—King Jayd is working on his air patrol. I might feel my way through this," he grinned.

"Awesome. If the pilots faint, you're in charge," I said.

"Stop talking about fainting pilots," Anita turned in her seat to glare at Kory.

"Stop acting like you can't get yourself out of here if it becomes necessary," Kory shot back. "If I knew where this place was, I'd have carried Lexsi and Kell with me. You could take the others."

Anita grimaced at Kory and turned back in her seat. She didn't like leaving Watson behind, even if he were with his sister, who was taking good care of him. I hoped Watson realized how much Anita cared and worried about him. I'd seen her lost look when she believed him dead.

"The boss says we have to get there using normal transportation," Davis broke in. "We'll be met by prison officials, who aren't pleased that we're questioning their security."

"You mean they think that we think those prisoners got out using mundane methods?" I asked. "And then substituted ten others, who look exactly like them?"

"You see the quandary we face," Davis shook his head. "These people are human, and don't believe in other races or other worlds."

"You think they'll let those people go, if we prove they're not the right prisoners?"

"It may take some string pulling," Davis said. "And not by us. The boss will have to go through channels to get them out."

"That's not right or fair," I grumped.

"Young one, very little is fair," Kell turned to speak with me. "No matter where you are. Is it wrong that innocents are suffering? Yes. Innocents suffer every day. We must do what we can to move around these officials; they hold the safety of these innocents in their hands until someone with more authority tells them that they may be released."

"You think they'll make these people suffer, if we cause a fuss?"

"Prisons can be strange places," Kell said. "Prisoners can become victims, just as anyone else can."

"You'd think if they were innocent, they'd let them go." I huddled into my seat, feeling cold.

"Yet innocents have been held in prisons for life, or even put to death, as you have seen already," Kell observed.

"Yeah." He made sense, I just didn't like that he spoke of the reality of things. I could almost hear my mother saying that ignoring reality was the wrong thing to do. You can't make something right, no matter how hard it is or how long it takes, if you ignore it in the first place.

The flight from San Francisco to Denver didn't take very long; my thoughts warred with one another the entire trip.

Three frowning prison officials waited for us when we got off the plane. *There is trouble already,* Kell surprised me with mindspeech. He knew, somehow, before any of the three opened their mouths.

He was right; one of the prisoners we'd come to check on had died that morning.

CHAPTER 3

"He was beaten by another prisoner; we don't know which one," Warden Jackson informed us.

Lie, I sent to all in our party. We walked behind the warden and two guards through a narrow, claustrophobia-inducing hall toward a room where the other nine prisoners waited for us.

"Are you investigating this death?" Kell asked smoothly as we rounded a corner.

"We're in the preliminary stages. Asking questions of the other prisoners," the warden claimed.

Lie, I sent.

Nine men, shackled to benches, waited for us in a white-painted, concrete-floored, sterile-scented room. Their eyes held no hope—they were resigned to their fate.

The dead one, I imagined, hadn't lost hope. He'd died for it.

"Stand here," Kell's voice dripped with compulsion as he ordered Warden Jackson and his guards to stay near the door. "You will watch," he added. "Young one, Kordevik, please step toward the prisoners."

Kory and I were at least twenty feet away from them. Kory took my arm and led me forward. We'd barely walked five feet toward the nine shackled men when their appearances began to change. One by one, their faces transformed.

Behind us, I heard one of the guards gasp.

"What the hell are you doing?" Warden Jackson began.

"You will remain silent unless we ask a question," Kell said.

Kell. I was beginning to have a mountain-sized respect for him. "You," he ordered one of the guards, "send a communication to someone, to fingerprint these men while we are here. Then, we wish to see the body of the dead one. Mr. Stone," he turned to Davis, "Are you recording this?"

"From the beginning," Davis nodded. Davis apparently had a tiny camera, or perhaps more than one—hidden on his clothing. "I'm transmitting everything directly to the boss. She has an outside team coming in to do the fingerprint scans."

"You will direct all your employees to cooperate," Kell informed the warden. Anita, who'd stood behind the guards, grinned—I could see it from where I stood halfway across the room.

Kell had to be an ancient vampire—the way he moved and the deliberateness with which he spoke told me that. He was also very, very experienced in dealing with humans who wished to hide something.

Kell could practically smell a desire to conceal things from him. I found him amazing—and just a tiny bit scary—as a result.

Oddly enough, the fingerprinting crew that arrived didn't work for the Joint NSA/Homeland Security Department. They worked for the FBI.

Kory's arm dropped around me while we stood nearby, nullifying the duplication spells so the FBI team could do their work.

"These fingerprints match those of the missing men from that bus in California," the FBI agent in charge announced shortly after running the electronic information through a database. "These are innocent men. Where is the body of the one who is now deceased?"

His gaze leveled on the Warden, who wanted nothing more than to leave and hide in his office. Kell's commands kept him where he was. Both prison guards stayed with him, gaping, while the prisoners were identified as missing migrant workers last seen in California.

One of you must remain with these nine while they are removed from the prison, Kell sent to Kory and me. *The other must view the deceased one.*

I'll go to the body—I want Lexsi out of here soon. I don't like this place, Kory replied.

I dislike it as well, and worry that these nine may not be the only ones who carry a spell, Kell informed us.

I hadn't considered that Laurel's pet warlock and Sirenali could become that devious. I should have known better, after what I'd already seen of their work.

Anita, do the Warden and these two guards have an obsession? I sent to her.

They don't, but I'm getting the shivers in this place, she replied. *I think the prison itself is ready to become a beast to devour and digest.*

She was right—I'd begun to feel as if unseen insects were crawling across my skin. *I think we should get out of here,* I whispered mentally.

The noise started then; it was only the beginning of one of the worst prison riots in US history.

"I can help deal with this," Kory's nostrils blew a stream of smoke as he took a step toward the door.

"Hold," Kell held up a hand, stopping Kory in his tracks. "This may be a trap. We will not fall into it. Mr. Stone," he turned to Davis, "Instruct your crew to shut off the cameras in this room."

"Done," Davis said after several seconds passed and the noise grew louder outside.

"You knew about this?" Kell lifted an eyebrow at Warden Jackson, who tried to back away.

He knew something; that much was certain.

"I trust you three," Kell nodded to Anita, Kory and me, "can get all of us out of here? They're coming this way, and they don't intend to let us live, if the voices I hear are correct."

"What?" the Warden blustered. "They're supposed to," he stopped short and snapped his mouth shut, much like a turtle would.

"They're supposed to take us while you go free?" Kell demanded.

"We need to go. Now," Anita interrupted. The noise had risen until it was deafening, and something large and metal banged against the door into our room. It bounced off with a metallic ringing, before rolling down the concrete hall outside.

"I can deal with this," Kory began again.

"You cannot be seen," Kell snapped. "Take us out of here—all of us," Kell swept out a hand. "We do not wish for the enemy to have our images in this place."

I went still. He was right. They'd laid a trap. "Go, Kory," I shouted at him. "I'll take these nine," I jerked my head at the shackled prisoners. "You help Anita with the others."

"How?" Kory yelled over the din. More objects crashed into the heavy door separating us from the mob outside.

"I'll mist them out," I shouted. "Go!"

There wasn't time to make plans as to where to go or what to do after we got there, but I was desperate. The military plane was my destination as I misted nine terrified men out of their chains and away from a growing prison riot.

I hesitated overhead for a moment, watching as flames licked one section of the prison. I'd bet anything that somewhere in that section, the tenth man's body was stored—they wanted to hide evidence of their crime and that was how they intended to do it.

It's all right, I attempted to soothe my reluctant passengers. *You'll be back to normal soon.*

I had no idea how prophetic my words would become.

Kory, Anita and the others were waiting aboard the plane when I arrived with my nine. They were just as shocked as I was when I let them go—I even stood farther away than necessary to double-check.

Somehow, riding inside my mist had removed the duplication spell completely. All nine were back to their original selves.

"Young one, you have made me happy this day," Kell stood beside me and patted my shoulder. "It will be much less difficult to prove to the authorities that these are not criminals." He turned to glare at the Warden, who quailed under Kell's stern gaze.

At least the Warden was safe—I had the idea that he might have died in the riot still happening at the prison.

"Is there anything we can do?" I asked, chewing on my lower lip. "People are going to die in that prison."

"People have already died," Kell breathed a soft sigh. "Our work is complete—we must rely on mundane agencies, now."

"I was told to expect the unusual," the lead FBI agent rubbed the back of his neck as he came to stand beside Kell. "If I hadn't seen this, I wouldn't have believed it."

"I hope you know how to keep secrets," Kell said, his voice dry.

"Oh, don't worry. This isn't going anywhere." The agent shook his head. "We'll have to debrief these—to determine what they recall of their kidnapping. We'll issue a new wanted list, which includes the drug lords they replaced in that prison. I don't think you'll have a job or a prison to go back to," he rounded on the Warden. "There may be some steel bars in your future, unless I miss my guess."

"Are you cooperating with the Joint NSA/Homeland Security Department?" Kell asked the agent.

"That's why we're here," he grinned.

"Then send Director Tadewi my regards," Kell smiled.

"I will," he said. "Damn, this is a mess," he added, gazing at the nine unfortunates at the back of the plane.

"Treat them as well as you can," I laid a hand on his arm. "They lost family on that bus and they're still grieving, in addition to the all crap they've been through in Warden Jackass's prison. They deserve respect, at the very least."

"Agent Blevins," he held out his hand. "I don't know how you did what you did, but it makes everybody's job easier. I'll do my best to see that they're comfortable and given every ounce of respect. We have interpreters waiting, and they'll be informed."

I shook Agent Blevins' hand and nodded my thanks to him. He'd given me truth, and I appreciated it.

Warden Jackass didn't like that I'd morphed his name into profanity, but he wasn't saying anything; Kory folded arms across his chest and frowned at the warden when he opened his mouth to protest.

"Turn around, Warden Jackass," Agent Blevins said pleasantly. "You get to make the trip to D.C. in cuffs."

"Are we going to D.C., too?" Anita asked. I knew what she meant—she wanted to go back to Watson.

"You can go home," Davis tilted his head at her. "If we need you, I'll call. Kell, Kory and Lexsi can answer the boss' questions."

"Thank you." Anita threw her arms around Davis' neck and hugged him before folding away.

"She, uh, didn't like leaving Watson behind," I mumbled.

"I get that," Davis grinned. "I'm getting word," he tapped his left ear, where a tiny communicator was placed, "The boss wants to have dinner with you tonight, after the debriefing."

Sighing, I looked down at my clothing. Yes, I was still clean enough, but I wore jeans and a pullover sweater. Kory was dressed much the same, in jeans and a polo. Kell—I could tell he didn't want to have dinner with Opal dressed as he was; he'd gone casual, like the rest of us.

"Stop worrying about your clothes. The boss likes pizza," Davis said.

~

Kordevik

Lexsi finished writing her report first, then went back to edit it, then edit it again. I'd filled out reports before, but I'd bet a lot of money that hers was going to look perfect while mine would only provide basic information.

Kell was still tapping away on his tablet; vampires had perfect recall, so I doubted anything would be left out of his report. I sighed and went back to my less than descriptive memory of the events leading up to the prison riot. The riot was still going on and had made every news program in the nation.

The National Guard had been called in to secure the perimeter, while local and federal agencies attempted to contact those inside. No images were available—the prisoners had destroyed all cameras and the recording systems in the prison offices.

The guards—many feared they were dead already.

"I worry that this is an attempt to distract us," Kell looked up from his work.

"It's working, if that's the case," Lexsi snorted. I watched in surprise as a tiny curl of smoke drifted away from her nostrils.

Baby, that's hot, I sent to her.

"Right," she whispered and went back to reading her report for a fourth time.

Kell hid a smile and returned to his report.

Lexsi

"There's still no word on the guards," Opal said as we read menus at her favorite pizza restaurant.

"Oh, I want the seafood pizza," I breathed.

"Where's that?" Kory leaned toward me. I pointed at a section of the menu, where the lobster and shrimp pizza was listed.

"Sounds good. Can they add anchovies and pepperoni?" he asked.

"I don't want either of those things on mine," I said, making a face at him.

"No problem. I can eat a medium by myself," he said. "With salad."

"Kell?" Opal turned toward him. He sat in the booth next to her, while Kory and I sat across from them.

"I will share whatever you're having," he said.

"I'm really hungry," she said.

"Then I will take whatever is left."

"Then we'll get a large sausage and mushroom," she said, setting her menu down.

"That is perfect," Kell declared.

I think he's saying she's perfect, Kory sent.

Honey, stay out of it. This is their romance, not ours.

Are you accusing me of something?

What are you talking about? I turned toward him. I should have known better. He was teasing me; a mischievous light shone in his dark eyes and a smile lurked at the corner of his mouth.

I so wanted that mouth on mine.

I was terrified of what would happen immediately after.

At that moment, I cursed the one who'd made High Demons the way they were. Yes, I realized the original ritual had recently been altered for the better. My mother was ill for days after Daddy put his teeth in her neck. My older sisters, too—with their husbands. Someone changed it so the illness was a thing of the past, but the thought of my unconsciousness; lying helpless while Kory's Thifilathi —I shivered.

"Baby, you cold?" Kory's concern was immediate.

"No." I hunched my shoulders. How could I tell him that the ritual terrified me in ways I couldn't explain? How?

Stop thinking about it, Kory's hand went to my back. His fingers gentle, he soothed away the tightness in my shoulders.

He knew.

Kordevik

I did my best to calm Lexsi while making conversation with Opal and Kell. "Do we have a schedule for the other prisons?" I asked.

"I wanted to get two out of the way tomorrow," Opal said, pointedly ignoring Lexsi's sudden silence. "I knew the one in Denver was going to be the most difficult," she added.

"The riot continues," Kell said, shaking his head. "They should realize that this will change nothing in the end, except to add years onto many sentences. Those who have died," he frowned at the thought.

"You can't reason with a mob," Opal said.

"I agree," Kell dipped his head in acknowledgment.

"Ready to order?" A perky waitress appeared at our table. The pizza restaurant had a theme—that of a 1950s pizza diner. She wore a pink dress with a tiny, white square in a fake pocket, and a white apron, tied at the waist. Her shoes were fashioned after saddle oxfords popular in the era, with white, lace-trimmed socks.

I could see why the nostalgic dress was popular—I found it quite attractive. We ordered our food, although Lexsi looked as if she'd lost her appetite.

"Baby, you need to eat," I leaned close to her ear. "You've had a long, rough day."

"I want a small, seafood pizza," Lexsi said, handing her menu to the waitress.

"Want something else to drink?" the waitress smiled at us.

"I would like a refill," Kell indicated his wineglass.

"Bring two strawberry shakes, one for me and one for her," Opal pointed at Lexsi. "They're excellent," Opal said before Lexsi could refuse. "You need the sugar—you look pale, young one," Opal continued as the waitress walked away.

"I don't like being the young one," Lexsi dropped her eyes and twisted her fingers together.

"I know." Opal's smile was bittersweet. "I don't really like being so ancient. There's not much I can do about it," she added. "After a while, everything gets old. It's difficult to surprise an Old One."

"Madam Director," Kell began.

"You surprise me, Kell Abenott," Opal turned toward him. Lexsi and I watched as wonder touched his features and a slow smile spread across his face.

~

Anita

I held back from touching Watson. Yes, I cared about him, but the girlfriend thing still rankled. He'd gone for her after rescuing his sister, and she'd nearly killed him.

Yet here I was, waiting on his every wish and whim.

I sighed.

At least he was asleep. Sleep had been difficult for me since the big fight. Tibby—I could see in his eyes he mourned Martin, the cousin he'd lost. He tried to hide it from Farin, though.

"At least Claudia's dead," Sandra whispered, placing a cup of hot tea in my hands.

"Yeah." I didn't add that Felicia was dead, too, and good riddance.

I expected that Felicia—and her death—would create a canyon between Watson and me. Lexsi was right, dammit. I couldn't be just a sex partner to him, no matter what I said to the contrary.

Besides, nowhere in the records had a Sirenali ever mated with a werewolf. I doubted that tradition would be broken by the two of us.

Klancy and Mason stepped inside Watson's bedroom, probably to ensure that we were there and safe. They'd awakened with the setting sun, minutes earlier.

"Is there anything you need?" Sandra half rose from her chair.

"No," Klancy held up a hand. "We have fed and all is well. We merely wanted news of the day's events."

"I can fill you in while you see the rest of it on TV," I said, nodding to Sandra and rising from the chair I occupied. "The others are safe, but the prison is destroying itself from the inside."

"It is most fortunate that those victims no longer appear to be the criminals they replaced," Klancy said after I muted the sound on the news program. News crews, forced to report from far a distance, had long lenses trained on the prison. Half of it was now on fire.

Speculation was running wild as to how many deaths had occurred inside and the fate of the guards who'd been on duty when the riot erupted. If Lexsi were still employed by a news station in town, I could imagine her being the voice of reason as she stood there, mic in hand, while describing the day's events. She wouldn't make any wild accusations while she did it, either.

Kell had handled the situation at the prison with smooth aplomb, keeping everyone from panicking when the inmates threatened to break into our space. It made me want to ask what he'd been given to walk in daylight—I wanted those things for Klancy and Mason, too.

"I've never really been close to any vampires before," I looked at both. "I'm happy that you're my first vampire friends." I hoped I could count Kell as a friend, too—he'd impressed me already.

Mason grinned and held out his hand. Klancy did one better, rising from his seat at the island and moving to kiss my cheek. So far, Watson hadn't offered anything of the sort; he'd only barked at us when he was hungry, thirsty or tired.

He may have to warm his own bed, I thought to myself, although I recognized it for the lie it was.

~

Lexsi

"I texted Anita, to tell her we're staying here for the night," I said. Kory and I had connecting rooms at a hotel in Silver Spring, not far from Opal's office. Opal promised that we'd have uniforms delivered in the morning, before we started our day on another plane ride—this time to Texas.

We were going to interview Loftin Qualls' family about the so-called copycat crime committed in Austin.

I suppose they thought themselves immune by now—with Loftin considered officially dead. At least Kell would be with us, if we needed compulsion. Anita would have been useful with her talent of obsession, but she was worried about Watson.

"I wish Klancy and Mason were like Kell," I said, pointing my newly purchased hairbrush at Kory, who lounged against the doorjamb separating our rooms.

"You mean able to walk in daylight and eat a normal meal?"

"Yeah." I let my shoulders droop. *If wishes were horses,* Gran always said, *beggars would ride.*

"Stranger things have surely happened," Kory pushed himself away from the doorjamb and walked toward me. "Give me a hug, baby, and I'll shut the door and let you sleep."

"Okay." More than anything, I wanted him to stay with me. I wanted to lay my head on his shoulder so I could feel safe while sleeping in a strange bed.

Things would be so much easier right now if he were human. He wasn't. He was High Demon, and we couldn't even kiss without complicating everything.

"Baby, you have the strangest look on your face." Kory pulled me into his arms.

"Why do our lives have to be so complicated?" I muffled against his chest.

"Shhh," he said, combing my hair with his fingers. "It'll all come right. You'll see."

~

Kordevik

At least the hotel had a bar. I tried to be as quiet as possible when I sneaked out of my room and shut the door. Lexsi didn't need to know that I wanted several stiff drinks before I even thought about sleeping. Lexsi was terrified of the bite—I could see it every time she thought about us together.

Why the fuck did a kiss have to be so messed up between us?

A kiss.

The first thing humans did when they liked each other.

No wonder High Demons were kept apart until their wedding. The whole mess was fucked up beyond fucking recognition.

"You look like a man with a story," the bartender set a double shot of bourbon in front of me.

"A story?" I shook my head at him. "I have a fucking set of encyclopedias."

~

Lexsi

I didn't say it, but Kory looked just as haggard as I did the following morning. Kell hadn't slept either, although he hid it well. I doubted he'd been able to see Opal past dinner—and he wanted to, I think. She'd gotten a call at the last minute, to attend an emergency meeting at the White House. She had to go, but got a driver to take us to our hotel.

Kory and I—we'd said good-night and shut the door between our rooms, when it was the last thing either of us wanted. If Kell were just as frustrated, then he had my sympathy.

"Ready for a plane ride to Texas?" The werewolf driver, Jorden Billings, was far too cheerful that early in the morning.

"You can sleep on the way," Kory lifted my hand and kissed it. "If you want to."

"I may have to," I said. "My brain is numb."

"Want coffee? We have time for Starbucks," Jorden grinned.

"I think we all need coffee," Kell replied.

~

Loftin Qualls' parents, in their eighties and richer than most people deserved, lived on the outskirts of Austin. They owned a ranch farther west, but chose to live closer to the city for health reasons.

Jorden explained that to us on the flight; Gerald and Anne Qualls weren't in the best of health—all their money couldn't buy younger bodies or better wellbeing. It could only make them more comfortable in their waning years.

Great. We're interviewing sick people, Kory growled in my head.

I felt as he did. A part of me understood how ill, elderly parents might come to make a decision concerning their incarcerated son; one that would release him while putting another in his place.

I wondered if they knew who'd been placed in Loftin's cell before the scheduled execution.

For now, I was grateful Loftin hadn't gone on another killing spree. It made me wonder if his parents knew where he was, or whether he'd been squirreled away by those who'd facilitated his escape.

If the latter were true, then Laurel and her Karathian counterparts had a torturing and killing machine at their disposal. Either way, it wasn't good.

"Baby, we'll get through this," Kory's hand gripped mine as the jet descended toward Austin-Bergstrom International Airport.

~

Kordevik

On the drive to the Qualls' home outside Austin, I watched Lexsi's face. She wasn't talking, but I understood Loftin Qualls' attack on a women's shelter still disturbed her. I had no idea what his parents would be like—they had to know their son was a monster.

Kell—he'd read about Qualls' conviction on the plane ride to Texas, which included files of material describing his victims. I'd discovered that Kell was a speed-reader—no surprise, since he was an old vampire.

What did surprise me was the way he'd accepted English as another language in his repertoire. I'd had to fumble my way through slang, idioms and colloquialisms for three months or more before feeling comfortable.

Kell had it already, and I could only salute his rapid adaptability.

"We're here," Jorden announced as he steered the car through a tall, metal gate. It was open because we had an appointment.

The wide, intricately carved front door opened before we could knock; a servant invited us into the massive home and asked if we wanted food or drink.

Jorden declined for all of us; I didn't want anything from anyone named Qualls. I knew Lexsi didn't, either. If I'd had my way, I'd have gone in with Kell, only, and we'd have done the questioning rather than putting Lexsi through this.

It's fine, Lexsi sent mindspeech. *I want to know whether they're at the bottom of this and if they know where Loftin is, now. Off the record, remember?*

That had been Opal's stipulation—that any information given by Loftin's parents would remain secret—they believed we wanted to ask questions about a copycat killer.

We were ushered into a downstairs sitting room, where Gerald and Anne were seated, waiting for us.

Behind them hung a painting of Gerald's father, who'd served in the state legislature. They were arming themselves against any accusations that could come from us, by dressing regally, jewelry included.

We were seated opposite them, much like an audience with royals. Frankly, I didn't care how much goddam money they had. Their son was a murderous lunatic, and they'd paid to get him out of jail.

That's when Lexsi's hand touched mine. *We'll get through this*, she reminded me.

Yeah. I wondered how long the royal couple's composure would last if my Thifilathi appeared and offered to take them to hell.

Lexsi

"Why do you think someone would copy your son's crimes?" I asked. I wanted to feel them out. If they didn't believe Loftin guilty, it would come out now.

It did.

"Loftin was convicted on purely circumstantial evidence," Gerald Qualls said immediately.

Lie.

"Do you have any idea who the real culprit was, then?" I asked.

"The police have files and files on possible suspects," Anne said.

Partial truth.

Her voice was rough—almost a gasp. She had emphysema, according to the reports. She'd chosen to meet us without her oxygen tank—it just didn't go well with her dress.

"It's my guess that whoever did the original murders killed those women in that shelter," Gerald insisted.

Lie.

"Where is Loftin now?" Kell broke in.

"Why, in Heaven," Anne snapped.

Big lie.

"Tell us the truth," Kell said, placing compulsion. "How much did you pay to get Loftin out of prison?"

"Two-hundred million, disguised as an investment," Gerald said immediately while Anne nodded.

"Where is Loftin now?" Kell asked.

"They took him. We had him in a safe place on our ranch, and guarded day and night. They took him." Anne wrung her hands.

"Is this before or after he killed those women in the shelter?" Kell demanded.

"After. He promised us he'd be good if we got him out. He did that," Anne wept. "That's why we sent him to the ranch. He came home as he always did, covered in blood and happy. We had to do something."

I wanted to vomit at her explanation. All along, they'd known their son was a psychotic murderer, and they'd done nothing to stop him.

"Where do you think he is?" Kell asked.

"I think he's in South America," Gerald answered. "That's where the investment was."

"I hope they're taking care of our boy," Anne continued to weep.

"Who died in his place?" I asked.

"Some homeless man, I think," Gerald said. "A drain on society. Deserved to die."

"I'm done." I stood and shook my head at two who'd become so wealthy that anyone else was expendable to them. Too bad the laws of state and country got in their and their son's way, most of the time.

Yes, they'd likely paid their way past many a smaller crime, but Loftin's murderous tendencies finally led to an arrest and conviction.

I didn't feel sorry for either of them.

"We can have you killed," Anne coughed as I turned to walk away.

"Try." Kory's smaller Thifilathi appeared before both of them. Anne coughed a shriek while Gerald scooted his chair back in alarm.

"You will forget you saw him this way, and you will never pay anyone to commit a crime again," Kell responded smoothly.

We walked out. Jorden, who'd waited outside the door and likely heard everything said with his sensitive ears, nodded to all of us and led us toward the door.

We'd see ourselves out, thank you very much.

CHAPTER 4

*L*exsi

"So Qualls is in Peru, if my guess is correct," Kory said.

Jorden had taken us to a restaurant in Austin for lunch. I wasn't hungry—meeting with Loftin's parents left me feeling queasy.

"You need this," Jorden came back to our table after a brief visit to the restaurant bar.

"What's that?" I asked when he set the bottle in front of me. "I don't drink beer," I added.

"It's hard cider. Crisp, sweet and alcoholic. I think you need at least two or six to get over what we just dealt with."

I sipped tentatively from the bottle. Jorden was right—the cider was good. If it would take the edge off, I was more than willing to drink it.

Kory sat so close beside me we could have been mistaken for one person at times—he knew I was upset.

"Want a taste?" I held the bottle up. Kory took it and drank half its contents.

"Good," he said. "Order more."

Jorden wasn't drinking—he was our designated herder/driver. He talked to Opal, too, while Kory, Kell and I sat at a table in an upscale restaurant at the airport and drank the bad taste of the Qualls away.

~

A second night in a hotel went as well as the first. When we arrived in D.C., Jorden informed us that we had a meeting scheduled with Opal the following morning. He didn't give particulars on the phone conversation he'd had with her, either.

"Do you think it has something to do with Loftin Qualls?" I asked Kory as we followed the carpeted hallway toward our connected rooms.

"Probably," he rolled his shoulders to get kinks out of them. We'd been stuck in chairs most of the day and I could tell it made him restless.

"Want to work out before we go to bed?" I asked.

He almost stopped walking as he considered my question. The alcohol we'd consumed had left our systems long ago—High Demon metabolisms tend to do that.

"Yeah," he said. "Let's see if the concierge has something we can wear to exercise."

They did—the hotel was equipped to handle visiting statesmen and foreign dignitaries, so of course they had something.

Clothes and shoes were delivered to our rooms quickly, too.

"Meet me downstairs," Kory said before closing his door to change.

Someday, I thought to myself, *I want to be able to change clothes while he watches.*

~

Kordevik

I'm certain she didn't intend for me to catch her thoughts, but I did. I almost didn't convince my cock to behave while I dressed in shorts and a tee. The athletic shoes delivered by the hotel were serviceable, but weren't what I would have chosen for myself.

It didn't matter. Lexsi wanted me. I wanted her. That's what mattered. I just had to convince her that the bite wouldn't be scary or awful, and that I was the High Demon she needed to spend the ages with.

When she walked into the exercise facility on the third floor, I was already lifting weights.

She went straight for the treadmill, to run off her frustrations.

"I'll give you a thousand dollars to take your shirt off."

I hadn't even noticed the woman who'd walked in after I'd been at it for half an hour. Deliberately, I allowed the four-hundred-pound weights I'd been lifting to drop to the floor with a clang as I turned toward her.

"I'll give you two seconds to leave me alone," I snapped at her. Most women would have recoiled at the anger in my voice. Not this one. She didn't even blink.

"You don't understand," she said, extending a card held between red-painted fingernails. "I'm a fight promoter. I can get you a high-paying job in less than a week."

"Lady," I growled at her, "I have a job."

"Something wrong?" Lexsi had gotten off the treadmill to join me.

"It's nothing," I said. "She offered a job. I declined."

"Oh. Are you the girlfriend?" Red nails turned toward Lexsi. "Your boyfriend here could be turning down millions in earnings as a wrestler."

"My boyfriend gets to make up his own mind," Lexsi said, her eyes narrowing as she frowned at red nails. "If he says no, he means it. Find somebody else."

"Is there a problem?" Kell walked in with Jorden. They'd come looking for us—had probably tried calling us in our rooms.

"I want to hire him," red nails jerked her head toward me.

"He has a job," Jorden pulled out his badge. Red nails' eyes widened. So that's what it took to get her attention—a threat from the authorities.

"My apologies," red nails held up a hand. The four of us watched her open the glass door of the facility and stalk through. I figured she'd have slammed the door shut, if it were possible. I released a pent-up sigh.

"That'll get your blood boiling late at night," Lexsi frowned, still staring at the door.

"Come on, you," I pulled her into the crook of my arm and planted a kiss on her cheek. "Let's get our exercise done, then listen to what Jorden has to say."

"I got this information after our interview with the Qualls," Jorden began. We sat at a table at the hotel bar, Lexsi's and my hair still damp from quick showers, while Jorden explained what he'd heard from Opal.

"Reports are coming out of Peru's border countries, with descriptions and images of women's bodies being dumped in remote places. The few photographs we've seen are of decomposing bodies, and without further evidence, we can't prove Loftin Qualls had a hand in it. Mind you, there haven't been any reports of missing women from those border countries, so these are likely from Peru."

"And with the new regime in power in Peru and no official information coming from there, this is all we have, isn't it?" Lexsi asked. She toyed with her napkin while waiting for the cocktail waiter to bring her a glass of cranberry juice.

"Yeah. The boss asked for permission to bring in some of our forensics teams, but we're still waiting for a response. She says that bodies of seals and other—well—creatures, are still washing up on nearby shores. I doubt Loftin is involved in that; we know it was going on in the Bay area before Loftin's miraculous escape."

"It's a Sirenali, you can bet on that," Lexsi snorted. "I saw pictures of the dead seals found in San Francisco Bay. The bites are roughly shaped like a human's mouth—but the sharp teeth," she shivered.

"We've seen the same thing," Jorden acknowledged. "The boss said the same word—Siren-what's-it."

"Sirenali," Lexsi repeated. "If you want to see a good one, ask Anita to change for you. You don't want to see a bad one," she added.

"The boss said something like that, too."

"We are dealing with at least two psychopathic killers, then," Kell said, his face expressionless, his words measured and even. "Sirenali love warmer, fresh waters and won't willingly go into cold saltwater. This one—he is ignoring the cold and salt his kind deplores, merely because he enjoys killing so much. A very dangerous thing. Tell me, Agent Billings, are there reports of missing sailors or fishermen in the same areas?"

"A few reports," Jorden rolled his shoulders, as if the information made him uncomfortable. "Mostly local fishermen in small, not-so-sturdy craft."

"Then he's turned to killing humans, too, and is clever enough to choose those whose absence could be explained easily enough."

"Yeah." Jorden wiped the sweat off his beer bottle with a thumb. I watched as a bead of moisture traveled down the bottle until it dispersed into the napkin beneath it.

"Cranberry juice," the waiter arrived and set Lexsi's drink in front of her. "Beer," he placed the bottle in front of me. "Anything else?" He was far too cheerful at midnight for my liking.

"We're good," Jorden handed him a credit card.

"I ran that woman's picture through our database," Jorden said when our waiter walked away. "The one who approached you in the gym?" His eyes locked with mine.

"What about her?" I asked.

"Charlene Devangi. She's an agent and fight promoter," he said. "She represents Tiburon's opponent in the upcoming match in Las Vegas."

"You think it was accidental, then, that she happened to show up while we're working out?" Lexsi asked.

"I hear they have spies everywhere," Jorden said. "Including outside private gyms and such. Who might have told her where you were?" he asked.

I went still.

"Farin," Lexsi breathed a disappointed sigh.

Lexsi

"She's crying, now," Anita reported. "She didn't realize they weren't just fans, standing outside Tibby's gym asking about the guy who'd sparred with Tibby awhile back. It's obvious they've been watching the gym for weeks and saw Kory go in and out."

"Oh, no." I had a headache, and it was getting worse by the second. Why had Farin felt it was all right to tell anyone that Kory was in D.C.?

"They must be really interested to get that bitch on it and to D.C. so fast," Anita grumped.

"I'm worried they're not only into fight promotion," I responded. "I don't trust anybody, anymore."

"Oh. I see what you mean," Anita said after thinking about it. We were having a face to face via computer, and she was now just as unhappy as I was about the situation. "They connect Farin to you, and Kory to you, and then Farin to Tibby, and presto—they're trying to wiggle their way in, so they can take you and kill the rest of us. Especially since they failed so miserably to do that a few nights ago."

"Yeah, provided Granger isn't so pissed he wants me dead with the rest of you, because they now realize we're working for the government. How's Watson?" I changed the subject.

I didn't know that would be the wrong question to ask her; Anita's face became a mask. "Eating. Sleeping. Griping. That's about it."

"Typical werewolf," I attempted humor. It fell flat. "Tell me he's not still pining after that two-faced bitch of a girlfriend," I began.

"Maybe we'll talk about that another time, okay?" Anita dropped her eyes. I'd hit the nail on the head. I wanted to hit Watson on the head, too.

"Look, tell Farin to stop crying—it would have happened eventually, I'm sure. Just tell her that information about all of us should be guarded carefully from now on."

"I will. She feels bad enough, I think, that she'll never open her mouth again."

"Tell her to be careful. Tibby, too. She's been kidnapped once. We don't need that kind of dangerous inconvenience in our lives again. It's how we lost Martin."

"Tibby's entire family is going to Vegas, and I think that's unusual," Anita said. "I believe they intend to act as bodyguards for him. For Farin, too. They're pissed about Martin, you can count on that."

"Poor Martin," I sighed. "We still haven't mourned properly for those we lost."

"When you come back, we'll have a memorial. How's that?" Anita asked.

"I think that's a good idea. You choose where and when. Okay?"

"Yeah."

"Look, I gotta go," I said. "I have an early meeting, and I didn't get much sleep last night."

"Then get in bed," Anita scolded. "We'll be fine—I'll make sure of it."

"Thanks," I said and ended the call.

Peru

Laurel Rome

"Laurel, my love, it is only a temporary setback. We'll make sure of his death next time."

"That's not acceptable," I snapped at Berke. "He was supposed to be dead. Dead-dead. Not pretend-dead."

"My love, Deris is consulting with his uncle. You have nothing to worry about."

"Fuck his uncle," I snapped.

"Dearest, Morgett Blackmantle is a very powerful warlock and a partner to Dervil for many, many years. He has placed Deris and Daris at your disposal, you know."

"Berke, don't make me regret letting my husband die," I fumed. Yes, Jamie was dead—I had several online newspapers that bore photographs of the burned pile that was once my home in LA. Jamie was hidden in the closet, away from human eyes. He'd died in that fire with nobody the wiser, until afterward. Federal authorities reported his death two days earlier, after sifting through the debris. I'd seen the report in an online newspaper.

I really didn't care—Jamie's money was the most attractive thing about him since the beginning.

The money was mine, now. All of it. Berke had no legal claim to any of Jamie's bank accounts, no matter how much he resembled my deceased husband. It made me glad we'd never had kids—I didn't have to share. The fucking Feds had locked up everything I hadn't already transferred, and that made me want to murder all of them, beginning with Kory Wilson.

The Kory Wilson I'd thought was already dead.

To take my mind off frozen assets, I considered Dervil's promise of wealth beyond imagining if I invested in his new drug. *People will kill to get it,* he'd told me.

I didn't care who died, as long as the money came back to me in the billions, as he said it would. So many people said love was the most important thing. They were delusional.

Money was the most important thing.

~

Lexsi

"So far, there hasn't been a mass exodus of people fleeing Peru," Opal said. We sat inside her office as she laid out information gathered in recent days. I found it difficult to believe that it was less than a week since we'd fought with Laurel, Granger and Claudia's bunch outside San Francisco.

Claudia was dead, but Granger and Laurel were alive as far as we knew. They had at least one powerful warlock at their disposal, and if my guess were correct, others, too. It made me wonder who'd brought them to Laurel's attention. Jamie only had limited information on all of it, beginning with Laurel cheating with the one called Berke Gillson.

"The majority of the Rome's liquid assets were diverted from domestic accounts before we froze them," Opal continued. "We're getting preliminary information that Laurel's name was on numerous offshore accounts—most of which disappeared before we could do anything about them."

"You believe the money has been funneled to Peru?" Kell asked.

"Yes." Opal nodded at Kell's assumption. "I'm working on getting cooperation from other countries to stop imports into Peru, but that, so far, has been useless."

"Money from Earth has no value elsewhere," I said. "So they intend to spend what they have here and sell all their product elsewhere? That really doesn't make a lot of sense."

"It doesn't, does it?" Opal turned dark, unblinking eyes in my direction. "Perhaps some untruths have been told to Earth's investors, to keep them onboard?"

"We figure it's drakus seed," Kory said flatly. "If you don't know what that is, Kell can probably explain it best. We don't need that stuff anywhere on Earth."

"Kell has already informed me," Opal sighed. Today, she'd left her long, black hair loose, and it hung in straight, shining swaths to her waist. She shoved part of it impatiently behind an ear and studied the tablet in front of her—it held information she'd passed on to us.

"For now," she lifted her eyes to meet ours, "We've been instructed to stay away from Peru. The bordering countries—those we can visit, except for Colombia. Word from the President is that this is a delicate situation the State Department should handle."

"What's going on with Colombia?" I asked.

"They're working on a private treaty with Peru. Money may be involved," Opal replied. "They've refused an envoy from our State Department, and the Colombian Ambassador has already declined to meet the Secretary of State. The last I heard, he was packing to move back home."

"Have you met with the Secretary of State?" Kory asked.

"Yes. Secretary of Defense Hunter thinks Secretary of State Hinson is an idiot, but he didn't come right out and say it. The President is siding with State for now, unless something blows up first."

"Something already blew up—in California," I pointed out.

"Yes, but we have yet to officially place blame." I could see that Opal wasn't happy about that. "For now, all fingers point to US citizens—Laurel and James Rome. We reported James as having died in the fire at his LA home, and Laurel as missing and possibly out of the country, but that's it. It still leaves Jamie as a guilty party—making him temporarily dead was the best I could do."

"So we can't convince them that Jamie had nothing to do with this?"

"Have you ever tried to convince a mundane human of the existence of other worlds and races other than human?" Opal's right eyebrow lifted. "The ones who say they believe are labeled as nuts and crackpots. They don't have real information to produce, so there's no good way to convince anybody."

"Well, no. And some of those races don't want to be outed anyway," I said.

"Very true. I can't get different species of shifters to agree on anything, let alone come out of the jungle or the cave."

By her statement, I knew Opal had attempted to unite the shifters. Perhaps was still trying to do so. Gran always said in a room full of twenty people, at least eighteen would have differing ideas on how to accomplish the same goal. The last two were probably in bed together and felt obligated to agree with their partner.

Gran wouldn't wait for the State Department to give the okay to go to Peru. This was something I'd have to think about, before siding with anyone.

"We still don't know what they were lobbing at Kory," I said. "In California. If those were magical blasts, he should have nullified them. That's what our kind does."

"Non-magical weapons," Kell considered my words. "That makes sense, but what sort of non-magical weapons would have an impact on your kind? Anything made on this world?"

"I'd say it would take a really big weapon, and I have to tell you, those blasts were coming from everywhere," Kory said. "Every time I went toward the location of the last firing, I'd be fired at from another direction."

Kell went still for a moment.

"Director, may I see you in private?" he asked, surprising Kory and me.

~

Opal

"You're sure of this?" I asked. I should have known better. There was no subterfuge in Kell's eyes or his expression.

"Yes. Those two—they've had the construction plans for millennia. I suspect this is a testing ground for their initial efforts at building these machines."

"Deris and Daris Arden," I raked fingers through my hair. I'd left it loose that morning, because—*because I was seeing Kell*. I may as well be honest with myself on that, at least.

As for a Fifth-level warlock and a Fourth-level witch building some of the most destructive weapons another world had produced; that was worse news than I expected. No wonder Kory was turning in circles, attempting to combat them. In fact, a single weapon could have done the damage in California.

N'il Mo'erti. Death machines, they'd been named. That was their sole purpose—to bring death to an enemy. They didn't give up, either, unless they were destroyed or recalled by the one who commanded them.

Earth wasn't ready for *N'il Mo'erti*. Wouldn't be for centuries, at the very least. "They're armed with ranos technology—the *N'il Mo'erti*," I said.

"Yes."

"We're screwed."

"In a most unfortunate manner," Kell agreed.

Lexsi

"I'm going to run a background check on Charlene Devangi and have her movements tracked," Opal said once she and Kell came back to her office. "I think Kell is right and there's more going on there than her desire to hire Kory. Too many coincidences."

"She'll be in Vegas during Tibby's fight," I said. "He could be in danger, too."

"I'm considering that," Opal nodded. I understood this was just a subject to distract us—she and Kell had talked about other things while they were gone.

"If Devangi is connected to those in Peru, and that could be," Opal tapped her chin with a finger, "Then maybe we can use our resources to get information from her."

"Anita? Or a vampire?" Kory asked bluntly.

"Either works for me," Opal said, taking her seat and frowning at her tablet. "I'll have some of mine following her and tracking her communications and expenditures. If anything connects her to Peru or those we're looking for, I think you'll be heading for Vegas. She's approached you once, Kory," Opal's dark eyes studied his face. "We may ask you to be a bit more cooperative this time—to draw her in. Let's face it—my hands are currently tied where Peru is concerned, so we'll work it from the States if we can."

"Sounds good," Kory slapped a knee. If that woman is connected, I really, really want my hands on her. They killed a lot of good people in California."

"You must let us get information, first," Kell advised.

"Don't worry. I have control of my Thifilathi. You can get as much as you need—it's just that my hand may be around her throat while she tells you everything she knows."

"Suitable," Kell agreed with a slight nod.

"There may be a problem if she's already obsessed," I said. "Anita says so."

"Then Anita should be with you," Opal said. "What is the status of the werewolf? Will he be recovered enough to take along?"

"Oh, I think so," I said, although I worried what Anita would think. "His sister could go, too," I suggested.

"Good. I'll ask you to carry job offers to them," Opal said. "I'd like Mason and Klancy to travel at night—I can arrange transportation for them."

"We can all travel at night," Kell said.

"True. I'll schedule a private jet. It's not a long trip from San Francisco to Vegas."

"The Colorado prison riot ended about an hour ago—they're counting bodies," Jorden informed us as he drove to our hotel. "We have two more to visit tomorrow, before the boss sends you home for a few days."

"What's the preliminary on that?" Kory asked.

"At least a hundred dead. I think that's conservative," Jorden shook his head as he turned a corner. "Word has it that some of the guards locked themselves inside a room somewhere, but I think the boss wants you to question them in a few days. Just to make sure they weren't part of the problem."

"Yeah."

"I'll let you know when it's set up," Jorden said. "Until then, just put it out of your mind."

"Easier said than done," I mumbled on of Gran's favorites while staring at my hands.

It's okay, baby, one of Kory's hands covered both of mine.

Kordevik

After another restless night and an early morning in the gym, Lexsi and I got ready for our trip to two prisons; one in New York, another in Virginia. Virginia was closest so it was first on the list. A helicopter was scheduled to take us there.

I almost wished they'd let Lexsi and me skip in with Kell and Opal, who was coming with us, this time.

Opal was determined to arrive by mundane means. I realized that many High Demons only had the talent to skip themselves; my ability to skip others, too, was very rare and secured a higher rank for me in the military. At times, I wondered if that ability alone made me a viable candidate as Lexsi's mate.

Lexsi had it, too, but I wasn't surprised, considering her lineage and her connections to royalty. Between her skipping and misting abilities, she could get anyone in or out of almost any situation.

Anita, Farin, Tibby and Diego owed their lives to her, merely for those talents.

As did I. I still hadn't considered what she'd done at the end of the battle; we'd have lost that round if not for her.

"I'm coming, too," Jorden announced as he opened a car door for Lexsi in front of the hotel.

"Good to have you with us," Kell nodded. Those two were becoming friends; that was obvious.

The helicopter waited for us at a small airfield outside Silver Spring, and, as instructed, we climbed aboard, buckled in and placed headsets on to muffle the noise and to enable us to talk to one another.

I'd ridden in an airchopper; this was an airchopper's great-great-great-grandfather, perhaps. Noisy as hell, too.

"Better than a ride at the amusement park," Jorden spoke into his mic. "Louder, too."

"Louder isn't better," I said. "You're a werewolf. You have sensitive ears, man. What the hell are you talking about?"

"Just making conversation," Jorden turned and grinned from his seat in front of mine.

Yeah, I was beginning to like him, too.

I suppose it was a good thing that our pilots were also werewolves; I wouldn't have said what I had if they weren't. I could see them grinning at one another as they lifted the craft off the tarmac and headed south.

"The prison population will be locked down while we're there, to avoid a repeat of Colorado," Opal interrupted. She sat beside Kell behind the pilots, and turned to look at all of us.

"I sure hope there's no repeat of Colorado," Lexsi replied. "We don't need more of that. Do you have updated information on the death toll?"

"Nearly two hundred," Opal said and turned back in her seat. Kell watched her closely, although he didn't say anything.

I think most of the guards died, Lexsi sent. Mindspeech was the only way we could hold a private conversation on the helicopter. She was telling me in a roundabout way how much the riot upset her. *I tried to get numbers of guards employed there,* she went on. *But that's not easy to find.*

Probably for good reason, I responded. *Put it out of your mind, love. It's over. We can't do anything about it now.*

I wish I'd done something about it when it was going on, she replied, surprising me.

What? I asked, shocked by her words.

I can mist, remember? All I needed to know was where those guards were and I could have gone to get them. I feel terrible, she admitted. *Gran wouldn't have waited. She'd have gone straight in there and done what needed to be done.*

You're not your grandmother, I pointed out.

Yeah. Thanks for the reminder.

Baby, my father is Lord Nedevik Weth. Have you heard of him?

She turned to look at me, before blinking twice. *The High Demon who's stood up for so many, even when it meant he was arguing with the King—not just this one but the two before him? Or even disagreeing at times with Kifirin? That Lord Weth?* I could tell she was impressed.

That's the one. I'm not my father, either, although I wish I were, at times.

Is he mad? At both of us? She sounded lost. I knew then that she idolized my father.

He was very disappointed when I burned down a bar in Veshtul. He said as much, too. That's why I was sent to Earth to serve five years punishment.

You burned down a bar? Why?

You really don't know? My eyes bored into hers.

Oh. That. She turned away and hunched her shoulders.

A few seconds later, I barely caught her mental whisper.

I'm so sorry.

CHAPTER 5

*L*exsi

Things were strained between Kory and me the rest of the day. I never expected him to react that way; I'd hoped he'd think the same as I did—that neither of us wanted a marriage to someone we hadn't met.

I never dreamed he'd get in trouble for venting his anger after I, well, there wasn't any other way to put it. I'd left him standing at the altar. Left him to explain to family members and guests that I didn't want any part of him.

The worst part?

The five-year sentence he was serving on Earth in the past. As I said, I had no idea.

None.

He was prevented from going home for at least five years.

I had to depend on Aunt Bree to get me away if things became too difficult. Would she? Or were Kory and I stuck here forever, until someone powerful enough took pity on us?

What if we died here? Kory had almost been taken down in a vineyard outside San Francisco. What if we weren't so lucky next time?

Fuck.

It was my gran's favorite curse word.

It could become mine as well.

Fuck.

Holy. Fucking. Hell.

Kordevik

I shouldn't have told her. The fault was mine for burning down that fucking bar, not hers. Yes, she'd been afraid. Afraid to meet me at the altar, because she didn't know me. I could have been the worst person in the universes, for all she knew.

Now, she was shouldering the blame for my five-year sentence.

Well, four and small change, now.

If I were my father, I'd march right in to King Jaydevik's throne room and demand that arranged marriages be outlawed. That High Demons be allowed to meet those deemed worthy of a High Demon female. Let her have a hand in the choosing.

Yes, I wanted Lexsi more than anything. Loved her more than anything. I'd be damned if another High Demon took my place. I hoped she felt the same way about me, if I were honest.

After all, how many times had she said it—when she thought I couldn't hear? That she wanted me. Wanted to go to bed with me. Wanted to undress while I watched.

Fuck.

I needed a cold shower; Lexsi was upset and I had nobody to blame except myself.

Lexsi

I studied the photograph while Opal told me about him. "His name is Vic Malone and he's considered one of the worst criminals in the country," Opal informed me as we walked toward a waiting van. The van would transport us to the prison, where I'd question the inmates. "Vic has ties to drug lords outside the country, as well as a multitude of others inside it. He's been acting strangely for weeks, and it won't hurt to check." Opal followed her statement with a shrug.

"He's the only one here?" Kory asked. I didn't turn to look at him. I felt too guilty to do so.

"The only one reported, yes," Opal replied. "If the real Vic Malone is running loose, we have a problem. He likes killing, although he doesn't discriminate between male and female."

"You mean he'd fit right in with Loftin Qualls?" I asked.

"Like a brother," Opal muttered and pulled her leather jacket closer about her. Fall was coming swiftly to the East Coast. I felt it to a lesser degree; High Demons aren't affected by cold temperatures as much as humans or many shifters are. It made me wonder (again) what sort of shifter Opal was.

Being cold wasn't the reason my arms were crossed tightly over my chest; it was because I felt uncomfortable. I wished Kory had waited to tell me what he had. I could interview prisoners while remaining oblivious for a little while longer.

How many times could I apologize?

Probably not enough to make it better.

For either of us.

Kory scooted into the van beside me and shut the door. Kell sat in the row of seats ahead of us with Opal, while Jorden sat in the front with our driver. The drive took half an hour, during which neither Kory nor I spoke. I leaned toward the window to peer up at the high, gray walls of the prison when we drove up to it, where razor wire curled about the top like a deadly embellishment. Lowering my eyes, I allowed them to settle on the armed guard stationed at the gate.

He didn't look pleased.

"It looks starker than the one in Colorado," I whispered.

"Built earlier," Opal replied. "It was designed as a deterrent to crime, in and of itself."

"I wouldn't want to live here," Kory mumbled, leaning in to look out my window. His breath was warm on my neck as he studied the structure. I shivered involuntarily at his closeness.

Baby, we'll talk when this is over, he promised in mindspeech.

I wasn't sure I wanted to talk. I felt bad enough—and guilty enough—as it was.

~

Kordevik

The inside of the prison reflected the outside. Nothing there felt welcoming. Even family photographs on the warden's desk did nothing to lighten the heaviness that oppressed as well as incarcerated.

"Vic's posse on the inside have had to defend him several times from attacks from other inmates," Warden Greene said. "Yes, that's usually reversed," he held up a hand when Opal started to say something. "We do our best to maintain a balance, but you understand, they outnumber us. We don't want a replay of what happened in Colorado, either."

"How did you know we were there?" Kell asked.

"Word gets around," the Warden lowered his eyes. I doubted he wanted to tangle with Kell, who was more than ready to defend Opal. I could see it in the tension that gripped his body the moment we walked inside the prison.

"What did you hear, exactly?" Compulsion filled Kell's voice as he spoke.

"We heard that the Director of the Joint NSA and Homeland Security Department sent several agents to the facility in Colorado, and then a riot broke out. I'm still not sure that what I heard about ten prisoners is true."

"What's that?"

"That somehow, ten innocent people replaced ten drug lords from South America. We've heard rumors that a devil witch and her demon are involved." Warden Greene couldn't look Kell in the eye any longer; Kell's eyes were dark and hard.

"That information will no longer trouble you," Kell gritted. "You will not recall it after we leave this day."

Opal could only shake her head. Somehow, the enemy in Peru was already spreading stories and lies about us, taking what little they knew and expanding on it. I marveled at how closely they'd come to the truth, however.

Lexsi had Karathian blood, through her grandmother. The enemy had no knowledge of that—how could they? Lexsi's grandmother wouldn't take the throne of Le-Ath Veronis for nearly three hundred years.

They'd invented stories to frighten the gullible on Earth, and managed to get close to the truth as a result.

Like Kell, I wanted to defend Lexsi. She was only twenty-three, for fuck's sake, and barely considered an adult according to High Demon law. While she behaved in a manner beyond her years, there were so many things she hadn't experienced for herself, yet.

I worried about her because of that.

Keep your mouth shut—it already bothers her, I berated myself.

"We're ready to see the prisoner," Opal said, interrupting my thoughts.

Yes, I wanted out of this hellhole already. Lexsi was upset enough as it was.

Lexsi

Four guards stood outside the room that held Vic Malone.

At least they thought it was Vic Malone. Warden Green swiped his badge across a reader to open the door for us.

Once inside, he closed the door and locked it behind us with the same badge. Across the room, sitting at a single desk with wrists and ankles shackled to bolts in the floor, sat Vic Malone.

Kory and I were still far enough away that any spell would still be active. "I'll go first," Kory said and strode forward. We all knew it the moment Kory came close enough to disable a spell.

Vic's features changed. Warden Greene stifled a gasp. The man—a hapless victim forced to take Vic's place, blinked helplessly at us.

～

"Fingerprints and blood type match our missing guard," Warden Green tossed a tablet onto his desk, rattling the photographs sitting there. "DNA will take a few days, but it'll probably match, too, goddammit."

"How long has he been missing?" Opal asked.

"About as long as Vic has been acting strangely," the warden admitted. "The guard disappeared while he was off during a weekend. Went camping, according to his sister, and never came home. Fucking hell." Fingers raked through the warden's thinning dark hair as he shook his head in disbelief. "How?" He raised his eyes to Kell, begging for an explanation.

"We cannot say at this time; we are still investigating it ourselves and have no accurate information," Kell replied smoothly. "What we now know for certain, however, is that Vic Malone is no longer incarcerated. We must add him to the list of escapees that we seek."

"Yeah." The warden blew out a breath and sat heavily on his desk chair. "How many?" he turned to Opal. "How many of these prisoners are we going to find aren't really the ones we locked away? How long has this been going on?"

"I don't have solid answers, and I don't wish to speculate. You'll be kept in the loop as far as Vic Malone is concerned."

"I appreciate that. I don't understand, but I appreciate any information you're willing to share."

My arms were crossed tightly over my chest again; Kell had been forced to use compulsion on the warden a second time after I'd taken the imprisoned guard into my mist to destroy the duplication spell.

He recalled who he was, then, and began to weep. All of it was very sad, but at least he was released from his chains and taken to the infirmary afterward, with Kell and Kory as additional guards to make sure nothing happened to him along the way.

As Warden Greene had said, we didn't want a repeat of what happened in Colorado. Kell made sure that the victim was placed in an ambulance and carried safely away from the prison before we regrouped in the Warden's office.

"What happens now?" Warden Greene asked, his eyes meeting Opal's for mere seconds before dropping again.

"This isn't your fault, or the fault of your guards," Opal said. "Neither you nor they could have prevented it with the resources you currently have. For now, we place Vic on the most wanted list again, but as you can probably guess, he may no longer look like himself."

"I don't understand how this is possible," the warden moaned, covering his face with both hands.

"As I said, not your fault. Stop beating yourself up about it. We'll keep you informed."

Warden Greene walked out with us and watched as we loaded into our van. Jorden had waited with the driver at the vehicle, just to make sure it wasn't approached or compromised while we were gone.

The prison in Virginia took five hours, when it was scheduled to take only one. We were far behind schedule when we climbed into the van to go back to the airport.

The sun was setting by the time we arrived at the prison in New York. Opal spent most of the trip by plane getting in touch with the Secretaries of Defense and State, in addition to the President, the FBI and the CIA.

Her conversations took place by cell phone at the back of the plane; that was fine with me—I didn't want to hear any part of it. Kory remained silent at my side; he'd refused to sit anywhere except in the seat next to mine.

How could he do that, knowing I'd caused him five years' worth of trouble?

We'd found another van and driver waiting for us when we landed, and he drove us to the prison in New York while the rest of us took our usual seating arrangement.

Jorden looked worried when we left him and the driver with the van like before. "Here," Opal handed him a communicator, which he immediately placed in his ear. "Anything goes wrong, you know what to do."

"Yes, Ma'am," he nodded.

Was she expecting trouble already? That ramped up my worry to a new level. So far, the day had sucked, as Gran said. Could it get any worse?

Kory's hand dropped onto my shoulder. It felt warm and comforting as we walked along an ugly, tiled corridor toward the Warden's office.

Kell

This warden wasn't as accommodating as Warden Greene. This one acted guilty from the moment we walked into his office. I wanted to begin questioning him then, but held off. We would see the three prisoners first, and then I would ask questions.

I should have asked questions at the beginning.

"Follow me," he said, his voice clipped and words short as he lifted a badge from a desk drawer and brushed past us on his way to the door.

We were led down two more corridors that smelled of antiseptic and hopelessness, until we arrived at another secure room. Like Greene, Warden Brackett swiped the badge to let us in and waited by the door until I stepped into the room.

The door was slammed shut the moment I was inside, the portal was locked on the outside and an alarm began to sound throughout the prison. Three prisoners were chained to chairs at the center of the room, but to our surprise, on the far side, four others appeared, as if walking out of the painted, concrete walls.

Two were Sirenali in their scaled forms; the other two were warlocks. That was easy enough to see.

The warlocks' first blasts toward us were nullified by Kordevik and Lexsi.

The Sirenali, without power of that sort, pulled out weapons and began to shoot. Kordevik changed immediately and with flames licking his black scales, he stalked them while they continued to fire.

Opal fought me when I attempted to shove her body behind mine; I turned us both to mist when she refused to cooperate. Lexsi screamed when the fire net was dropped over Kory's Thifilathi; he screamed, too, when the net began to burn through his scales.

Without thinking of herself, Lexsi changed to Thifilatha and dived toward Kory, grabbing the net in her silver-scaled hands to pull it away while the fools in the corner ran behind the firing Sirenali.

Kell, get us to the Sirenali, Opal snapped in mindspeech.

She was right—they'd caused this trouble. Now it was time for them to die.

Lexsi

Tears of flame dripped down my cheeks—tears for Kory and for me. The net burned my hands whenever I touched it, but I couldn't let it harm him any more than it already had. Kory's wings, with burn-holes between ribs, beat to help me get the net off him. That's how I missed the events surrounding the four who'd attacked us—Kell and Opal went after them.

Kory screamed as the net sunk farther into sections of his back—it was designed to burn flesh until it had completely passed through whoever it was dropped on. I shook my hands to rid myself of the wad of net I held to reach for the part that was burning Kory so badly.

I felt as if it took hours to clear the net off him and then knock it from my own hands. Likely, it was minutes at most. Otherwise, it could have killed both of us. Burns sunk to the bones in my hands, but

I was determined not to pay attention to that. I had to remove the net from Kory, first.

Once the net was off and piled near the door, Kory and I limped toward the corner where the warlocks were, only to discover they'd gone to hide behind the Sirenali. Likely, it was because Kory and I together neutralized their ability to fold space out of the prison.

Had anyone told them that might happen? Were they expendable, to disable or kill Kory with a fire net?

How the hell had they gotten a fire net to begin with?

Fire nets were terrible things, used only on the worst High Demon criminals to subdue them. They were taken off immediately, once the High Demon was subdued, lest it kill them. It normally took very little time to subdue someone with a fire net—that's how badly it would burn a High Demon. It would continue to burn until the victim died if it weren't removed.

Kory's back, sides, arms, legs and face were scored with net burns. My hands, arms, and chest were also scored, because I'd pulled the net to me to get it off him. Together, we were a burned, bloody mess.

I couldn't look at my hands. Instead, I lifted my gaze to see what happened to Kell and Opal.

With eyes that merely recorded instead of analyzing, I watched as Kell, his claws extended, appeared from mist, Opal with him. In less time that it took to blink, he had the heads off our four attackers, while three shackled prisoners screamed and shouted from their chairs at the center of the room.

Kell shook blood and gore from his claws and retracted them. Opal bent down to examine all four bodies, searching for identification.

Eventually, the prisoners realized it was over and quieted. When Jorden and a mass of other agents broke into the room, it was almost peaceful inside.

Opal

"Pain medication doesn't have much of an effect on High Demons —you'd have to give them a massive dose just for it to touch their pain," I said.

Kell ended up misting Kory's Thifilathi and Lexsi's Thifilatha to a nearby safe house; if they changed to humanoid, the severity of the burns and the subsequent pain could kill them.

They needed to heal as they were if they were to survive.

"We need a fucking pool," I swore softly as I watched them breathe with difficulty as they lay on the tiled floor of the safe house.

"Then we will find a fucking pool," Kell snapped. "I will place compulsion if I must. The young one weeps in pain when she wakes. Kory's injuries may be worse and I am terrified for him."

"Hold on," I said, pulling my cell phone from a pocket and hitting the Secretary of Defense's private number.

"Colonel Hunter," he said when he answered.

"Colonel Hunter," I said, "I need a very private residence with a swimming pool, and no questions asked."

"I'll get one for you," he responded. I heard him barking commands at an underling. In less than thirty seconds, he rattled off an address roughly five miles away.

"Thank you, Colonel. We'll be there in ten minutes."

~

Lexsi

"What's this floating in the water?"

It was Kory's voice, saying something strange. I almost opened my eyes, realized I must be dreaming and allowed sleep to capture me again.

"Ground oatmeal," came the reply, as if it were from far away. I ignored it and went back to sleep.

~

Kordevik

Kell's eyes met mine; he sat at the other end of a rectangular pool, cross-legged, as if he'd been meditating. "Why ground oatmeal?" I asked. Yes, it was difficult for my Thifilathi to form the words, but not impossible.

At least my back, arms and chest were no longer on fire, although I could still see the dark indentations left by the fire net on my skin—when the layers of oatmeal parted, the water was clear enough to make them out.

Lexsi lay against me in the crook of my arm, her forehead resting in the hollow between my neck and collarbone.

Her net marks were more pronounced, since her Thifilatha was silver and the net burns were black. I was grateful they weren't crusted with blood; someone had likely seen to it that the pool filtered all that out of the water before filling it with ground oatmeal to help with the burns.

Lexsi had slept most of that time, until I'd almost wakened her when I spoke.

Fire net burns were serious. Fire nets could kill. Somehow, the enemy had gotten one, when that shouldn't have been.

Those in existence were closely guarded by the High Demon army on Kifirin.

Except this was Kifirin in the past, I reminded myself. A time when both Croth and Drith Houses were in full flower. Many of them were in Kifirin's military, and long before Jaydevik and Glinda took the throne.

Fuck.

Croth and Drith had almost destroyed Kifirin. Would almost destroy Kifirin, in less than three hundred years from when I currently was.

Have you identified the warlocks or the Sirenali? I sent to Kell. Hell, he was a mister. Made sense that he could also be a mindspeaker.

No identification on them, Kell's mental voice was clear. *Impossible to tell from where we are.*

True, I allowed my eyes to close as I breathed a weary sigh. Earth wasn't even aware that there were vampires and werewolves living among humans, let alone know that there were other planets with other races living upon them.

Where are the bodies now? I asked.

Opal sent them to a guarded facility for examination, Kell replied. *The Secretary of Defense is helping her as much as he can. The President and Secretary of State have their heads up their posteriors,* he added.

No surprise. I breathed against Lexsi's damp hair, hoping she didn't feel cold in the water. The pool wasn't heated. As far as the burns went, that was a good thing. Cool water was the best solution for a net-burned High Demon.

When she woke, I intended to thank her for getting the net off me so fast. If she hadn't, I could have died. She couldn't have turned to mist to get me out of it, either. The net burned into the skin and had to be ripped out at times, just to separate it from the High Demon in question.

Legend had it that Kifirin himself designed fire nets. If that were true, I was ready to curse his ingenuity. Certainly, no High Demon that I knew could manufacture them. They were practically indestructible, from everything I'd heard in the past about them.

What happened to the net? I asked.

Ask Opal. She knows. I wasn't there when she had the thing removed. As you've probably guessed, the warden was obsessed. He and many underlings are now imprisoned for this attack on a government official.

I hope it's buried deep, wherever it is. I never want to see another of those things touch Lexsi's skin or scales.

I never wish to see another touch either of you. Opal told me I couldn't have extricated you from it by turning you to mist—that it had already burned into your scales and skin. Turning you to mist would mean turning it to mist, too.

Yeah. I get that. Lexsi burned her hands pulling it out of my skin.

We will see that the young one receives the best of care. You, too. Without your particular talents, the warlocks would have gotten away. The Sirenali were determined to kill all of us; it makes me think that they may have been young, too, and had obsession placed by an older one. During the entire debacle, they never spoke.

Check to see if they still have their tongues, I snorted, watching the smoke I'd breathed drift away on the cool air. At least the pool was enclosed, even if the wood and brick structure around it wasn't heated in any way. It kept Lexsi and me away from prying eyes.

If you are well enough in a day or two, we will return to California. I believe Anita has been calling the Director every half hour to check on you and Lexsi.

Tell her we're fine. Lexsi's sleeping and I don't want to disturb her. While she sleeps, she heals, I said simply. It was an old High Demon saying, and a very, very true one.

~

Lexsi

I'm hungry. The words formed in my mind before I recalled that others could hear them.

"Baby, we'll feed you if you'll open your eyes," Kory's lips grazed my ear. "Tell us what you want and we'll do our best to get it for you."

My eyes opened; I blinked several times so I could bring everything into focus.

Kory and I—we were in a swimming pool filled with what looked and felt like oatmeal.

"Better for you to heal with," Kory's warm breath informed me before pulling away. I realized then that he'd been keeping the rest of me warm; cold water rushed in to replace his warm body against mine.

I wanted to pull him against me again and cling to him like a barnacle on a rock.

"Where did the fire net come from?" I asked instead, my voice rough as I shivered in cold water.

"Baby, we don't know. The four that brought it in are dead, so they can't answer any questions," Kory said, standing and stretching before pulling himself out of the deep end of the pool.

Water dripped from his wings and body as he accepted a very large towel from someone.

"If you can climb out, now's the time," Opal said behind me.

My Thifilatha's silver scales couldn't show embarrassment. If I were humanoid, my face would be flaming. Kory stood above me, completely naked, while I huddled in the pool, just as naked.

Instead of attempting to climb out of the pool, I dropped my face into my hands. The pain that surged through me had me yelping and dumping both hands into the water again.

They hurt—as if they were still burning.

That's when the tears came.

"Baby, no," Kory was back in the water, getting wet again just because I couldn't behave like an adult and not cry at the state of my hands. "Sweetheart, it'll take time—you handled that net, over and over, to get it off me. Your hands will heal, it'll just take time." Kory rocked my body against his.

What if he were wrong?

What if I could never cook again?

I wanted to wail louder at the thought. Instead, I sniffled and shook against Kory, while he tucked hair behind my ear and kissed the top of my head. I knew I looked a mess, my hair and wings draggling in the water while Kory did his best to stop the tears.

"Kell, we'll have to feed her; her hands are so bad she can't hold anything to feed herself," I heard Opal say.

"We will feed her for as long as it takes," Kell's voice answered.

I felt helpless as I collapsed against Kory and sobbed.

"This is a natural, aloe-based gel," the werewolf physician informed me as he wrapped my Thifilatha's hands later. Kory had fed me soup and a sandwich; I was still Thifilatha to ensure a faster healing. And, as he was Thifilathi for the same reason, the soup bowl was a large, stainless-steel bowl with a half-gallon of chicken noodle soup in it, while the sandwich was a large French loaf cut in two, lengthwise pieces and piled with ham and turkey.

"Soup and sandwich, High Demon style," Kory called it and fed me with the largest cooking spoon Opal could find.

Then the werewolf physician arrived, assessed the situation and opted to wrap my hands with the healing gel and gauze. He said our other burns were healing quickly on their own and with one or two more sleeps, we should be well enough to go back to humanoid.

"Leave your hands wrapped," the physician said. "I'll allow a bath tomorrow. We'll remove the gauze then, check the burns and re-bandage, as necessary."

"Baby, will you let me comb your hair?" Kory asked, once the physician packed his things and left.

"I feel like a mess," I hung my head. "I can't even brush my teeth or anything."

"We have mouthwash for now," Kory gave me a lopsided grin. "Teeth brushing is for later."

It took more than an hour for Kory to comb out my hair, which still held bits of oatmeal in it. He was so gentle during the process that I fell asleep after the first half hour.

CHAPTER 6

*K*ordevik

"Her hands were burned repeatedly, when she pulled that net out of my skin and scales," I explained to Anita. Lexsi was asleep in her bed and had been since we'd arrived home an hour earlier. "Some of those burns went to the bone," I added.

We were back to humanoid, although Lexsi's hands were still wrapped in the healing gel provided by the werewolf physician in New York.

"That hurts, just thinking about it," Anita grumbled.

"How's Watson?" I asked.

"Hmmph," Anita snorted.

"Please tell me he's not still hung up on that fucking, two-faced girlfriend," I said.

"I don't know what's up with him. I just cook and clean around him, that's all." Anita tossed up a hand as if to say she'd given up on him.

"I can rip an ear off—or blister it when I yell," I offered.

"Don't intervene on my behalf," Anita said. "If he doesn't wake up and smell the bacon frying after a while, then we're done."

"How's Sandra?"

"Sandra's fine. She and Mason are getting along like a house on fire. Sorry. Didn't mean to use that particular saying," Anita winced.

"No problem. Just don't say fire net, okay? That's what caused the problem. Ordinary fire is nothing to a High Demon. Tell me about Sandra and Mason. I need a good, cheerful story." I lifted the bottle of beer I'd hauled from the fridge after getting Lexsi settled in bed. The cold liquid felt good as I swallowed it.

"Not much to tell, yet, but there have been lots of long conversations between those two, followed by plenty of glances and sighs, if you know what I mean. If her now-deceased husband weren't so deceased, Mason would probably deal with that problem himself."

"I see." I took another swig from the bottle. "What about Farin and Tibby?"

"Tibby's in constant training mode because this is a championship fight. Farin follows him to the gym every day and stays until he's done. Most of the time, that's late. Two more cousins and Tibby's brother have joined Diego in providing bodyguards for both Farin and Tibby. After that debacle you had with the opponent's fight promoter in D.C., they're making sure nobody approaches Farin that they don't know."

"Good for them," I said emptying the bottle and rising from my barstool to get another. "The way I feel right now, I'd probably kill Charlene Devangi if I saw her. Tibby's family can keep her away from all of us."

"Tibby's abuela is coming to the fight. I hear that's a big thing with all the rat shifters."

"Maybe she's a legend or something in their community."

"Maybe." Anita pursed her lips and considered that for a moment. "Tibby's never said her name—he just calls her Abuela."

"Have you looked him up by his real name?" I asked.

"Everybody knows Tiburon Snark Demonio Diaz. You don't have to look him up."

"Maybe somebody mentions his mother in all that. If that's true, maybe you can go backward and get to his grandmother."

"You know, you're pretty good for a thickheaded High Demon," she pointed a finger at me.

"Wow. That's faint praise if I ever heard it." I popped the top off my second bottle of beer and drank a third of it in two swallows.

"Sunset in two hours," Sandra walked into the kitchen. "Any more of that?" she nodded at my bottle.

"Plenty. Somebody restocked," I said.

"Mason went shopping last night—I gave him a list," Anita said.

"Good for him," Sandra sighed and headed for the fridge.

"We can't let people starve while Lexsi is recovering—especially Lexsi," Anita said. "She needs good food to get better."

"I hear that," Sandra agreed as she bent down to search the rows of bottles at the bottom of the fridge. "I'm a decent cook, but I've never seen anybody who can turn food into a masterpiece like she can."

It made me chuckle as I considered telling Anita that I'd fed Lexsi's Thifilatha soup from a large, stainless-steel bowl, to get enough food into her. I decided to save it for later—when I could tease Lexsi with it.

"What about the three prisoners in New York?" Anita asked, changing the subject.

"Petty criminals, exchanged for bigger and badder," I said. "They should be in jail, just not on life sentences," I added. "Opal and Kell took care of it after the warden and a few guards were arrested."

"Sick," Anita shook her head. "I hope they're not thinking about asking either of you to go to another prison. Ever."

"They're not. Opal says they have to come to us from now on, at a place of our choosing and they won't know the location until ten minutes before they arrive."

"Good. No more of this attack shit. If I had my hands on Laurel Rome, I'd," she pounded the kitchen island with a fist.

"I feel exactly the same," Jamie walked in wearing sweats and a T-shirt. The T-shirt was soaked in sweat—he'd been working out.

"Tibby and his family hauled equipment to the house. Said we could make use of it, as it was cluttering up his gym," Jamie shrugged. "Treadmill, weights, that sort of thing."

He'd done it for Lexsi and me, because that's how we exercised, for the most part. I was glad others in the house were getting some use out of it, too.

"Keeping yourself busy?" I asked, holding up my bottle and silently asking Jamie if he wanted a beer. He nodded and took a stool beside Anita. I rose to get him a beer.

"I'm busy enough. Checking stocks and investments. Winnowing out good from bad. This way, when I can access the money in my hidden account, I can build up my portfolio again. Laurel destroyed what I had."

I popped the top off the bottle and set it in front of him. He nodded his thanks and drank.

"Was that letter you got the insurance check for your Jeep?" Anita asked as I took my seat again.

"Yeah. I guess I'll go out and find something new," I shrugged. "I'll need something besides Lexsi's TinyCar to get around in."

"I'd like to go with you, if you don't mind," Jamie perked up.

"No problem, man," I said.

~

Lexsi

The last four days had settled into a new routine. I slept until my growling stomach woke me. I'd be forced to let Kory feed me, because my hands were still swathed in gauze. Then I'd let someone remove my bandages, take a shower, get re-bandaged and go back to sleep.

At least while I slept, I didn't worry about not being able to use my hands, which still looked awful. Instead, I dreamed of my family. Of Bel Erland, my Karathian warlock half-brother, who'd somehow gotten himself engaged to a winged woman.

At least he was engaged in my dreams. I had no idea whether it was real or not. I'd spent my last year on Avendor before the wedding date at SouthStar. Nobody gets in or out of SouthStar without the owner's permission. An impenetrable boundary lay about SouthStar's groves and without the owner's or the Second's permission, nobody could get through, no matter how strong or talented they were.

I'd guessed that Mom and the others knew I'd try to run, so I'd been hauled from EastStar to SouthStar the year before the wedding without any warning beforehand.

News had been spotty as a result. I admit that I could have sent mindspeech to Mom, Dad or Uncle Edward, but I was pissed at all of them and didn't try. I still got my training from Uncle Sal at SouthStar—his best friend owned those groves, after all, although he was seldom there for anything, including meals and harvests.

Shoving covers aside with bandaged hands, I headed for my closet to find a robe. Fixing rumpled hair was out of the question, so I shrugged into the robe and left it loose over my pajamas before skipping into the kitchen.

Kory was having a beer with Jamie and Sandra while talking to them and Anita. "Baby, sit, I'll find something for you to eat," Kory rose from his seat.

I wanted to tell him I wanted steak and pasta, but there probably wasn't anything in the house to make either.

"Yeah." I held up my hands, frowned at the thick bandages and allowed Kory and Anita to herd me toward Kory's barstool.

"Here," Anita set a glass of juice in front of me. Kory lifted it to allow me to drink. *Enough*, I sent after a few swallows. Kory set the glass down.

"What do you want for dinner, onion?" Kory asked.

"Steak with mushroom sauce and pasta," I sighed, lowering my forehead to the granite island and letting it settle there. My hands were useless. If I were whole, I'd already be working on what I wanted. Nobody here knew how to make what I wanted.

"I think we have T-bones, will that work?" Anita stood at the fridge with the door open while she turned back to ask.

"Good enough. What about mushrooms?"

As it turned out, we had everything we needed. I had to walk Anita, Sandra and Kory through the making, though, while Jamie watched. After a while, when the scent reached Watson wherever he was in the house, he wandered in.

"You need your furry tail pulled," I snapped as he sat beside me.

"I probably do," he agreed. "Is there more beer? Please say yes," he said.

~

Peru

Laurel Rome

"What do you mean, they're all dead? All four of them?" I narrowed my eyes at Berke. I hadn't told him, but I was beginning to regret that he had Jamie's body. The Berke I'd fucked early on had a younger body. Now, he only had a younger brain.

"We're beginning to see what he's capable of—Kory Wilson, that is," Berke spread his hands as he attempted an explanation. "Yes, we lost four, but they were unimportant, as Deris will tell you. The Sirenali were young—V'ili made sure they weren't able to speak, you know, before he sent them to do his bidding. Shame, though; V'ili should have told them to fold the warlocks away at the first sign of trouble. He was so sure the fire net would work that he didn't add safeguards. We won't let that happen again, dearest."

"With another fire net? Why didn't the first one work?" I demanded.

"We, ah, don't have another net. That was the only one we could acquire for now. As you see, it wasn't as effective as we'd hoped. Somehow, they managed to defeat it and kill our four servants. V'ili felt the obsession die when they did; regardless, no information could be gotten from them."

"Where is Hannah?" I asked. "I want to ask her questions. She knows both of them. I want to know how to kill Kory Wilson and that trollop of a girlfriend he has."

"I'll find Hannah. She's probably out sunning herself by the pool," Berke replied.

"Tell her to get her ass in here, or I'll think twice about saving it next time," I snapped. "She has what she's wanted for a long time—a younger body. I did that for her. She owes me."

~

Lexsi

"No more," I held up a gauze-swathed hand. Kory fed me steak, mushroom sauce and pasta until I felt as if I'd pop with one more bite. He'd fed himself while I chewed, so we could have dinner together.

"I'll be done in a minute," Kory said. "I'll take the bandages off then, so you can get a shower. Your hands looked much better the last time."

Lie.

"Do they still hurt?" Sandra asked, turning me away from Kory's untruth. He'd said it to make me feel better. There was no need to accost him over it.

"No. I just have trouble flexing them," I admitted. Yes, the net had burned through muscle and sinew on both hands; they looked skeletal at best and I secretly worried they'd never be the same. Automatically, I hunched my shoulders at the thought.

"It'll be fine," Kory laid an arm over my shoulders. "High Demons are tough. My Lexsi is tough."

"I don't feel tough," I mumbled.

"But you are," he kissed my hair. "Trust me, ninety-nine percent of the High Demon army would have watched me burn rather than pull that shit off me and risk injury."

"Ninety-nine percent of the High Demon army are idiots and they don't love you," I sighed.

"My baby loves me," Kory pulled me into his arms.

"I am pleased to see you home," Klancy declared. Sunset had come and the vamps were awake.

~

After my shower and the rewrapping of my hands, Kory settled me on the sofa next to him and crooked his arm about me while we answered Klancy and Mason's questions. Watson, Anita and the others came, too, in case there was news they hadn't already heard.

"You call this a fire net?" Klancy was curious.

"Yeah. It's a way of controlling High Demon criminals. No idea how they got their hands on one," Kory shrugged. "They're all guarded like your proverbial Fort Knox. You have to handle fire nets by the narrow edges only—everything else will burn what it touches."

I watched their faces as they digested that information. "Where is Kell?" Mason asked after several seconds.

"He stayed behind with Opal. She appreciates his advice," I said. "Plus, I watched him behead two warlocks and two Sirenali in about a blink. He was pissed, I think, that they'd attacked us like that."

"Do you think the enemy knows those four are dead?" Sandra asked.

"Probably. They've been a step ahead of us most of the way," Kory rumbled. I snuggled farther into his warmth as he explained what we'd seen and heard since our visit to the Colorado facility.

"They attempted to kill you during the riot in Colorado, then again in New York. Why wasn't an attempt made in Virginia?" Klancy asked.

"We don't know," Kory combed fingers through my hair. I closed my eyes and didn't open them again while the others talked. Eventually, I fell asleep.

~

Kordevik

When I carried Lexsi to her bedroom to put her to bed, I found Li'Neruh Rath waiting for me.

"I'm here to help her hands heal faster," he said as I laid her gently on the bed. "She shouldn't have to suffer like this."

I watched as he removed the bandages from her hands as if it were something he was used to doing. I was afraid to pry, so I didn't ask.

Lexsi's hands looked small and knotted, crisscrossed with net burns as they were.

His hands were careful as he held hers, while light formed around them. Under his guidance, fingers straightened as flesh and muscle grew about healing bones. That's how her hands had been until now—nearly skeletal as they slowly recovered.

When he finished, her hands looked so much better I felt tears prick my eyes. She was worried enough that I hadn't added my worries to hers.

With Li'Neruh's assistance, I felt optimistic for the first time in days.

"Thank you," I breathed, once the light dimmed and he laid her hands on the blanket covering her chest.

"It is deserved," Li'Neruh shook himself as he stood. "Do not let fear defeat you. Either of you," he nodded and disappeared.

"Whatever you say," I sighed and gently touched the hands he'd healed before rewrapping them. I'd let Lexsi discover for herself just how much they'd improved.

~

Lexsi

I skipped into the kitchen early the next morning, hoping somebody would be awake to make coffee. I found Tibby and Farin in the kitchen. Without a word, Tibby pulled a mug from the cabinet and poured coffee for me.

At least I could hold the mug between bandaged hands and sip. "Thank you," I sighed after getting my first taste of the hot brew.

"Lexsi, I am so, so sorry," Farin began.

"Lesson learned," I set my mug on the island and took a seat. "Stop beating yourself up about it. They're trying to get information on us, and that's how they did it."

"Car's ready, man," Diego walked in.

"Diego, I want to hug you," I said. "You and Tibby both, for what you did inside that wine cave."

"I'll take a hug," he grinned. I gave him a kiss on the cheek, too, while I was at it, but refrained from kissing Tibby.

Farin was watching, and he was her man.

If I'd thought Tibby looked tough and muscular before, well, he'd improved in a matter of days. He looked as if he could take on bigger and badder and make them cry before he was done.

"You know, I never asked who your opponent is in Vegas," I said, sitting down again and lifting my cup carefully to drink.

"Lyle, 'Lover Boy,' Landon," Tibby shook his head.

"Lyle wishes he were lover boy," Diego huffed. "That one—only his mother would love him."

"He's ugly?" I asked, curious.

"Not ugly. Mean and nasty," Tibby replied. "He married twice. Both left him because he wasn't a proper husband."

"What Tibby's saying is that Lyle likes to hit and cheat," Farin said. "The money was good; otherwise neither would have married him in the first place."

"Money covers a lot of sins, huh?" I asked.

"Yeah. I guess," Farin shook her head.

"Stop worrying about that pendejo," Tibby pulled Farin against him. "He is nothing to us."

"I don't want him to hurt you," Farin mumbled against Tibby's shoulder. Diego snorted at her words.

"I take it Tibby doesn't intend to get hurt by that pendejo?" I lifted an eyebrow at Diego, who laughed.

They left a few minutes later, Tibby pressing a kiss against Farin's temple as he pulled her along with him. I was in the kitchen alone and had almost reached the bottom of my coffee mug.

"Want more?" Anita's house slippers scuffed across the kitchen tiles as she wrapped her robe tightly about her and tied the belt around her waist.

"Yeah. And some bacon and eggs, if we have any."

"I think we do," she said and pulled my mug away to pour more coffee.

"Did you leave any for me?" Kory walked into the kitchen, followed closely by Watson.

"I'll get the plates," Watson offered before Anita could say anything. I wasn't going to be the one to tell him she wasn't planning to say anything to him—her words would be for Kory, while she pointedly ignored Watson.

Watson wore a grim expression as he laid out plates, flatware and cups for Kory and himself. Kory's setting was next to mine as Anita placed a platter of bacon and another of scrambled eggs on the bar so they could help themselves.

She then took the barstool next to mine, while Watson sat beside Kory. Kory didn't say anything aloud. *We're the divider between them*, he dipped eggs onto his plate, then reached for the salt and pepper.

"Bacon, please," Watson held out his plate. Anita had placed the bacon on her end of the island.

"Dude," Kory reached across me, lifted the platter, snagged four slices for himself and passed the rest to Watson. Anita sat beside me and fumed.

"Look, about that tail pulling," I began.

"You don't have to say anything—or pull my tail," Watson admitted. "I know I fucked up. I just—I was in love with her since we were kids. And to have her do that—Anita, I owe you a big apology, but I have to get this shit out of my head, first. Okay?"

Watson turned deep-brown eyes in Anita's direction, pleading with her to understand.

"Then why didn't you say that to start with?" Anita demanded. "Instead of this pining away shit, like I didn't fucking matter to you. I thought you were fucking dead, you asshole."

Watson stopped chewing bacon for a moment as he considered what she'd said.

"Yeah. I get that now."

Anita began to sniffle beside me.

"It's not your fault," I put my arms around her. She turned, dropped her head on my shoulder and began to sob. I shot Watson the nastiest of looks while I awkwardly patted Anita's back with a bandaged hand.

"Want me to kill Watson for you?" Kory asked almost pleasantly. "I can. Won't take much; my Thifilathi can burn just about anything, especially when it's this close."

"What?" Watson scooted his chair back in alarm.

"I'm not kidding. I can do it now if you want," Kory went on.

Anita's head flew off my shoulder. She blinked tear-filled eyes at Kory. "Please don't," she whispered. "I love him."

"Baby, I," Watson began.

"I'm still mad at you," Anita wiped tears off her cheeks. "Really, really mad." She folded space before I could attempt to stop her.

"Dude," Watson blinked at Kory. "Would you really have done that? I thought we were friends."

"We still are. I just wanted to point out the reality of the situation. Anita thought you were dead. I offered to make you really dead, just to make her realize how much she cares. And to show you how much she really cares about your sorry, furry ass." Kory lifted another piece of bacon, folded it into thirds and stuffed it into his mouth.

"You need to get your priorities straight," I said, waving a gauze-swathed hand at Watson. "Anita is here, now, cooking and waiting on you while your ex tried to kill you. She's been depressed for days because, well, you're an asshat."

"Hey, are you forgetting that I almost did die?" Watson demanded.

"See this?" Kory grasped my right wrist and lifted my bandaged hand so Watson could see. "Lexsi pulled a fire net out of my skin with these hands, over and over, so it wouldn't kill me. The pain of a fire net is indescribable. It burned her to the bone, man, and she did it because she loves me. Anita is doing the same for you, you stupid shit, because she loves you. I'm beginning to wonder why." Kory laid my bandaged hand gently on the island and patted it.

I was blinking tears away when he did so.

"Yeah. Well. I guess I ought to go find her," Watson slid off his barstool.

~

Opal

"Colonel Hunter, I know you're more accepting of this sort of thing than the President and the Secretary of State," I said. He, Kell and I agreed to meet over lunch, not far from both our offices.

"I find it interesting that there wasn't an incident at the Virginia facility. It's as if they were waiting to see who showed up there, to put their plans in motion in New York," August Hunter replied.

Colonel Hunter never minced words and had more insight than most people I knew. Yes, I realized that he still dealt with the occasional racist opinion on the Hill, but he was one of the sharpest men I knew.

It was something I'd dealt with myself often enough, as old as I was. Not just as a female, but as a native to the continent, before the Americas were called the Americas. When I was asked if I wished to stay on Earth and hold a position that could make a difference, I'd accepted it.

Yes, I could have gone off-world and anywhere else I wanted to go. I'd chosen to stay on Earth. At least for as long as I could make a difference.

Perhaps Colonel Hunter guessed I wasn't completely human. I didn't care that he might know—that secret would remain with him, hidden behind eyes that were darker than his skin.

He knew of the vampires and werewolves employed by several security agencies—he had to, to consider the best ways to approach any security issue involving the country and its government.

I also understood that he'd died once, and I knew what had brought him back and the cost of that miracle.

Someone else had paid that price.

I missed her.

"I'm thinking about a trip to Ecuador," I said, shoving those thoughts aside.

"For a vacation?" Colonel Hunter's eyebrows rose. If I said yes, he wouldn't believe it for a minute. He also would never say otherwise, if asked.

"Sure. I hear the beaches have interesting things washing up from time to time."

"You wouldn't mind shipping souvenirs back, would you?"

He was telling me that he wanted evidence, if we found any. That included bodies we found ahead of the local authorities.

"Sure thing," I shrugged.

I had another reason for going, too, but I didn't want to say it here. I wanted to search for shifters in the area, both on land and in the water. They'd have tales to tell, and I needed that information.

"Let me know if you need money before you buy my souvenirs," Colonel Hunter nodded.

He was giving my attempt at espionage a green light and funding, too.

"Thank you, Colonel Hunter," I nodded my acceptance.

Peru

Laurel Rome

Hannah was young, dark-haired and sultry-eyed. She owed that to me. "What do you want?" she asked petulantly.

"I want you to go to Las Vegas," I said. "Charlene may not be able to do this by herself, so you'll have to help her."

"Help her with what?" Hannah examined her fingernails. She'd just had them painted a neon-pink. It looked good against her tanned skin and she knew it. Word had it that she'd warmed Deris' bed a few times, but then Hannah never discriminated if a willing cock were involved.

"Help her get rid of that colossal pain in my ass Kory Wilson, that's what," I hissed at her. Really, could she get any more obtuse than she already was?

"Kory Wilson?" Hannah perked up immediately. She wanted to bed him—I understood things better, now.

"Yes. That's the one. I don't care how you and Charlene do it, just get rid of him, all right?"

"Sure," a slow smile spread across her lips. "When do I leave?"

"Start packing now. Charlene's already there, getting things ready for the fight between Lover Boy Landon and Snark Demonio."

"Ooh, I interviewed Lover Boy once," Hannah gushed.

"Look, I don't care who you screw while you're there. Just get rid of Kory Wilson. Deris and his Uncle say he's the biggest threat to our operation, so we have to get him out of the way."

"All right." Hannah turned and swished her hips as she walked out. I began to wonder how many times I'd regret saving the ass that she swayed so seductively at anyone willing to watch.

~

Lexsi

"Kory," I said as he unwrapped my hands so I could take a shower.

"What, baby?" He kept his eyes on his work, unwrapping the gauze as carefully as he could.

"I'm really sorry. About the wedding. The bar. Everything."

He raised his head and looked at me, then. "Onion, an apology isn't necessary. If I'd had any sense at all back then, I'd have realized how uncomfortable you'd be. I'd have gone to the King myself and demanded that we meet ahead of time, just to make you more comfortable. If my dad ever speaks to me again, I'm still going to ask him to present a modification of the laws at a Council meeting. People need to meet before they're forced to marry. And they need a say, in case marrying that person is the last thing they want to do."

"I love you," I sighed. I watched his mouth as a slow grin developed.

"I love you too. If we could, I'd kiss you right here and now. But that scares you, so we won't." He went back to unwrapping bandages.

"People have sex without kissing," I said, causing his hands to stop. Slowly he lifted his eyes to mine again. I will never forget what he said to me, then.

"Onion, I love you. More than anything. Unless I am very, very wrong, this will be your first time. A High Demon's claiming marks do more than just mark a female as his, did you know that?"

"What else does it do?" Somehow, I'd never heard this part. I'd been willing to have sex with him, as long as we didn't kiss on the mouth. I was about to learn something about it that I didn't know.

"It creates the linking." He went back to unwrapping my bandages. "The linking," he explained before I had to ask, "Is a mental bonding between the pair. It feeds off the desires of the mated High Demons, and bounces back five or tenfold. I've heard that once the linking starts during foreplay, that the sex that follows is the most intensely satisfying you could ever hope for. Baby," his eyes bored into mine, "I want that for your first time, all right? That you find it not painful, but highly satisfying. We're not having sex until then. Okay?"

"Okay." My reply was small. Almost a whisper. I had no idea.

None.

"Look," Kory touched the flesh on my left hand.

My gaze dropped and I gasped. My hand—it looked almost normal.

"Flex," Kory instructed. I curled my fingers, then straightened them. Everything worked perfectly. Tears of joy ran down my cheeks as he unwrapped my other hand.

I wasn't going to be crippled or scarred for the rest of my life. I flung my arms about Kory's neck when he finished; he held me, murmuring soft words of love.

CHAPTER 7

"Take it easy for a day or two," Kory cautioned as I considered what I wanted to cook for dinner.

"All right," I made a face at him. I was so excited to have the use of my hands back that I wanted to do everything at once. "What do you suggest?"

"Soup and bread?" He sounded hopeful. "You know, that seafood stew and homemade bread you make?"

"That's easy enough," I agreed. "You can shell and devein shrimp, then chop tomatoes, celery, peppers and onions. I'll use the mixer to knead the dough. We need to go to the store, though," I said, pulling out my cell phone to make a list. "I'd really like to go to that fish market down by the wharf. They usually have crab claws. I want those for an appetizer."

"You just got a free skip to the fish market," he grinned at me. "Put a jacket on, baby, I'll take you."

Kory stayed close the whole time I picked out locally caught drum, then added crab claws and shrimp. After a quick skip home to put that in the fridge, we went to my favorite supermarket in the city for the other items on my list, including fresh tomatoes, celery and peppers.

"I got the check for my Jeep," he said. "Want to go out tomorrow and pick out something new to replace it?"

"Really? I've never picked out a vehicle before."

"Then you get to help," he pulled me close while I bagged up green and red bell peppers.

"I think I'm more excited about that than cooking dinner," I said, turning to pat his cheek. "And I'm really excited about cooking."

"Did they just not let you out much?" he asked quietly, dark eyes narrowing in concern.

"Dad always said it was dangerous to let me go places unless I had a huge crowd with me, half of which were guards," I sighed. "That carried over while I was in the Advanced Academy on Wyyld II. I never got to shop for groceries by myself until I came here. Yes, I know I'm related to royalty," I held up a hand. "But every once in a while, I just wanted to feel normal."

"I'm about as normal as you can get, for my race," Kory shrugged. He looked good in his zippered fleece jacket, his wide shoulders filling it out completely, while muscles rippled beneath.

"You worked hard, didn't you—while you were in the army?"

"As a Captain of the Guard, it's sort of a requirement," he said.

"Well, Mr. Normal, you've turned my head, that's for sure." I watched his grin as it flashed briefly.

"You turn everybody's head," Kory leaned in to whisper as I placed a bunch of celery into my basket.

"Everybody will have to be disappointed," I teased. "I found what I wanted."

"Stop selling syrup and let somebody else in," the man behind us demanded.

"Oh, is there a problem?" Kory rounded on him.

"I need celery. Like yesterday," the man insisted, although he did back up two steps. Kory was taller, broader and much more imposing.

"Baby, give him the best celery they have," Kory turned back to me. "He's in a hurry. Looks like he works for the guy you interviewed awhile back."

When Kory stepped aside, I saw the hotel restaurant's name on the man's jacket. "Yeah, he needs celery, all right," I grabbed six good bunches and handed them off to him.

"You interviewed Luigi?" the man gaped while clutching the celery to his chest.

"She did. She worked for News Seventy-Four until they shut down," Kory said.

"Are you looking for work?" he asked. "The hotel has an opening in PR."

"No," I shook my head. "I have another job already. But thank you."

"What do you think of Luigi? Honestly?" he asked.

"She'll never say it, so I will," Kory said. "He's an overbearing ass."

"Yeah. I hear that a lot. Look, thanks for picking the celery for me," he said. "I hope I get to see you again."

Kory and I watched Luigi's assistant walk away for several seconds before he pulled a ringing cell phone from a pocket. "I'll be there soon," he said and broke into a trot toward the registers.

"My mother is a hundred times the cook that Luigi is, and she never acted like a tyrant." I shook my head.

"Luigi can't compete with you, onion. Your mom is awesome. I think you're just as awesome."

I had no idea where Watson caught up with Anita, but they came back to the house together, with Watson's arm linked with hers.

Anita looked as if she'd been kissed a few times.

I hoped Watson could sort out his priorities well enough, so that neither suffered through the process. My guess was that Watson was also very worried about rebuilding the local Pack, and that wouldn't be an easy thing.

"Fish stew?" Watson begged me to say yes.

"With crab claw appetizers," Kory grinned. "It'll be ready, soon."

"That bread smells like heaven," Anita sniffed.

"I don't know where you learned to cook, but you must have passed with flying colors," Jamie observed as he walked into the kitchen. I smiled—the scent of good food cooking or baking always brought people together.

"I learned at my mother's and my uncle's restaurants. In Targis," I said.

"Targis?" Jamie asked.

"The capital city on Tulgalan," I said.

"Another place I've never been," Jamie chuckled. "Maybe you should take me there, sometime, so I can eat at both places."

"We'll have to ask," Kory said. He was thinking the same as I—that it was Tulgalan in the future and not now.

Kory's cell phone rang as we were getting dinner on the table.

Tibby was calling, asking him to go a few rounds.

We all went to Tibby's gym after dinner—Jamie included, because he wanted to watch. "Are you sure?" Kory asked Tibby as Diego placed boxing gloves onto Kory's wrapped hands and tucked the Velcro fastener snugly across the bottom.

"You're the only one who's given me any competition—and ended up beating my tail," Tibby grumbled. "I need to know where I stand, brother."

"Is he serious?" Jamie turned to me to ask.

"It's what Kory and I are," I attempted to explain. "Most humanoids and shifters can't move as fast. Only a vampire would give Kory a hard workout. If the vampire brought his claws into play, that would be the end of it, unless Kory turned. Kory doesn't have claws so long and sharp they can split hairs."

"Are you serious?" Jamie revised his question while looking worried.

"Yes, but we don't have a vampire in this fight. With Tibby, Kory will probably hold back—Tibby needs his full strength and no injuries for the fight in Vegas."

"Lover Boy isn't that tough," Jamie sniffed. "I've seen him fight."

I think I began to suspect something was up then, but I kept it to myself. Tibby and the rest of us would leave for Vegas in three days. I'd tell Kory then, and we'd decide what to do about it. It made me wish Kell had come, or that Klancy had been awake to come to the gym with us; Klancy was a martial artist before he was vampire. Maybe he could give us advice.

Nevertheless, the beginning of an unnamed fear crawled along the base of my spine and I didn't like it at all.

Kordevik

Tibby was in top shape for his fight in Vegas and I told him so when we were done. In my opinion, the fight with Lover Boy Landon would be a short one, with Tibby's hand raised by the referee over an unconscious opponent.

"I wish I had your speed," Tibby said as Diego removed his gloves. Tibby's brother, León, worked on the borrowed ones I still wore, pulling the Velcro straps up before taking them off my hands. The hand wraps I could remove myself, once the gloves were off.

"Man, you'd have to be born into my race," I shook my head. "As much as you might want that, you could have second thoughts on some of the drawbacks."

"Perhaps you will explain that to me soon," Tibby nodded. "After the fight."

"Sure. Anytime," I agreed.

"We wondered where you were." Mason, Klancy, Davis and Thomas arrived and came to stand beside us. Klancy, like an old pro, began to unwrap my hands. I held the one he'd started on higher, so he could reach it easier.

"I asked for a short bout, to gauge my strengths and weaknesses," Tibby explained. "Kory says I'm fit."

"You train?" Klancy asked as he unwrapped my left hand in record time and motioned for my right hand.

"The uh, High Demon army has tournaments every year. Rules are almost the same."

"Do you place highly?" Klancy was now finished with my right hand.

"Usually," I admitted. I didn't tell him that High Demons used their fists—no gloves were allowed. High Demons healed easily. Humans and some shifters didn't. Gloves were a good idea, in the long run.

"Good," Klancy nodded. "Perhaps you will agree to spar with me, sometime? I promise to keep my gloves on and claws retracted." Klancy smiled for a brief moment.

"Sure. You'll probably lay me in the dust in no time," I said. "I don't think I've ever taken on a vamp before."

"Uncle Aurelius taught me a lot about hand fighting." Lexsi made her way to my side. "He's vampire."

Klancy turned to Lexsi, then. "Aurelius? There are stories about an Earth vampire named Aurelius. Dead long ago, of course," Klancy observed.

"Maybe we should discuss Uncle Aurelius sometime," Lexsi smiled up at him. "I think he'd like you a lot."

"What's up?" I turned to Davis and Thomas.

"We have some intel on the Devangi woman. Her high-roller suite in Vegas got a bit more crowded yesterday. We have some photographs, but don't recognize two of the people. Not in any of our databases, either."

"We'll take a look," I said and lifted myself off the stool I sat on. "Can it wait until we get home? Lexsi made enough food for an army earlier, so there's a good meal in it for you if you want it."

"They both give me the shivers," Lexsi said as we examined the photographs together at the kitchen island. "I don't know why," she added.

The woman looked Hispanic, with honey-colored skin, dark eyes and darker, straight hair that hung nearly to her waist. Pretty enough, but the sour expression she wore made her ugly, in my opinion. The man was taller, with brown hair, green eyes and wore an expensive, dark suit.

"I wish we had video," Lexsi mumbled.

"Why?" Davis looked up from his bowl of fish stew to ask.

"Mannerisms—the way people move—if these have a duplication spell on them, we might be able to tell who they are from another standpoint," I answered for her. I'd learned that from Kell, in the brief time I'd known him.

"I'll see if our agents tailing them can get video," Thomas pulled out his cell phone and tapped out a text.

"Have you seen them during daylight?" Klancy peered over our shoulders at the two individuals.

"Not yet, but I'll ask about that, too," Thomas tapped out a second text. "Damn, why didn't we think of this?" he turned to Davis.

Davis, whose mouth was full of food, merely shrugged.

Tibby, Farin, Diego and León ate with the others, but listened intently as we discussed the happenings in Vegas. I hated that information was being handed to them in this way, but there wasn't any help for it. Charlene Devangi was plotting—although there wasn't anything concrete to accuse her of at this point.

"You know," Lexsi pulled the photograph off the island and held it up for a closer inspection, "Hannah used to hold her mouth that way when she was pissed about something."

"Holy fuck," Davis growled and dialed Opal on his cell phone one-handed. Before the conversation was over, Opal informed Davis that she and Kell were meeting us in Vegas.

Lexsi

Jamie and I went with Kory in the TinyCar to a Jeep dealership the following morning. Kory was intimidating enough, but Jamie evidently knew everything there was to know about buying a new car. Between them, they had a new Jeep purchased for a reasonable price before an hour had passed.

Jamie drove the TinyCar back to the house while I rode with Kory in his new vehicle. No, it wasn't the top of the line or the fanciest, but it was new and I learned how to negotiate for a vehicle.

Kory took me to lunch, and when we got back to the house, Davis and Thomas had arrived with video of the woman I'd pegged as Hannah. The man, oddly enough, was nowhere to be seen in the early-morning hours in Las Vegas.

Kory and I watched the video several times. Every time, all I could see was Hannah's mannerisms and the way she spoke rudely to a valet as Charlene's car was brought to them at their hotel.

"I just get chills every time I hear her speak or see her move," I shook my head. Sure, somebody else could move and speak like Hannah, but not that much like her.

"We'll keep tabs on both, and have someone track the guy if he leaves the suite," Davis took his tablet back. "We're providing a private jet for your flight to Vegas in two days. I hope Tibby doesn't mind—Opal is concerned about him just as much as she's concerned about the rest of you."

While the weather was usually chill in San Francisco during late October, it was ideal in Las Vegas. Anita and I surveyed the clothing spread across my bed, attempting to decide what I should take.

"I'd say nice jeans and blouses, with one dress for a night out—have you ever seen a big fight in Vegas?"

"No. Have you?" I turned to her.

"Only on television," she pursed her lips. "But the people who show up for those things can get really dressy. It always amazes me that they want to look as fancy as they can to watch two men beat each other up."

"I don't want to see Tibby get beaten up," I said. "Farin will faint."

"What would you do?"

"Be pissed enough to go after his opponent."

"Not good," Anita frowned. "We don't want the world at large watching a short blonde beating the hell out of Lover Boy Landon."

"At least you acknowledge that I can do it."

"Hell, I can do it," Anita snorted.

"True. What are you packing?"

"Watson made me pack two dresses," she huffed. "I'm not fond of dresses."

"Since when can Watson make you do anything?"

A slow smile curved her mouth. "Oh. Never mind," I turned away to study my clothes again. Since Watson admitted he sort of cared about Anita, they'd been to bed together every night, while Kory and I, well.

Mason, too, was slowly working his charm on Sandra, so it probably wouldn't be long for them, either.

Everybody got sex except me.

It had to be good, right? Everybody was doing it every chance they got. I wanted to do it; Kory wanted to wait until I wanted the bite that went with it. Honestly, being High Demon and female sucked most of the time.

"Take that red dress." Kory walked in and weighed in on the clothing situation while I silently bemoaned the race of my birth.

"I've never worn it. Red looks good on other people, but I always feel like I'd look like a neon light," I said.

"Nah, take it. I'll take you out for a nice dinner, somewhere, if we can get away." He pulled me against his chest and wrapped arms around me from behind, while breathing on my left ear. *Wear it for me, onion,* he pleaded.

I'll wear it for you, I promised. *You have to dress up, too, you know.*

Davis brought me a suit. It'll have to do.

Okay.

"What if that woman really is Hannah? What if she isn't under a duplication spell?" I wondered aloud. "If that's a brain transfer, I'll bet she's pissed they didn't find a body with blonde hair for her to exploit."

"And the body everyone thought was Hannah's was an innocent victim," Anita sighed. "Just as Lexsi thought."

Kory hugged me tighter for a moment.

"I'll take one pair of heels," I said, pulling away from Kory. "Not too high—I hate running in heels."

"Who said you had to?" Kory looked disappointed.

"Just in case. You never know about these things," I said. "I sure as hell don't want to beat the crap out of Hannah while wearing heels."

"Oh, no," Anita chuckled. "Wear those heels. Put some holes in her ass while I watch."

"Take these," Kory lifted the black pair of three-inch heels with the narrow straps that went around my ankles and buckled with tiny, gold buckles. "They'll cause some righteous holes."

"We don't know for sure it's Hannah," I pointed out.

"What does your gut say?" Watson wandered in and put his arms around Anita.

"It's her." I hung my head and sighed.

~

Tibby, León and Diego were more than happy to board a private jet with us to fly to Vegas. Farin was so excited she vibrated with joy. Not only was she riding in style with Tibby, but she had a huge, new engagement ring on her finger.

Yeah, if Tibby won, it would add around a hundred million to his bank account. "Maybe we should rethink your employment as a fighter," I teased Kory.

"No." He rubbed his nose against mine and settled into the seat beside me.

"Okay." I wanted to kiss him. Really, really kiss him.

Right. Then.

I sighed and dropped my head against his chest. Perhaps he knew what I was thinking and kissed the top of my head before gently pushing me upright in my seat and checking my seat belt.

"You know, between you, Anita and me, we could get everybody off the plane if it were necessary."

"You'd let it crash with nobody on it?"

"No. I think," I turned to him and blinked. "I think I could turn the whole thing to mist and put it in a safe place while you and Anita got the others off."

"Let's not talk about emergency measures," Anita turned in her seat to look back at me. "Flying makes me queasy enough."

"Sorry." I understood she'd rather fold space than ride in a jet, even for such a short flight.

"We have news," Davis stood beside Kory's seat. "A recon plane flying near Peru's border just got shot down. Word is that it was obliterated before the pilot and crew could eject."

"One of ours?" Watson turned in his seat to ask.

"UN," Davis replied. "Sort of makes it worse—they weren't armed while they investigated one of the passes, where bodies have been piling up."

"There are bodies piling up? I only heard about women," Kory began.

"This looked like a mass grave. We didn't tell you, because we had no solid information. The images sent back from that plane before it was shot down are pretty damning."

"Sounds like the Peruvians didn't like the takeover of their country."

"We think that, too, and the Secretary of State is demanding answers. He's as likely to get a reply as he is to fly to the moon in a motorboat."

"We'll have a meeting after we land in Vegas," Davis said before heading back to his seat. "Opal and Kell will be waiting for us."

"Too many things happening at once," Kory grumbled as the jet lurched forward.

~

Watson, Anita, Sandra and Mason went with Tibby to the hotel hosting the fight; Kory, Klancy and I went with Thomas and Davis to meet with Opal at a different hotel.

Kell and Klancy nodded at each other when we arrived; they liked and respected one another already.

"This is what the UN Peacekeeper plane sent back before they were blown out of the sky," Opal tapped a tablet to bring images onto the screen.

"That's inexplicable," Kory blew a smoky breath.

It was inexplicable. I'd seen similar photographs from the past in countries that engaged in genocide, killing off large portions of their populations because of race, beliefs or other, equally as disturbing reasons.

"These bodies are mostly intact," Klancy observed.

"Yes," Opal agreed.

"This means that the weapons turned on that plane—and upon Kory recently, were not employed in these deaths, otherwise, there would be very little left to photograph." Klancy spoke, but Kell nodded his approval; they'd reached the same conclusion.

"That's why we need to go in—while there are still bodies left," Opal's eyes were dark and unblinking. "We need to collect a few at least, to determine the way in which they were killed. It'll give us better ammunition when we approach the President and the Secretary of State again."

"When?" Kory asked.

"Tonight. Kell and I are prepared to go with you. We have special suits and body bags ready."

"You think they'll get rid of the evidence, don't you?" Kory asked.

"That's exactly what we think. You can skip us down," Opal added.

"Then let's go," Kory said simply. I nodded at his words.

I took Opal, Kell and Davis with me; Kory took Thomas and Klancy with him. Opal had given us detailed photographs of where she wanted each of us to land, and, as all would stay within a few feet of Kory and me, they'd be protected from any spells lobbed in our direction.

The plan was as sound as we could make it on such short notice. Kell and Davis held two body bags apiece, as did Klancy and Thomas.

Opal checked her weapons before we left Las Vegas for the mountain pass on the border of Peru—she was armed to the teeth, as Gran would say.

The first part of our plan was executed flawlessly. I set my crew down at the designated point; Kory did too, about a hundred yards away.

The stench from rotting corpses assaulted my nose; it had to be a hundred times worse for Kell and Davis.

Bodies had been tossed carelessly in a heap, like a fallen game of stacking logs. "Probably been here close to a week," Opal covered her nose with a hand and strode after Kell and Davis.

"No!" I shouted before Davis could reach out with a gloved hand to pull a body off the pile and stuff it into a body bag.

He stopped immediately.

I heard Kory's Thifilathi roar from yards away as the mass of bodies exploded into a seething pile of snakes.

Kell was ahead of me, turning Davis and Opal to mist. I misted toward Kory, whose Thifilathi held Klancy and Thomas in his arms while huge snakes lunged and bit at his scaled legs and wings.

No poison can harm a High Demon, I reminded myself of that while enveloping Kory and his burden inside my mist.

Rising above, I could see that only the edges of the enormous pile of corpses hid snakes.

Kory, can you skip home with the others? I sent. *Kell has Opal and Davis in his mist, but he can't transport them back to Vegas.*

I will. What are you going to do?

Gather a few bodies in my mist. I'll be there in a few, just—get a space ready for me to dump them.

Baby, no, he objected immediately.

I don't think they'll harm my mist, I said. *Opal needs them. Just—make sure everything is locked and quarantined before you tell me where to drop them.*

Kory cursed in the High Demon language—for what felt like

forever. He didn't like the idea that any corpse could come in contact with me—even my mist.

I felt ill at the prospect, but what else was there to do?

Just do it for me. Please?

I'll do it, Opal's mental voice intervened. *I'll get them back; show up here,* she sent a mental image of a forensics lab located at a military base outside Las Vegas.

I'll be there in a few, I said, stunned that Opal would be the one to get the others back. I was learning that there was more to Opal than I originally thought.

Perhaps she and I needed to talk.

After I took bodies to a lab, then heaved into a toilet after a long, hot shower.

～

Kordevik

I wasn't sure how she'd done it, but Opal folded space to get the others and me back to Vegas. We landed at a military facility in Henderson, a suburb of Las Vegas. I hit the ground cursing. She didn't attempt to stop me.

The others blinked as my smaller Thifilathi stomped from one end of the room to the other, waiting for Lexsi to arrive with the bodies.

"What kind of snakes were those?" Davis stretched his arms and shoulders, as if folding space caused them to cramp.

"Not native to here," I snapped in guttural English. My Thifilathi, when angry, has difficulty forming words. I didn't want to change in front of the others, either; I'd be naked.

One of the downsides that I hadn't yet told Tibby about.

"The bodies are here." A voice sounded over an intercom. "Do we ah, need to provide you with anything else? There's a naked girl in the hallway outside, puking her guts out."

"We'll take care of it," Opal said. "Kory, let's go get her."

I sheepishly followed Opal out of the room, breathing smoke the whole way.

CHAPTER 8

*L*exsi
"I'm not dying. I just can't stop gagging," I said.

I had a cold, wet cloth covering my eyes and forehead, as I lay flat on my back on a hotel bed. I'd dry heave every time I thought about carrying decaying corpses in my mist, so I had to attempt to block those thoughts.

"I told Opal I'm not going anywhere until you feel better," Kory insisted.

"You have to go help Tibby and the others," I mumbled.

"I'm calling in sick."

"You're not sick."

"How did they get those snakes from Verbaan?" Kory asked, changing the subject.

"The same way they got their sorry asses here," I snapped. For a moment, I sounded like Gran. Verbaanese adders weren't the most poisonous snakes in the Alliances, but they came close.

Somebody had gone to a lot of trouble to stuff dead bodies with nasty snakes who could kill humans in moments. Werewolves or shifters could take longer, but they'd be just as dead—it took a special antivenin to counteract the poison.

The snakes didn't make me sick, although the memory of snakes crawling from bloating, rotted bodies could.

I barely hung my head over the side of the bed before I began to heave into the wastebasket again. Nothing was coming up; I felt like crap and Kory rubbed my back, hoping I'd stop heaving soon.

"Look at it this way," he said, sounding philosophical. "If we ever have kids, we'll be well-prepared for morning sickness."

"You want kids?" I coughed out between dry heaves.

"Well," he shrugged. "I might. Plus, Dad would love to be a grandfather. He's never been one, you know. My mother would dance a jig and taunt Jaydevik Rath for hours."

"Because Jayde's daughters have never had children?" I breathed a sigh and flopped back on the bed—looked like this bout of heaves was over.

"Not yet," Kory grinned at me.

"I didn't realize it was a contest."

"It's not. I'm just speculating."

"Would your parents be that happy?" I asked.

"I'm being conservative, in my estimation."

"Kory?"

"What, baby?"

"We need to plan our kiss."

His eyes widened at my statement. "But," he began.

"I think we should plan it. Set a date. Look at it this way, if we'd gone through with our wedding, it would have already happened, right?"

"Probably," he nodded after a moment.

"I love your eyes," I said. "And your mouth. I want to know what your kiss feels like. We just have to get over the initial—bump in our relationship, first. How long will I be out? Will it disable me in any way?"

"I'm not sure how long you'll sleep. You shouldn't be disabled— that's supposed to be how it works."

"Because I can't afford to be disabled in any way—not while this mess is going on."

"I hear that." Kory slid off the bed to stand and stretch. "We'll think of something, all right? Come on, onion, get fresh clothes on and let's go help the others."

❧

Opal

"Looks like those victims were hit with several black spells," I said, sitting across the table from Kell. We were waiting in the coffee shop downstairs for Lexsi and Kory to arrive. I hoped Lexsi was over the dry heaves—I felt bad enough about that as it was.

"Using power to cause organs to explode is the cowardly way to kill. That alone would garner an immediate death sentence, were the one responsible standing before the King of Karathia."

"Either one—the current King or the King of the future," I agreed. "Although Rylend wouldn't waste time asking questions, I think."

"We know how things turn out in the future, although we also know the past can alter those events, should it change in any way." Kell's dark eyes were unreadable as he toyed with his mug of tea.

"Yes. I've seen it happen before," I agreed. "I've seen sacrifices made to make things come out right, too—when the timeline was altered too much."

"At least these bodies the young one transported for us did not contain snakes. That is also as vile as a witch or warlock can get, defiling the dead in such a way."

"I can't believe we have to hunt those snakes down—they don't belong on this planet," I complained. "The only good thing is that they're used to warm weather. Here, they're high in the mountains. I hope they freeze to death before they bite anybody else."

"My dear, there are many things they have brought here that do not belong," Kell said quietly. "We will handle this."

My breath caught when he called me dear. Somehow, Kell Abenott made me feel young again, and I hadn't felt young for centuries.

❧

Lexsi

Tibby's suite was huge and sat atop the casino hosting the fight. When Kory and I walked in, people were everywhere. We were introduced to Tibby's agent and his agent's assistant. Tibby then led me to the ones he considered most important in the room—his mother and grandmother.

"Abuela, these are the ones who saved Farin and me," he introduced us, first.

I blinked in confusion for a moment at his grandmother. Yes, I knew she was a Packmaster in San Diego. What I hadn't realized was that she was also a ranking member of the California State Legislature.

"Mrs. Riveras, it is such a pleasure to meet you," I held out my hand. I couldn't help smiling at her; she wore a huge smile in return.

"You are both members of my family, from now on," Maria Riveras announced as she refused my handshake and pulled me into a hug instead. "My Tiburon has explained that without your help, he and Farin would be dead."

"It was the least I could do," I shrugged. "They're my friends and I love them."

"They are your family, now," she said. "Jenita, help me welcome your new daughter and son into the family."

Jenita, Tibby's mother, looked so much like Tibby. She smiled shyly and hugged Kory and me while speaking softly in Spanish. She welcomed us into the family in her native language.

"My husband wished to be here, but he had to work—he is the Chief of Police for the city," Jenita explained.

"And the local Packmaster for our kind," Maria winked at us. "Come, sit. Drinks and food are coming."

"Think you can eat?" Kory lifted an eyebrow at me while we followed Senator Maria Riveras to sofas set beside floor-to-ceiling glass walls. The view of Las Vegas from those windows was spectacular. Yes, I'd seen images on television and in movies, but this was my first time to see it in reality.

Casino City on Gran's planet was smaller, but glittered in much the same way. "I think my stomach has settled," I whispered as I sat on a sofa beside Tibby's grandmother.

"I hear you're an amazing cook," I turned to her. "Tibby says you make amazing enchiladas."

"I'll teach you sometime," she smiled and patted my hand.

"I would love that," I said, my words sincere.

"Tomorrow is the weigh-in," Tibby said. He settled Farin on the sofa opposite ours before sitting beside her. His drink was juice; everyone else had something alcoholic at hand. Farin looked as if she were in a daze—as could be expected of a sudden engagement, followed closely by a championship fight involving her new fiancé.

"That PR nightmare where you're expected to stare down your opponent?" Kory asked while accepting a glass of Scotch from Diego.

"That's the one. I hate those," Tibby shook his head. "Save it for the fight, man."

I didn't want to tell him what concerned me; that Charlene, Hannah and whoever was with them planned a nasty surprise for Tibby by employing a duplication spell and putting a bigger, nastier opponent in the ring.

"Is there some way I can get close to Lover Boy Landon?" I asked. "Not tomorrow, but just before the fight?"

"What the hell are you suggesting?" Kory demanded.

"I'm just concerned that somebody could make a substitution, that's all," I said.

Tibby cursed softly. His mother and grandmother looked at me in alarm.

"I think this is something to discuss with Opal," Davis said, handing me a glass of wine. "After the big blow up in San Francisco, we're a little worried ourselves."

"Do we have more information on the man with Charlene?" I asked Davis, who settled cross-legged on the floor at the end of our sofa.

"Nothing yet. He hasn't stuck his nose out of her suite again. Maybe he's worried they're being followed—because they are."

"If he's vampire, he'd know by scent," Klancy volunteered.

"Is this something I should be aware of?" Maria was suddenly acting in a governmental capacity.

"Mrs. Riveras, there are strange things happening. People are reported as dead who aren't really dead, because, well, they've traded places in a disguised sort of way, with someone else, leaving innocents to die in their place," I explained. "Loftin Qualls isn't really dead. We don't know who died in his place."

"*Madre de Dios*," she sighed. "Not what I wished to hear, you understand, but good information to have. I will keep this to myself."

"It's better for now if you can," Davis said. "Our special paranormal division is investigating this. If word got out, the population could panic. They're worried enough about the recent events in San Francisco. They don't need to worry that the same thing could happen anywhere."

"Is this tied to the Rome family?" Maria had hit it perfectly with her speculation.

"Mrs. Riveras," Jamie walked over to stand in front of her. "I'm living proof that what Lexsi says is true. I'm James Rome, Jr.," he said, extending his hand to her, "I'm very pleased to meet you."

Jamie was invited to a private meeting with Maria; Kory and I were included in the invitation.

"This is difficult to believe," Maria shook her head for perhaps the fourth time after studying Jamie's face. "Some other man, wearing your body? That is incredible."

"It feels that way at times," Jamie admitted. "I don't recognize myself in the mirror, I forget the sizes of my clothing; it's going to be a long battle," he acknowledged.

"They're in Peru, now—the ones responsible," I said. "Things are going on there that will terrify just about anyone."

"I miss you on the news," Maria patted my hand. "I believed what you said, because you spoke the truth. Those others," she waved her hand in dismissal.

"At times I miss it, too, but I'm needed more where I am," I said. "These people—I don't know what their plans are in Vegas, but I don't trust them."

"Me, either," Kory agreed. "Whatever it is, it isn't good. You can count on that."

"If Laurel is behind it, it will be bad," Jamie confirmed.

"She came from behind and did this to you?" Maria was still having difficulty with Jamie's situation.

"I realize now that my money was the most attractive thing to her. I came in a distant second, until Berke Gillson arrived to turn her head."

"All a part of the same plot, you think?" Maria's guess was a shrewd one.

"Yes. I think this was the way to get to her and to my bank accounts," Jamie agreed. "By the time I realized something was wrong and confronted her, they were ready for me. I still held important information, so they kept me alive by switching bodies." He tapped his chest.

"Does this mean you are penniless now?"

"Practically. I'm just waiting for this to be over, so I can begin to invest again. I don't intend to remain poor for long."

"I don't think you will," Maria agreed. "Meanwhile, we must protect your secret and my grandson's life. Yes?"

"Yes." Jamie nodded. "After all, if certain people see me here in Vegas, they'll know I'm not dead."

"You mean the enemy," I said. "Laurel. Those she's backing. Nobody else knows Berke Gillson or what he looks like."

"Stick close to me," Kory said. "I'll do what I can to keep them away from you."

"I think she wants both of us dead," Jamie leveled his gaze on Kory.

He'd said exactly what I was thinking.

Kory was worried, or he'd never have asked to sleep in the same bed. I said yes, and honestly, I didn't care if he ended up asking for sex without a kiss.

He didn't, though. He just wrapped his arms around me and I fell asleep with my head on his shoulder.

We skipped to Tibby's suite the following morning to have breakfast with him; the weigh-in was scheduled at eight in the evening and there was still training to do before then.

Jamie stayed at our hotel, with Thomas and Sandra acting as guards for him, Klancy and Mason. The vamps had to be protected during the day, while they slept in darkened rooms.

Peru

Laurel

"Granger?" I held the phone tighter against my ear, attempting to get better reception.

"We have seen him," came through, but it was garbled.

"Who? Kory Wilson?"

"No. We saw germy."

"Germy? Who the hell is that?" I demanded.

"No need constipate."

"Constipate?"

"Concern yourself."

"Concern myself about what? What did you mean, constipate?"

"(Crackle) deal with germy."

"If germy makes you constipated, then deal with it," I shouted and ended the call.

Opal

"We ah, intercepted a call," Davis reported.

"From?"

"From the device in Charlene Devangi's hotel suite."

"What did you find out?"

"First, the call came minutes after sunset."

"All right," I said after thinking about it for a few seconds. "By a male?"

"Yes."

I spoke with Davis over the phone; we'd had a listening device planted in Charlene's room for barely a day and a half, by one of our agents posing as housekeeping staff.

"You think it's Granger, don't you? What was the message?"

"Somebody in their party has seen Jamie. They have plans to take care of the situation, if I heard right. Didn't have time to get a fix on where the call went, but we're working on that."

"If we had Granger's phone, it would be easy," I pointed out.

"You ready to take him on?"

"I see your point. Let me work on this, while you find a safe place to stash Jamie."

"Will do, boss."

"Kell," I said after Davis ended the call, "I need your help."

Kordevik

"We need someone to transport Jamie to this location," Davis showed me a map and photographs of the safe house.

"I can do that. When?"

"Now?"

"All right. This means I won't be at the weigh-in," I cautioned.

"I know. Lexsi will be there. I hope that's enough."

"Watch out for her," I said before skipping to our hotel to find Jamie.

Opal

"What did you just say?"

Davis was on the phone again. It wasn't good news.

Jamie had left the hotel suite, when he'd been told to stay put.

According to Davis, Sandra was doing her best to explain to an angry High Demon that she hadn't thought anything of it when Jamie said he wanted to go downstairs to the casino for a few minutes. That had been half an hour ago. Sandra stayed behind, for no reason other than she wanted to talk to Mason after he woke.

I wanted to pound my forehead with a fist. I held off. "Tell her and the others to put their noses to work and find him. Pronto. If Granger finds him first, he's a dead man."

"Yeah. Got that, boss."

~

Jamie

It had been months since I'd had a cigar, and the wait for vampires to wake was boring enough. Nothing was on television worth watching, so I told Sandra I wanted to go downstairs for a minute or two.

No, I hadn't intended to stay gone so long, but the gift shop didn't have anything I wanted. The clerk told me that the brand of cigars I liked was sold at a casino six blocks away.

I hadn't had a long stroll in months, so I made the decision to go.

Halfway there, I realized I didn't have a phone or anything else on me. All I had was a temporary credit card that Opal had given me, in case I needed something.

I felt like cursing myself, but I was more than halfway to my destination when all those things finally hit me.

It's one thing to be young and stupid. It's worse to be old and stupid.

~

Kordevik

"Kory, stay here in case he comes back," Thomas said. "The rest of us will try tracking him by scent."

"Fine by me. I might consider punching him if I found him first," I said. I didn't try to hide the curls of smoke drifting from my nostrils. Lexsi would be at the weigh-in without me; Charlene and Hannah would certainly be there, and nobody knew who or what they could be bringing with them.

Yeah, I was pissed. One human could screw everything up and make everybody scramble, just to save his thoughtless ass.

Fuck.

I was mad enough to punch somebody through a wall, already. Therefore, when the door to the suite blew in and a vampire stepped into the room, I laughed as flames bloomed about me.

The laugh became a roar as my Thifilathi beckoned Granger forward. He wanted a fight?

He was about to get one.

~

Lexsi

"They strip down to their boxers?"

"Just watch," Anita soothed. "It may look like two roosters facing off after they weigh, but it's all a show."

"Right. Can we get any closer?"

The press of bodies around us thickened as Tibby shucked his jacket, shirt and warm-up pants before stepping on the scales.

"One hundred fifty-seven pounds for Tiburon, Snark Demonio, Diaz," somebody announced.

"Can you see?" Anita asked.

"I can't see anything," I huffed, attempting to wriggle forward in the crowd. I wasn't close enough to Lover Boy Landon to see if he were the real thing or whether he'd been replaced by someone else.

Go to mist, Anita suggested.

"Huh?" I blinked up at her as someone shoved into my back.

"Here." She jerked me in front of her, so nobody would see. I went to mist immediately and flew forward, to hang over Lover Boy's head.

He was the real deal, all right. I watched him remove his clothing before stepping onto the scale.

"One hundred fifty-nine for Lyle, Lover Boy, Landon," the man announced after examining the scale carefully.

The weight limit was one-sixty—Tibby had already explained that on the walk from the training facility.

Next came the stare off, while cameras were shoved in both faces.

We have a dilemma, Kell's voice sounded in my head. *The hotel suite is on fire, and well, Kory is chasing Granger through Las Vegas in his smaller Thifilathi, which is on fire.*

Kordevik

"Can you bury yourself more in a cliché?" I growled as I climbed a replica of the Empire State Building following Granger, whose claws helped him scale the vertical walls. I'd shut off most of my flames with much effort; my Thifilathi was so angry it wanted to burn half the city to kill Granger.

By this time, most of the city's news crews were likely on the scene, recording everything.

Fuck.

Here came another five-year sentence.

Granger reached a decorative window, pulled off chunks of it and threw them at me. My Thifilathi flamed again in response.

Climb faster, you idiot, someone spoke into my mind.

Opal.

Don't let him escape, someone else broke into the conversation.

Kell.

My claws on hands and feet bit into the façade of the building as I struggled up its height, following a vampire determined to elude my Thifilathi.

More detritus rained down on me as Granger became desperate. At least he had to stop for a second or two to claw out more of the façade to toss in my direction. I took the opportunity to leap and claw, leap and claw, digging my claws deep on the second leap to keep from falling while loose debris rained onto the ground far below.

I'd made up some distance between Granger and me, though.

Vampires seldom show emotion. I could almost see the fear in Granger's eyes; that's how close we were.

The trouble was, we were nearly to the top of the building; it was angling inward, bringing new sets of obstacles before we reached the top. Many yards away, another casino tower jutted, but it would be a terrifying leap even for a vampire, from such a height.

One the other hand, I could *fly*.

I snapped my wings open. Fire outlined their edges. Shoving away from the building, I flapped furiously to hold myself aloft at my current elevation.

Granger looked back in alarm.

Yes, he was at the point where he'd have to jump. Having settled myself in the air, I made my body into a flying arrow and went for him.

He leapt toward the other building and screamed while he did it.

In midair, before I could reach him, he disappeared.

I have him, Kell shouted mentally.

I have you, Lexsi's voice surrounded me. Her mist extinguished my fire as I relaxed inside her invisibility.

Somewhere, far below us, a crowd cheered.

This was Vegas.

They'd just seen the show of a lifetime.

～

Lexsi

"Don't ask. If you don't, I don't have to answer," Opal held up a hand as I stared at the powerlight cage that held Granger. It took a powerful warlock or witch to build a powerlight cage. Once built, it would hold another witch, warlock, or a vampire, even. Granger would be electrocuted if he touched any of the glowing bars surrounding him.

"It's a gift—from a friend," Opal admitted. "That's all I can say right now."

We were back at the military facility where I'd dropped bodies a day or so earlier. With everything that had happened since then, it felt like weeks had passed.

At least Kory was back to normal, although he was dressed in borrowed sweats provided by the military facility.

"Don't worry, we're calling the whole thing a publicity stunt," Davis explained to Kory, who was concerned about what he'd done.

Truthfully, Kory had done what he could—all he could—to keep Granger from getting away. Granger hadn't gotten away, either. He was right there, trapped in an inexplicable powerlight cage.

Kory and I were surprised we hadn't nullified the thing when we stood close to it. Opal merely shrugged and didn't explain that part.

Frankly, I thought Kory should be commended for his tenacity in chasing down Granger, even if he did end up climbing a scale model of the Empire State Building and gouging out chunks of it with his claws while doing it.

Granger had done the same with his vampire claws, plus his claw marks were deeper. He frowned at me from his cage; I doubted he wanted to see me again like this—him in a cage while I stared and shook my head.

"Boss, call from Sandra and Mason," Davis held his cell phone out for Opal to take.

Opal said hello and then listened for several minutes with Davis' phone pressed against her ear.

She doesn't look happy, Kory sent.

I'd already figured that out—a tight frown tugged at her mouth. Whatever Sandra and Mason told her wasn't good news.

Opal stabbed the end call button with a finger before handing the phone back to Davis. "Photographs were just delivered to Tibby's suite," Opal said. "They're of Jamie. They have him, and they want to trade for Granger."

CHAPTER 9

*L*exsi

"How and where did they find Jamie?" Kory asked.

"Sandra said his scent was mixed with two others—one of them vampire—outside a casino several blocks away from ours," Opal replied. "The scents disappear after that, so a car was likely involved in taking him away."

"We can get inside Charlene's suite," I offered.

"He's not there; we've got eyes inside and out of that place," Opal waved off my suggestion. "He's somewhere else, and who knows what shape he's in right now."

"I really don't want to let that bastard Granger go," Kory snorted smoke. "But if we have to, I want to make sure Jamie's alive and well, first."

"We're attempting to set up a location for the trade," Opal shook her head. "They'll kill him if we try anything other than a prisoner exchange."

"This is awful," I raked fingers through my hair. It was a tangled mess halfway down. No, I hadn't bothered looking in a mirror—too many things had happened since the weigh-in.

"You look fine," Kory pulled my fingers from my hair and set about combing his through it instead.

"We still don't know what they intend to pull during the fight," I began.

"Let's find out, shall we?" Kell walked past us to approach Granger's cage. Granger hissed at Kell the moment he came close—he knew by scent what Kell was.

Kell.

It hit me, then.

Kell was ancient. Very ancient as a vampire. The older the vamp, the stronger the compulsion. An older one would have a younger one doing cartwheels if he commanded it.

I doubted cartwheels were on Kell's mind, though. "You will do everything I say from this point forward," Kell's eyes locked with Granger's. I held my breath and watched as Granger's head dipped in an unwilling nod.

~

Opal

I sent everyone else out of the room except Lexsi and Kory, while Kell questioned Granger.

He didn't know specifics—he was centuries old as a vampire and wasn't ready to accept that people from other worlds had actually invaded his, with destruction on their minds.

Sure, somebody who Deris and Daris Arden worked for wanted to produce drakus seed. Granger didn't even know the name of the drug. He only knew it would fatten his bank accounts, none of which I could easily get to with mundane resources.

The name that troubled me most, however, was Morgett Blackmantle.

He was supposed to be dead. Currently and in the future. In fact, his death was reported long before his younger brother Hegatt died, more than twenty-thousand years in the past.

I figured he'd manufactured his death to escape the price the Reth

Alliance had on his head. I needed information about Morgett, but had the idea that Kell could know more than I in this matter.

Kell.

Born on Hraede who knew how many thousands of years ago. He intrigued me in ways I couldn't describe.

What we did learn is this; Granger said that Laurel wanted Jamie brought to her in Peru. He'd had plans to do that for her.

I hoped we could interrupt those plans; Jamie would be very, very dead if he ever crossed Peru's borders. *Laurel would see to it*, Granger said.

Laurel was becoming more of a problem every day. I wondered how she felt about innocent civilians in Peru being tortured and killed by Loftin Qualls and Vic Malone. Granger also didn't know where the N'il Mo'erti were—he barely had information on them, other than they were some kind of new weapon to use against the enemy, although he did confirm that a single N'il Mo'erti was used in San Francisco.

There was a huge crater, still, on land outside San Francisco where a peaceful vineyard should be.

I still didn't know exactly how Lexsi had managed to destroy the thing, or if she were responsible for the crater and not the N'il Mo'erti.

Granger, we also learned, was of the lazy sort, who preferred to place compulsion on minions to do or get what he wanted. Kell had less respect for Granger after the questioning than he did at the start; therefore, that ran into negative territory at the end.

Planning an ambush, I think, Kell turned to look at me after he'd asked his last question of Granger.

During the exchange? I returned.

I believe so. Whoever goes with Granger to make the exchange will have to be wary.

I suggest somebody who doesn't mind that his allies are mist behind him, I suggested.

Yes, Kell's eyes nearly closed, acknowledging my assessment.

My worry is this, I said. *That they won't bring the real Jamie.*

That is my worry as well.

I'm also concerned that they may want to make the exchange while the fight is happening. We can't have our resources in two places.

True. It is something I would do if I were they.

You think Morgett is calling the shots?

Perhaps in the background. I doubt he will make himself visible for long. The Reth Alliance will search him out, no matter where he is—even on a non-Alliance world.

I'm not sure involving the Alliance Security Detail is a good idea. I didn't explain why, but that had already been attempted in the past, with disastrous results.

You're thinking in the past. Shall we consider the future? A slow smile spread across Kell's features. My breath stopped for a few seconds as I committed the sight to memory.

Let me think on that, I said. I knew whom I'd like to ask for help, but didn't know if it were even possible. Many, many strings would have to be pulled, but then again, we had Morgett Blackmantle to deal with. This was a rift in the past that definitely hadn't happened the first time around.

Or the second.

~

Lexsi

Kell and Opal held a private conversation in mindspeech after Kell questioned Granger. I didn't want to interfere with that, so I studied Granger while Kory's arms went around me and his chin settled on top of my head.

Granger knew less than I'd hoped about the business in Peru with Laurel and the others. I was beginning to suspect that each of the players from Earth knew some things but not all.

Granger had no idea that Deris and Daris were a powerful warlock and witch, although he'd seen them do things he couldn't explain.

I really, really needed Anita's opinion, since Granger could be obsessed by a Sirenali. Nobody currently in the room could tell.

Granger could be centuries old and still susceptible to a Sirenali's words; not once had Granger mentioned anything about anyone capable of such things, although they had to have one at their disposal.

Kory and I stood close enough to Granger's cage to nullify any hidden spells placed on him. I worried that the information we'd gathered was obtained because we'd been that close. I surmised that hidden spells and an obsession could lie about Granger like a second skin, and we couldn't see or feel them.

More than enough to worry about, with Jamie in the hands of the enemy.

"I may ask for more help," Opal turned away from Granger's powerlight cage to look at Kory and me.

"Who?" I asked.

"I have to ask, first. I don't want to get any hopes up, especially my own."

"Yeah." I understood that, all right.

~

Kordevik

"It's just as we feared. They're demanding that the exchange take place during the fight," Kell informed us two hours later over dinner.

"And we can't be in two places at once." A tiny curl of smoke escaped my nostrils before I could stop it. Lexsi scooted closer against me. She liked Jamie and worried about him. As did I.

"What about the people we need to help?" Lexsi directed her question at Opal.

Somehow, Lexsi and I had begun to suspect that there was much more to Opal than we'd originally thought.

Much, much more.

A part of me worried that this fight—these events—had little to do with my punishment and more to do with placing Lexsi and me in a place and time when we were needed.

"I've got messages out. We'll know more in a few hours. One has to have permission. The other—is sort of held back—loosely, by the rules of noninterference." Opal smiled when she made her last statement, however, so I imagined that the one she spoke of had flaunted those rules in the past.

"What can they do for us?" I asked.

"It's just to fill in the holes to combat what we're facing," Opal said. "We don't have a warlock or a witch. I'm hoping to fill those vacancies in our army with a witch and a wizard."

"Anyone we know?" I asked, toying with my fork. A bit of crusted chocolate clung to the tines—Lexsi and I had shared a dessert. If we'd been alone, I'd have fed her from my fork and she'd have smiled at me.

Those thoughts were pushed aside as I considered that we were building an army.

It made sense, though. Laurel Rome and her cronies were an army and so far, they'd caused plenty of deaths and destruction on their way to mass producing the worst drug known to the Alliances.

"What are they doing in Peru—to get drakus seed to harvest?" I asked.

"We can't say for sure," Opal replied. "Recon planes are either shot down or come back with their recording devices fried. We haven't gotten images since the debacle in San Francisco."

"So we don't know how far along they may be, then."

"Yes. It's aggravating in the extreme."

"I understand they want to ship this off-world, but you know some of it will make its way onto the rest of this planet," I said. "Humans will die, because they won't be able to deny the visions and the addiction of the drakus seed."

"Yes. I know that all too well," Opal agreed as she set her napkin beside her plate and rested her hand there.

It didn't surprise me that Kell's hand covered hers for a moment, or that he squeezed her fingers gently before letting go. I think if they'd been alone, her head would be on his shoulder while he comforted her.

We can leave if you'd like, I sent to her.

It's all right, she said. *I have people to contact and arguments to make so I can get the help we need.*

~

Lexsi

"Hard to tell," Anita sighed as she turned toward me. I'd taken her to see Granger after dinner. Before, she and Watson had been guarding Tibby and his family with Mason and Sandra. Klancy was doing reconnaissance at Charlene and Hannah's hotel with Thomas and Davis.

"What does that mean?" I asked as she grabbed my arm and pulled me out of the room. Our walk along a lengthy hallway seemed to take forever; Anita waited longer than that before she spoke again.

"He can hear for miles, and he's obsessed. I'm worried there may be an implant," Anita whispered. I stared at her in alarm. We hadn't thought of that. A mundane implant could be passing information to who knows what—or to whom.

"And they may have heard all of Kell's questions and Granger's answers," I mumbled, hanging my head. Yes, I was a difik.

A big difik.

I hadn't realized I'd said it aloud until Anita asked me what difik meant.

"It's High Demon for idiot," I shook my head. "Which is what I am."

"You're not an idiot; they have a physician who can do a brain transfer. It makes sense that he could use not-so-legal technology to gather information through an unsuspecting host."

"I can't believe he may have done this with a vampire," I hissed.

"You know how much money may be at stake. They'll stop at nothing," she pointed out.

"Yeah. Damn. I'm just not thinking big picture enough," I rubbed my forehead.

"You're worried about Jamie. So am I," Anita frowned. "We just have to worry about ourselves, too, you know?"

"Yeah." I hunched my shoulders. I suddenly felt more uncomfortable than I had before, and a headache formed behind my eyes.

I wanted Kory. I wanted his arms around me and I wanted all this mess over with. That wasn't going to happen. Not anytime soon, anyway.

Love, affection and all that went with it took an unwelcome back seat to the troubles lying before us. I'd begun to realize just how sheltered my life had been before. Nothing threatened me, then. My past worries weren't even classified as worries compared to this.

"First things first," Anita said, pulling me into a hug. "We have to get Jamie back. Then we have to find a way to deal with the mess in Peru."

"We have to protect Tibby and Farin, too," I sighed, pulling away. "They're vulnerable. She's completely human, and we've already seen that he'll risk everything to protect her."

"Yeah. Nice to have that in a man," she said.

"Please tell me Watson isn't being a difik again," I begged.

"He's—well, every spare moment, he's on the phone with the Grand Master and other Packmasters, asking for help and advice to put the San Francisco Pack back together."

"If my head didn't already hurt, it would start now," I shook my head at her. "The world is falling apart and he's worried about the unrelated details."

"I thought I might find you here," Opal walked down the hall to join us.

"Granger has an obsession, and he may have an implant," Anita sighed.

"That's—not good," Opal said. "I have two people coming to help. Come on, we'll go meet them—they're waiting at our new hotel."

Yes, the old hotel had asked us politely to leave after our suite inconveniently suffered scorch marks and a shattered window when Kory's Thifilathi went after Granger. At times, I wished I'd been there to see Kory's smaller Thifilathi throw Granger through the plate glass before going after him.

Word had it that Granger ran down the sloping sides of our casino before digging in his claws to stop the hurtling descent.

They'd raced so swiftly in and out of traffic past that point that few could accurately describe what, if anything, they'd actually seen.

They'd ended up climbing the walls of a scale model of a famous New York landmark. It surprised me that Kory had so much control over his Thifilathi—I imagined that most male High Demons would have been flaming while they chased a criminal vampire through the streets.

Opal chose a limo as our method of getting to our new hotel. It was comfortable and, to be honest, I needed the time to get my thoughts in order. The dilemma with Granger had brought my worries about Jamie to a peak—what if they'd already hurt him? They couldn't obsess him; we already knew that, but there were other ways to harm him—and us through him.

"Why couldn't he just stay in the room?" I muttered.

"Thinking about Jamie?" Opal opened a small refrigerator in the car and handed me a bottle of water.

"Yeah."

"We can't lock everybody up that we want to keep safe," she said and turned to look out the tinted window. Outside our moving vehicle, glittering casino after flashing façade passed by. Another time, I'd have gazed at all of it in curiosity, eager to soak up the visual information. Now, it was unimportant, compared to Jamie's life.

"Yeah, but," I responded to Opal's comment.

"Yes, in this case, his common sense should have kicked in," Opal agreed. "You understand, though; he was locked in a closet and starved for months. He wanted to exercise what little freedom he had. It ended up harming him."

"I hate that this happened," I shook my head. "I really need half a bottle of ibuprofen right now."

"We'll find some for you, if you still need it after we meet our new recruits," she said. "I hope you like them."

∾

Kordevik

"Look, I know I'm fucking things up, but there are a thousand things on my plate right now," Watson defended himself.

"Anita and the war going on around us should be items one and two," I snapped.

"Opal has arrived," Kell walked in. "She expects us in her suite in five minutes, to meet our new recruits."

"All right," I nodded at Kell. "Watson will be there, too, even if I have to carry him."

"What?" Watson's voice betrayed his alarm.

"Look, I can carry you or drag you by the ear," I said. "Or, you can walk with me, like a rational, dignified werewolf Packmaster."

"I'm undignified?"

"And clueless, unrefined, oblivious—should I go on?" I asked, snorting smoke.

"At least I don't breathe smoke," Watson pointed at me.

"That's who I am. You grow fur and a tail. I breathe smoke. Any questions? No? Class dismissed." I grabbed his ear and hauled him toward the door while Kell watched.

Anita

I had no idea who Opal had convinced to help us. Lexsi drew in a breath when we were introduced to a Grey House wizard first.

Yoff was Lexsi's cousin. He grinned at her before pulling her into a swift hug. Dark-haired, dark eyed, with the wings he'd gained at adulthood folded tightly against his back.

His grandfather, after all, was a winged vampire and a consort to the Queen of Le-Ath Veronis. His father was married to the only female Grey House Master Wizard and also had the rare vampire wings.

"Didn't expect me, did you, cousin?" Yoff grinned after setting Lexsi down.

Lexsi wiped tears away before wrapping her arms around Yoff's waist to hug him again.

"This," Opal said after a moment, "is Zaria."

"Hello," she said. I blinked at Opal's second recruit. Black hair hung in waves down her back, while piercing blue eyes assessed all of us.

My breath caught as one word went through my mind.

Q'elindi.

There was a reason her eyes seemed to pierce all of us. She could see straight through us. Read us like the proverbial book and understand more about us than we did about ourselves.

She saw my secret.

She nodded. At that moment, I understood I could trust her with my life.

"I want to stop Deris and Daris just as much or more than you do," Zaria informed all of us. "Because I know exactly who they are and what they're capable of doing. I'm related to both of them, after all."

I swallowed with difficulty. She and I—we had more in common than anyone would think.

~

Lexsi

Yoff—I never expected him to come—not in my wildest imaginings. He'd made First Level just before my wedding was scheduled, and would probably make Master Wizard in a few years.

Pitting a Grey House wizard against a warlock was perhaps a delicious idea. Fifth Level was the strongest level one could reach on Karathia.

Wizards ranked their levels exactly the opposite. Fifth Level was weakest, First Level, strongest. Master Wizard was even stronger, and Yoff was a prime candidate.

As for Zaria—I had no idea what her rank was as a Karathian witch, but Opal respected her, that was evident. I felt it rude to ask, so I kept my questions to myself.

Stop gaping, Anita sent. *Does the word Q'elindi mean anything to you?*

I gaped more at Anita. Zaria was Q'elindi? They were so rare they almost didn't exist. New respect dawned as I turned back to Zaria. Did Uncle Ry know about her?

He knows, Zaria sent while smiling at me.

My breath caught. *You know Uncle Ry?*

And his father and his son, your half-brother. Her smile widened.

"I can't believe they haven't locked you up and forced you to stay on Karathia," I blurted.

"Zaria isn't the kind you can lock away," Opal said gently. "We're lucky she's here to help."

Opal

Zaria watched as Granger paced the short distance in his cage, from corner to corner.

Is Anita correct? Is there an implant? I asked in mindspeech.

Yes, but it's vision only—they can't hear. That doesn't mean they won't read lips and gestures, she replied.

Damn.

I hear that and raise you a fuck.

I've missed working with you.

I know.

Look, I need to take you to see Tiburon and his family, I said. *There are a few others with him that I want you to meet.*

All right, she nodded. *Want me to take us?*

Sure.

It was nice to be transported by someone else for a change. We stood outside Tibby's suite in barely a blink.

Yes, she'd taken the information straight from my mind. A Q'elindi's talent was formidable. If I hadn't trusted her completely, I might have worried.

Zaria would give her life before betraying those she cared for.

She'd already done it, after all.

I knocked on the door. Mason answered, with Sandra standing

right behind him.

Mason's eyes widened at the sight of Zaria; he'd drawn a breath, first, and scented nothing.

Sandra, too, couldn't get a scent off her, she was so tightly shielded.

"This is Zaria—she's a new recruit," I said, introducing her. "Zaria, this is Mason and Sandra."

"King Vampire," Zaria shook with a blinking Mason. "Lady Wolf," she shook with Sandra. "You go well together."

"How?" Mason began.

"Ask me later," I shrugged. I just wanted Zaria to come in and meet the others.

Diego was in lust the moment he saw Zaria. Poor man didn't have a chance with her, although she smiled and shook his hand. She complimented Tibby on his fighting techniques and record when I introduced her to him.

"Weather woman," she said, shaking hands with Farin.

"Wow. I like that. Weather woman. Makes me sound important," Farin laughed.

"And this," I said, ready to introduce Klancy.

Zaria stopped. Her breath stopped, too. Klancy glided forward as if he were afraid Zaria would disappear.

"I am most pleased to meet you," Klancy lifted Zaria's hand to his lips to kiss it. Zaria blinked at Klancy.

Several times.

"It, uh, is a pleasure for me as well," Zaria breathed.

Kell

Before tonight, I had a concern for Klancy.

He was two centuries old, and had reached the stage where very little held any interest for him. Opal's offer of a job had kept him occupied for the moment, but I worried for the time when that interest would also fade.

Until Zaria Keppler walked into his life.

Yes, I knew about her heartbreak, and that there were others. I doubted Klancy would have a care about any of that.

This would be interesting.

Most interesting.

Lexsi

Sometimes, when I look at Anita, I see someone older.

Far older than what she appears.

Sirenali were mostly immortal, unless you managed to kill them. They could be killed—I understood that.

I had no idea how old Anita was.

"You said you had a cousin in L.A., once," I said. She and I stood at the window of our suite, looking out over Las Vegas.

"I still do," she nodded. "She's working things from a different angle."

"Care to expand on that?"

"Not really, no."

"All right."

"At least we're not having fights with strangers in parking lots," she teased.

"Day's not over, yet."

"True."

"I wouldn't mind punching Charlene and Hannah," I said.

"I wouldn't mind helping."

"What would happen if we took them? You know—just grabbed them?" I asked. "Instead of just trading Granger for Jamie."

"We won't know it's Jamie until we see him," Anita pointed out.

"Yeah. That's a problem."

"It is."

"Where would they take him? Do you think they'd send him to Peru already, without waiting for Hannah and Granger to go back?"

"No idea. Something to think about, though. I'd really like to get my hands on Hannah, not to mention that Charlene bitch. They're planning something, you know."

"I know," I agreed. "I'm really worried about what they intend to do to Tibby in the ring."

"I hope Zaria can help with that. You nullify spells, but she can tell if there's a spell to begin with."

"Like you can tell if somebody's obsessed?"

"Yes. Except she's better at it than I'll ever be."

"Why haven't I heard of her?" I grumbled.

"You know about her, now. I think that's enough."

"You sound like my mother," I grumbled.

"Maybe you sound like her daughter right now."

I bristled because I had no retort for that. Anita was right—I was whining. She just didn't put it quite like that.

"I'll stop whining, now."

"Where's the fun in that?" Anita was back to herself. "Just be glad we were able to get good help in dealing with all this—I'm worried. Not just about all this, but about things farther south. My cousin, Esme, is in Ecuador right now." She'd decided to tell me about her cousin after all.

I went still for a moment. "She's checking on those bodies in the water, isn't she?" I asked.

"Yeah. I get mindspeech now and then. None of it's pretty. She's made contact with some shifters, there, too. Some of their kind have been hit and they don't like it. Esme's doing her best to keep them out of harm's way, but you know how those things can go at times."

"A lot depends on Packmasters, how they handle the situation, but then again, there's always a few who go off the reservation if they really don't like something," I agreed.

"Well, they have no idea how much danger they're in," Anita grumped. "Esme's trying to reel them in and convince them to go elsewhere for a while, but she's getting a lot of resistance."

"Not good. Rare shapeshifters?" I expected her to say yes. Shapeshifters who became water animals were extremely rare—at least on Earth.

"Yeah. Unfortunately." Anita studied her shoes. They were sturdy, short-heeled boots covered mostly by the jeans she wore. She was dressed well enough to get into a restaurant or a brawl, if necessary.

"Does Esme need help?"

"She could use some help, but these shifters are so suspicious of everybody else. The only person who might have any sway with them is Zaria."

"You planning to ask her?"

"Hell, I want her to take us both to Ecuador so I can talk some sense into those people, too. I just need—Zaria to help me convince them."

"How can Zaria help?"

"I think Zaria has some talents that most folks don't or can't see. She'd convince me in no time, if I saw one or two things she can do."

"Are you going to tell me about that?"

"Those are her secrets. She'll have to tell you herself. I want her help, so I won't be talking for sure."

"You think Esme is in danger, too," I guessed.

"Yeah."

"You could have told me before," I said.

"Are you whining again?"

"I guess."

"I didn't tell you because you have enough to worry about already, okay?"

"And you're one of those people who keep their worries close to their heart. If you say it out loud, it makes it worse, doesn't it?"

"Yeah. You're extremely perceptive. It's annoying. Stop it."

I laughed—I couldn't help it. Her arm came around my shoulders and she hugged me close.

Another worry nagged at my mind, though. Anita's cousin and rare shapeshifters were in danger from those in Peru; Laurel's Sirenali, or perhaps more than one, was hunting off the coasts of Peru and Ecuador.

"There has to be more than one, right?"

"More than one what?" Anita pulled my hair back so it would fall where it should.

"Sirenali. They have more than one, don't they?" I turned to gaze into Anita's eyes.

"Bingo," she tapped her nose. "It's why some can go hunting while Laurel and her cronies remain blissfully away from prying eyes. You can't search for them using any sort of power if a Sirenali is nearby. It's why they couldn't see you right now, even if they wanted. You're with me."

"This really, really sucks, you know that? Not that I don't appreciate what you're doing for me. For us," I amended.

"I know. You provide your own sort of protection, as does Kory. No spell cast by the enemy will survive within a certain range of either of you; while you're close, it's nullified."

"I uh, got rid of some spells completely when I turned fake prisoners to mist," I admitted.

"You did what?" Anita was shocked.

"I don't know. The spells disappeared, once I turned them to mist. When I set them down, they looked like themselves again, and kept looking like themselves, even when I moved outside the nullifying perimeter."

"Do you know how fantastic that is?" Anita shook her head as if she still couldn't believe what I'd told her.

"I guess it's a really good thing." I turned my gaze back to the view out the window.

"It's an amazing thing," She sighed. "Maybe the most amazing thing I've heard or seen today."

"Zaria, Kell and I will be at the exchange site," Opal announced in our short briefing before the spectacle of the fight began. "Kory, Lexsi, Anita and Yoff will be in seats close to the ring. I expect you to take appropriate action if it looks as if something has been done to give Lover Boy Landon an unfair advantage in the fight."

"Or whether it's Lover Boy at all," Kory said.

"True. Thomas, Mason and Sandra will be stationed near the entrance, in case someone attempts to get away." Opal pointed at the holographic image of the venue, which was splashed on one of Tibby's hotel suite walls.

"Watson, Davis and Klancy will be with Tibby's family in their box seats, protecting them while the fight is going on. We don't want anybody getting away and we don't need more hostages," Opal stated flatly.

She was right about that; we didn't need more hostages. They already had Jamie, and they could force us to run in circles if they gathered even more hostages. The mere thought of it angered me in ways I couldn't accurately describe.

Kory, who sat beside me, was just as upset; tiny curls of smoke escaped his nostrils occasionally as Opal described our roles in the fight and the prisoner exchange. "Do you have more agents in the background?" I asked.

"Scattered through the crowd, in disguise and watching everything," Opal nodded. "They'll identify themselves to you if necessary."

"What's your plan for the exchange?" Mason asked.

"That's need to know," Opal hedged. I figured it would have to be. I imagined that she, Kell and Zaria would wait until they knew whether Jamie was real or not, then go on from there.

We didn't need everybody in a panic, simply because they didn't believe the real Jamie Rome would be handed over at the exchange.

Where is he? I leaned against Kory.

Jamie?

Yeah.

No idea. Stop worrying so much, onion. We'll find him.

Opal

We were headed to the desert outside Vegas, between the city and

Primm, where other casinos cropped up from the barren ground like plants after a brief rain. There, Nevada butted against California's border, and it was a place to stop for those driving from one state to the other.

Along a narrow road, heading east from Primm, was where we were to meet for the exchange.

The three of us were extremely wary as a result; not only were they asking for Granger, but they'd upped the ante, asking for Kory, too.

We hadn't told Kory or Lexsi about their additional demands. What did they think to accomplish by attempting to corral a High Demon male?

How did they think they'd capture a High Demon male?

Zaria was already preparing for this; a replica of Kory would walk beside us. If I knew Zaria at all, and I did know her a little, at least, not only would it look like Kory, but could also gesture and speak like him.

They want to see how important Jamie is to us, Zaria had said.

It angered me that we had to stoop to these measures. I wanted to tell Charlene and Hannah to fuck off, as Zaria so delicately put it.

She suspected there was more to all this than even I could imagine, and I could imagine much.

Charlene, after all, was supposed to be at the fight. I couldn't imagine her being anywhere but there.

Was someone coming in her place?

Hannah, too, wasn't prepared for this sort of thing. Why was she coming? It made no sense to send an inexperienced woman to do the exchange, when it could turn into a fight, with or without weapons.

Jamie.

What would his part be in this—would it be him or one of Laurel's allies in disguise, ready to shoot at us the moment we arrived?

Where was Jamie? Really?

I doubted we'd find him on the other side of this exchange. I believed that Laurel wanted him completely dead, this time. So much so that she probably wanted to witness it for herself.

Fuck Laurel. Too many people wanted her throat in their hands, so they could watch her die from close range.

Jamie might be one of those people. I still wondered at the fact that not only was she alive, but those who'd invaded Earth appeared to be listening to her and catering to her whims. Most criminals I knew would have blasted her to bits long ago, rather than listen to her whiny voice.

It comes down to DSG Enterprises, Zaria's voice sounded in my head. Or, rather, the DSG in DSG Enterprises.

You know who that is?

I have a good guess.

Who? I countered.

Dervil San Gerxon. You know, Divil and Arvil San Gerxon's father?

I went still.

Has he fathered those two, yet?

Unfortunately, yes, although they're very young—Arvil's still in diapers. They come from a long-lived bunch. Actually, they have a line of wizards in the family, somewhere in the past. That lineage gives them extended life—far beyond what is normal for either Alliance.

How? I thought for a moment before it hit me.

Who?

Ah, there's the question, huh? Somewhere in the past century, the Belancours married into the San Gerxon line. You and I know that the San Gerxons are also distantly related to the Cayetes Clan. Not many know of that connection.

You're giving me a headache. How did you find out? I doubted many of the San Gerxons actually knew.

I did research. Remember, Hegatt, Morgett's brother, hired Marid of Belancour for a rather illicit act in an attempt to take the Karathian throne. I decided to research that connection, which obviously led to other connections. The criminal streak runs through the San Gerxons, the Cayetes bunch and the Belancours like molten lead through plastic.

I agreed. At that point, I wanted to toss a hand in the air and go have a drink or three with Kell in a bar. The Belancour line was almost dead in the future, or so I'd thought. To learn that they were related, albeit distantly at that point, to the San Gerxons?

Not good news.

All that was unimportant, as far as Charlene and Hannah were concerned. Unless more family members of the San Gerxon variety showed up in disguise as their replacements.

At this point, nothing would surprise me.

Lexsi

I hated that we had to make our way into the audience like everybody else. The crowd was thick and overwhelming at times. Kory and I were bumped and jostled as we made our way toward the seats near the ring.

Those seats weren't cheap. Somehow, Opal had arranged for that, using her position to obtain those favors.

Kory and I would be in range to nullify any spells placed on Lover Boy. We weren't far from his corner, after all.

Kory's broad shoulders formed a wake for me to follow, although one of his hands gripped mine from behind. He didn't want me to disappear in the wash of bodies that swayed one way then another as the noisy, talkative crowd pushed into the arena.

His hand was a lifeline as I learned a valuable lesson that night; crowds frightened me. If someone took control of the entire crowd, they could cause a tremendous amount of damage just by startling it.

That was a nightmare, Kory's mental voice gritted as he settled me in my seat before sitting beside me.

It scares me, I responded. *What if they get spooked? People could die.*

Hmmph. I saw video of a much smaller crowd trampling people to death just to get one of five televisions on sale at the electronics store last Christmas season, he replied. *This could be a thousand times worse.*

How did you get here before I did? I asked. *To Earth, I mean? We should* have arrived at roughly the same time.

People who can bend time and fold space have their own agendas, he shrugged, attempting to settle his long legs into a more comfortable position. There wasn't much legroom to be had, this close to the ring. If we wanted out of our seats quickly, we'd have to skip out of them.

Do you feel it? I asked as I shivered. *Like something isn't right?* I glanced at the people who sat around us. All of them had blank looks in their eyes, as if their conscious minds had been temporarily removed.

If you're asking if the hair on my neck is prickling, then yes. Something is definitely going on.

What can cause that? I asked.

Not sure, he replied, turning in his seat to study the people sitting behind us. All of them now sat rigidly in their seats, fingers gripping the armrests on their chairs as if they were waiting for something, or were seeing something we weren't seeing.

What could do that?

I drew in a breath.

Why had I been so stupid?

Most of these people had stopped for drinks at temporary bars set up outside the arena. Many still had drinks in their hands, although they no longer realized they held anything.

I felt as if a switch had been flipped, suddenly, giving them blank looks as they sat, unmoving, in their assigned seats.

Kory, I'm worried, I informed him in a small voice. *It won't matter if we reveal who or what Tibby will be fighting. These people are already hallucinating. Somebody's drugged them with drakus seed.*

"What?" he turned to me and spoke aloud.

"It won't matter. If the police ask questions later, they'll get a thousand different stories from a thousand different people. We aren't close enough to the cameras recording the fight to affect the spells placed there. What are they planning?" I was terrified—not just for Tibby and his crew, but for the crowd in the arena. Depending on how much drakus seed they'd consumed, they could die in their seats or later, in their beds. Drakus seed didn't discriminate; it was merely a matter of individual metabolism.

"Send mindspeech to Opal," Kory rose from his seat while smoke poured from his nostrils. "I need to get to Tibby. I'll come in with him and his crew for added protection. You know to skip out of here if things get dangerous, don't you? Baby, tell me you'll be safe."

He lifted my face in his hands and kissed my forehead.

"Yes. Go. I'll be fine." I was determined to be fine, one way or another, although my fear of the crowd had been ramped up exponentially, once I realized they were under the influence of drakus seed.

Opal, I sent, *we have big problems. I think most of the crowd has been given drakus seed*, I reported.

CHAPTER 10

*O*pal

Lexsi's troubles only added to our own. Zaria, Kell and I faced not three but seven Ra'Ak.

Yes, in the future, these would be whittled down, but not now. Not where and when we were. I suspected at that moment that Morgett Blackmantle was involved in criminal activities on more planets than I could begin to name. I was beginning to worry that growing drakus seed wasn't his only objective.

Seven Ra'Ak had been sent to corral one High Demon. It would require four, at the very least, to attempt to take Kory down.

Zaria, who stood next to Kory's replica, stared at what looked to be seven men. As I suspected, Charlene and Hannah weren't there.

Neither, as it turned out, was Jamie, although the Ra'Ak had created a credible likeness of him.

Yes, they were powerful. Very, very powerful.

They had no idea what had come to meet them, however. Zaria, Kell and I had already seen through their humanoid disguises—Kell by scent, Zaria because she could see straight into their minds and I because I had the ability to *Look* to see what they were.

Granger hadn't a clue and chafed in his manacles next to Kell.

The Ra'Ak secreted a poison in their natural form so powerful it could kill a vampire. Would these turn to their giant serpent forms in an attempt to take what they believed to be a High Demon?

A small fact niggled at my mind. *Unless you belonged to the hierarchy of the gods, only one race was immune to Ra'Ak poison. That race was the High Demons.* I breathed slowly, to calm my heart. This had implications.

It meant something.

I needed more time to sort out exactly what it meant, and I was forced to deal with the crisis in front of me, first.

"Who sent you?" I demanded of the one who stood at the forefront, with the duplicate of Jamie Rome standing beside him. This was nothing more than a golem, made of who knew what, that the Ra'Ak had employed power to animate.

"You know who sent me," the lead Ra'Ak growled. "He dies if you fail to cooperate." He jerked his head toward golem Jamie.

Opal, Lexsi's voice interrupted. She sounded hysterical. *They've sent a High Demon to fight Tibby. Kory says he recognizes him—Geldivik Croth, from the Croth family.*

Tell Kory to do what he has to, I snapped back. *I know Tibby wants this fight, but he's overmatched and he ought to realize that.*

I think he's already planning to do that—Kory, that is.

Don't panic, I sent as I stared down the Ra'Ak in human form. *We have our hands full, too.*

There are more of them, siding with the bunch in Peru, Zaria informed me.

Can you see where Jamie is?

I can. He's in the crowd at the arena, and like most of those people there, he's high on drakus seed. We don't get to him soon, he'll die with the others.

Can the day get any worse? I wanted to curse aloud, but that would give us away.

If I get rid of these, the others will know, Zaria went on. *They're watching through their eyes.*

Any suggestions, then?

I have something.

Go ahead. I have nothing from where I'm standing.

All right. They'll try to kill us the moment Granger's in their hands, but I have a short-term solution for that, too.

Sure. It can't be any worse than what I'd like to do, which is shoot all of them with my ranos pistol.

Save that for later. I watched as a corner of Zaria's mouth twitched into an almost-smile.

"Very well, we will send Granger forward first, followed by the High Demon," I announced.

"Once they are with us, we will leave this one on the ground for you to pick up, like the garbage he is," the lead Ra'Ak laughed.

"If you insist," I agreed.

"Go." Kell shoved Granger forward. Granger's steps were measured, although he wanted to run to get away from us, I could tell. When he was halfway to the waiting Ra'Ak, Zaria released her copy of Kory. He strode forward, blowing smoke, just as one would expect a High Demon to do who'd been forced into a hostage situation.

One of the Ra'Ak at the back took a step forward, a hungry expression on his face.

They haven't fed, Zaria confirmed my fears.

"Stay the fuck back," Kory's copy breathed a cloud of smoke at the one who'd shown his impatience.

Zaria had done an amazing job at copying Kory, right down to his speech and mannerisms.

Three Ra'Ak fell on Kory's duplicate the moment he was in range; Granger shrieked unnaturally high and began to run as Ra'Ak, in their normal, serpent form, boiled about Kory's duplicate.

The golem posing as Jamie was trampled in the dust beneath thick, fifty-foot snakes as four of them lunged in our direction.

I found myself hanging over the destruction inside Kell's mist, watching as duplicates of all of us screamed and died in the attack.

Now we find Jamie, Zaria's voice was grim as she folded space while we were still caught in Kell's mist.

~

Peru

> *Laurel*

"Oooh, that went perfectly," I clapped to show my appreciation at the images displayed on the large screen in the hacienda's media room. Morgett, whom I'd only seen once before, smiled at my pleasure. He'd arranged the whole thing and it had unfolded flawlessly.

"We have to find Granger," I pouted. He'd taken off running into the desert at the sight of the giant serpents.

"No worries, my dear, he will be located. We will have our vampire back quite soon," Berke soothed.

"Did you see all the blood?" I felt like clapping my hands again. The three they'd sent to meet Morgett's troops hadn't had a chance. It pleased me greatly to watch them die alongside Kory Wilson.

> *Lexsi*

Farin ended up sitting beside me. Like me, she was concerned about all the blank, intent stares of those about us.

Tibby was in the ring, but serving in the trainer's capacity for Kory, who now had gloves laced and taped onto his hands.

From the other corner, assisted by Lover Boy Landon's crew, stood Geldivik Croth. Had the enemy reached that far—to convince Drith and Croth to ally with them in this endeavor?

I knew the history from the future, and what had happened to Drith and Croth then. In this time, their houses were still strong and thriving.

Had Kory been a part of that—in the future? Had he fought alongside others in the High Demon army, to defeat the alliance between Drith, Croth and Ra'ak?

How did Deris, Daris and Morgett Blackmantle figure into all this? What roles had they yet to play?

I wanted to shiver again, but worried that it would upset Farin more than she already was. The crowd—at least seventy percent of it, was high on drakus seed.

How good would Kory be against Geldivik Croth?

If my mother or grandmother were here, they wouldn't settle for anything less than Geldivik's death—that's how badly his family had betrayed Kifirin and the High Demon race. Geldivik was betraying all, now, in a pact to bring drakus seed to the Alliance and, as the evidence about me was mounting, to Earth as well.

Farin's fingers twisted together as she sat beside me, moving restlessly in her seat as Kory and Geldivik prepared to fight one another.

Did Geldivik know Kory? Did he know Kory's weaknesses when he fought? My heart began thumping in my chest. If they went to Thifilathi (and it could easily go that far quickly), they'd fight to the death.

Should I interfere? I could turn to mist and then—no. Kory wouldn't want that. It was a desperate measure and I should save it. Hide it from prying eyes and recording cameras. My mist was a weapon of last resort, although I fully intended to employ it if Kory's life were in danger.

I prayed to any listening that Kory would survive.

~

Opal

I didn't bother taking time to ask why Granger was still with us; he stood in a corner of Tibby's suite while Kell growled if he breathed too loudly.

I, on the other hand, watched as Zaria began to glow before putting her hands on an unconscious Jamie.

She'd transported us to the fight arena, picked Jamie out of his seat easier than a child plucked a daisy and rushed him to Tibby's penthouse suite.

He was already unconscious when we found him, his breathing shallow and his heartbeats irregular.

The drakus seed he'd been forced to swallow was killing him.

Zaria had a talent for healing, and I'd never been more grateful for something in my life. In the arena near the lowest level of the casino, Kory and an enemy High Demon prepared to fight.

I hoped Lexsi would know not to interfere unless there were no other options. Yes, I understood that cameras would be filming the debacle.

Unless—I sent out a call. Someone had to realize what this could do if images were displayed of this fight across Earth.

So many people would be watching.

For saving my brother, came a familiar voice.

My shoulders sagged in relief as I watched Zaria's hands move swiftly over Jamie's body, neutralizing the drug that coursed through his veins.

~

Lexsi

Those gloves won't last five seconds if they turn Thifilathi, I sent to Anita. She was close to the ring, hoping to keep the unwary away if the Croth difik turned first and burst into flame.

You'd know, Anita replied. *If both turn up the heat, anybody near ringside will be roasted, toasted and crispy.*

Have any of them succumbed to the drakus seed?

Two are dead, she confirmed. *One's on the floor after he collapsed. Those around him are so high, they haven't noticed.*

Fuck.

Look, we'll need to get the living out of here. The dead won't matter as much, she reminded me.

Yeah. I get that. Do you want me to come now?

Stay where you are and keep Farin from freaking. I'll get Tibby and his crew out in the first batch. You get Farin and anybody else left at ringside that you can haul.

Got it. Farin's already having a meltdown.

Keep her calm. Tibby's more worried about her than he is about himself.

Nice to see that in a man, huh?

I could tell by the tone of her voice that she'd been thinking it. I refused to ask where Watson was; he obviously wasn't there, worrying about Anita. Surely, he and the other werewolves could scent the changes caused by drakus seed consumption in the seething press of bodies.

If they had mindspeech, I could have asked them, but my thoughts were redirected when the announcer stepped into the ring.

Was he under the influence, too, or was he obsessed or delusional? He acted as if nothing were wrong as the fighters were introduced—as Tiburon *Snark Demonio* Diaz, and Lyle *Lover Boy* Landon.

I held my breath as Geldivik Croth threw the first punch.

Opal

"He'll be fine, he's sleeping, now." Zaria employed her formidable witch's talent to float Jamie to a bed. "Is there a safe place to keep good old Granger, there, so he'll be out of sight and mostly out of mind?"

"Who was that who went screaming off into the desert?" I folded arms over my chest and blinked once at Zaria.

"Those Ra'Ak knew where Charlene and Hannah were. I merely substituted Hannah for Granger."

I blinked again before dropping my arms and shaking my head at Zaria. "Half the time you blow me away with what you can do. The rest of the time, you scare me to death with what you can do."

"Glad to be of service. Let's get Granger settled somewhere and we'll see about helping that bunch in the arena downstairs."

"You think you can help them?" I whispered.

"Not all of them. A few. Maybe a third. The ones who aren't too far gone already. I'm not prepared to change much if anything, today. We'll heal what we can and leave it at that. It's time the President and his cronies woke up to the dangers presented by what's taken over Peru."

"Yeah. What about?" I began.

"The innocent will be protected."

If anyone would know who that could be, it was Zaria. "Then I trust your choices," I said.

"Yeah. Life sucks at times, doesn't it?"

"It sure as hell does."

Lexsi

The fight went on for two minutes, tops, before Geldivik became his smaller Thifilathi and burst into flames. By that time, the crowd was so far under the influence of drakus seed there was barely a murmur running through it.

Kory's smaller Thifilathi appeared quickly, while those in Kory's corner disappeared.

Anita had already acted to save lives. It was my turn, now.

"Farin, we have to go," I said.

Farin, who couldn't tear her eyes away from the fight in the ring, didn't respond. Turning to mist quickly, I pulled her in, then flew toward the ring to rescue those I could.

Kordevik

I knew Croth and Drith would side with the worst of the worst in the future. I had no idea they'd started their betrayal centuries earlier, or that they were involved in the drakus seed trade up to their hair follicles.

The moment Geldivik turned to his smaller Thifilathi and burst into flame because I'd gotten in a jaw-breaking punch, I was forced to do the same.

Cameras and recordings be damned, this was a fight for my life. Already the mat at our feet was on fire, and it was only a matter of minutes before everything would be blazing around us.

I hoped our crew was getting people out of the arena—if they didn't leave, they'd die. Especially if our full Thifilathis became involved.

We fought naked and covered in fire by this time, Geldivik throwing a punch, me deflecting or ducking before throwing one of my own.

I had no idea who'd taught him to fight, but he was quite poor as an adversary. My counterpunch hit him square in the face, almost knocking him down. More fire bloomed about us as the mat collapsed in a towering rain of sparks.

Geldivik almost fell again when we dropped to the concrete beneath the ring. He roared as he stood, his full Thifilathi forming and towering over me for a moment before I concentrated on becoming the same.

It concerned me that the crowd wasn't shrieking or running by this time—with fire raining down and setting clothing ablaze, they should be doing both.

Tearing my gaze from the crowd, I barely ducked to avoid another of Geldivik's right hooks. I had control of my Thifilathi—he didn't. He roared again and wasted time by beating his chest.

I took the opportunity to leap and kick him into a section of mostly empty seats. He crashed into it, his fire and weight destroying the section in seconds. He was slower to rise this time, and I was confident the fight was all but over.

Until he was joined by two others, already in full Thifilathi.

What the holy fucking hell was going on?

There are more of them, I sent desperate mindspeech to anyone listening and waded toward my new opponents, prepared to fight until I fell.

Lexsi

Farin was crying on the sidewalk while Tibby fought against a crowd of casino-goers to get to her.

That's when Kory's mindspeech came.

There are more of them. For him to say that meant only one thing—more High Demons had arrived. One or two he might be successful—if they weren't as strong or as well trained as he.

Three? Too many, even for one of the best. Two could keep him occupied while the third could employ his skipping talent to come in from an unprotected side and deliver a killing blow.

"I have to go," I shouted amid the noise of the crowd and sirens coming close. The casino, thanks to Kory and Geldivik, was now on fire.

"But," Farin wept.

I had to let her hand go. I had to leave her. Kory needed me worse. Tibby was near, but being shoved back by frightened gamblers.

I skipped away, leaving Farin curled up against the casino's facade, hoping Tibby would reach her.

I had to help Kory, and I only knew one way to do that.

Anita

"There!" I pointed at Farin, who'd curled up against an outside wall of the casino, while Tibby, still yards away, struggled to reach her through the crowd.

I'd landed atop a shorter building across the street so I could assess the situation easier. That's how I'd found Watson, Sandra, Klancy and Mason. I'd folded space to scoop them from the crowd before returning to my vantage point.

By that time, the crowd escaping the casino was so thick it was nearly impossible to tell friend from foe. Finally, I'd spotted Lexsi and Farin in a space between doors—it was an island where they wouldn't be battered while others screamed and ran.

Before I could do anything else, Lexsi disappeared, leaving Farin alone. That spelled one thing; Kory was in trouble.

"Take us down," Klancy's voice was calm. Deliberate.

"Yeah." Shoving my worries for Kory and Lexsi aside, I folded space with all four.

Lexsi

Long before I was born, my grandmother was involved in the battle for Kifirin. Without her help, the planet would have fallen to the rogue High Demons, the Ra'Ak who'd recruited them, and the Elemaiya, who, as a race, had sunk so low there was no saving it as a whole.

I'd read an actual history of that battle, although parts of it were still kept from me. My Amterean Dwarf tutor had allowed me to read it when I was fourteen. Old enough, according to Master Morwin, to know it for myself.

My grandmother had employed her mist to do terrible things to the enemy. At the time I'd read the history, it had revolted me with the violence of it.

I understood my grandmother's motives better, now. It was a desperate time, and she'd done desperate things to save Kifirin.

I was about to do the same thing.

Already, Kory fought two opponents while the third—Geldivik Croth—had disappeared. Planning the killing blow, no doubt.

Except I was there to even things up.

Turning to mist, I dived toward the nearest of Kory's opponents. I misted right into his head. Mentally gulping at what I was about to do, I wound my mist as tightly as I could before releasing it in less than a blink.

Kordevik

At the same moment I attempted mindspeech to warn Lexsi away, one of the two Thifilathis I fought exploded.

Yes, I'd seen that phenomenon for myself, centuries in the future.

He didn't completely explode—just his head.

Enough to kill him instantly. While I hesitated for a moment, Geldivik reappeared and attacked from behind, sinking his fangs into my neck. I roared in pain as the second Thifilathi's head exploded in front of us.

I'd been taught that this could be a killing attack if something weren't done quickly. I leapt straight into the air, before coming down on my back.

Yes, I felt as if my neck had been ripped apart when we landed, but Geldivik hadn't expected my weight to land on him when we hit. Using an elbow, I repeatedly slammed him in the ribs in an effort to loosen his teeth.

My last blow, as I felt myself falling into blackness, caused him to grunt and release the bite.

I barely heard—or felt—it when his head exploded beside mine, blasting bits of bone, flesh and blood into my face and hair.

~

Opal

"Zaria's exhausted. I wish Lexsi would stop puking," I sighed and took the chair offered by Kell.

Lexsi was throwing up in a toilet down the hall; I'd gathered my forces after Zaria did what she could to save roughly a third of the crowd in the arena. Once Zaria left the living with paramedics and the local police, I'd taken my bunch back to the military facility in Henderson.

Area hospitals were past capacity to treat the wounded and affected, so tents were set up on a blocked-off street while the National Guard flew the worst of the injured to Boulder City and Barstow.

Word was already getting around that some kind of drug was responsible for deaths in the arena. Las Vegas' Mayor was already calling for an investigation into the situation, while casino owners claimed innocence.

The casino owners were innocent—they were victims, albeit live ones.

Many hadn't been so lucky. Those who hadn't been burned in the fires were being hauled out by the hundreds. The arena had been packed to its capacity at nearly seventeen thousand. Only six thousand or so escaped with their lives.

I'd already been on the phone with the President, the Secretary of State and Colonel Hunter, the Secretary of Defense.

Colonel Hunter hadn't been surprised that I'd linked those in Peru with this disaster. The Secretary of State wanted more proof. The President was waffling over the debacle. I wanted to slap my forehead, but that wouldn't solve anything. Besides, Kell was beside me the whole time; I think he'd have stopped me from harming myself.

At least Kory's High Demon attackers were dead—Lexsi had seen to that, although she was now dry-heaving in a toilet because of the messy blood and brain matter involved.

The last thing Zaria did before she fell into a deep sleep at the Nevada facility was heal Kory. That fucker, Geldivik Croth, had bitten him and almost ripped out his throat. If Kory hadn't been such a seasoned fighter, and if Lexsi hadn't killed Geldivik there at the end, we could have had four dead High Demons instead of three.

"Dearest, would you like something?" Kell appeared with a tray of coffee and sandwiches in his hands. I had no idea how he'd managed to do that, but I was grateful.

"Yes, thank you," I pulled a wrapped sandwich and a cup of coffee off the tray. "Sit here and eat with me, please?"

"It will be my pleasure. The others are already eating, with the exception of our vampires and Miss Lexsi. The vampires have been provided with blood, so they are cared for. I wish we could do something for the young one, however."

"It'll take a while, but she'll get used to this." I bit into the sandwich. It was ham and cheese—standard fare. It contained protein, which I needed, so I ate it.

"I know." He leaned back in the chair next to mine and studied the sandwich he held before biting off a corner.

"I assume Granger was included with the other vampires?"

"Yes, although he hissed at me when I took the bag of blood to him."

"No surprise. He's the sort who'll continue to bite the hand that feeds him."

"What are your intentions where he is concerned?"

"I intend to turn him over to the Vampire Council. Wlodek can deal with him. We've proven he's a rogue, so he won't be allowed to live."

"As expected," Kell agreed. "The Rith Naeri would handle this the same. Will this Council provide transportation?"

"Yes. They'll be here tomorrow evening to collect him."

"Good."

"We need sleep and a planning session, so we'll be occupied until the Council's jet lands and they take him into custody."

"Do you think they'll attempt to rescue him?" Kell asked before taking another bite of his sandwich.

"Doubt it. We can't find Charlene, either, and the last we saw of Hannah, she was running wild in the desert while disguised as Granger."

"Too bad for her, then," Kell shrugged. "When will the disguise fall away?"

"No idea. Maybe never—Zaria is pretty powerful."

"I understand that. Those we met in the desert—they believe us dead. Does that continue to give us an advantage?"

"I hope so. I hope they think Kory's dead again, too; I had help scrambling the cameras inside the arena. I figure there are a bunch of people worldwide who are demanding their money back because they paid to see the fight on their televisions."

"High Demons and Ra'Ak," Kell mused before turning back to his sandwich.

"Yes. Exactly my thought. If there are more High Demons involved in this operation, then it makes sense that they really, really want Kory dead. Since Lexsi is female, they really aren't worried about her. In their experience, female High Demons don't turn. She can be a bargaining chip to get to Kory, but to them, he's their biggest threat. High Demons were created to keep the Ra'Ak and the other dark races in line. Their obsession to kill Kory isn't just because he can nullify spells, as I originally thought."

"Treachery from within is always the worst kind," Kell said. "This Dervil San Gerxon and Morgett Blackmantle have a far-reaching grasp if they can pit High Demon against High Demon."

"That grasp goes farther if they can pull in Ra'Ak. You know what that means, don't you? The Ra'Ak are already slavering over the population of Earth. If the people are devoured, it leaves the entire planet free to grow drakus seed."

"Yes, they are always hungry, these serpents." Kell rose from his seat and walked a few steps to the nearest wastebasket, where he dropped his empty cup and sandwich wrapper. "Planets become feeding grounds, unless someone stops them."

"There are few who can stop them," I said, my voice soft. "The one who planned this has thought of every angle."

Lexsi

"I found chicken noodle soup. In the chaos that covers the city, that wasn't an easy thing to do," Anita said.

She was right—I needed something in my stomach, but the thought of it made me want to puke again.

"Just a few bites?" She waved the bowl beneath my nose. At least it smelled better than fresh blood and bits of brain.

Gran was a vampire. Maybe she was better suited to those smells than I was. I closed my eyes and hugged myself as Anita produced a spoon. "Eat a little bit. That's all. Dry heaves can't be any fun."

"Chunky heaves aren't fun either," I muttered.

"If you'll eat a few bites, I'll tell you how Kory is doing." Yes, she was dangling that particular carrot in front of me.

After closing my eyes and mentally preparing myself for food that would probably make a second and not so pretty appearance quickly, I held out my hand for the spoon. Anita waited until I'd swallowed three bites of chicken noodle soup before telling me that Kory was fine; Zaria had healed him before she fell unconscious.

"She all right?" I studied the soup, wondering if it were safe to put another spoonful in my mouth.

"Opal says yes, she's just tired. Had a busy day, or so I hear. Eat another two bites and I'll tell you about Hannah."

"What about Hannah?" She had my immediate attention.

"Well, the way I hear it, Zaria managed to disguise Hannah as Granger. The last time anybody saw her, she was running through the desert, screaming loud enough to wake the cactus."

I had to lay my head on the table after a while, I was laughing so hard.

CHAPTER 11

Opal

"What the hell?" Davis handed his tablet to Thomas, who went still while reading it, then handed it to me.

I hadn't prepared myself for this.

The nut jobs in Peru were selling off ancient treasures to the highest bidders. That included blocks of stone from Machu Picchu. By the time I read that part, I was so furious I could have killed the ones responsible bare-handed. All of it was listed on the black-market portion of the deep web, and the buyers who frequented those sites had money coming out of their ass, ill-gotten or otherwise.

"Gold only," Davis tapped the screen after I'd tossed the tablet onto the kitchen island.

We were back at the house in San Rafael. The others were sleeping; I'd stayed awake for a conference call with Colonel Hunter. Once the Vampire Council arrived in Vegas to pick up Granger, there wasn't any need for us to stay.

Everything we needed to do could be done from San Rafael. At least I knew the house was protected against anything the enemy might throw at us. I thought it best to get the others away; Las Vegas

163

was in mourning, as was the entire country. No state was spared in the deaths that occurred in the arena.

Many foreign countries also mourned losses of citizens; the fight had sold out worldwide in less than five minutes, once the tickets were made available months earlier. At least three small countries lost royalty in the drugging. The fire hadn't killed them; the drug did.

At least there were no working cameras during the fight between Kory and—ultimately—three High Demons. Lyle Landon was found later, sleeping off a hangover in his suite while Tibby released a statement to the press, saying his team managed to get him away the moment the arena caught fire.

That left plenty of fodder for the press, sports related and otherwise, many of whom went so far as to blame Lyle for a conspiracy to burn down the arena.

I figured they weren't far from the truth, although it was Charlene Devangi they should be blaming and not Lyle. Nobody had heard from Charlene, and Hannah hadn't shown up on anybody's radar, yet. I imagined that the Ra'Ak, who had the ability to fold space, managed to get both to Peru.

Hannah probably didn't know much about the operations in Peru, but I doubted Charlene would be satisfied with lounging by the pool and handpicking her bed partner for the night. She was too much of a control freak to allow that to happen.

My guess was if she didn't know it already, she was working on the ones who did know the information she wanted. More than anything, I wanted to capture her and let Kell ask questions.

~

Peru

Laurel Rome

"It's Hannah." Deris was angry. He'd already set fire to the plants and trees surrounding the flagstone patio. While it appeared that Granger stood before us, it wasn't Granger. The real Granger would have burned to a crisp in full daylight.

This wasn't Granger, although whomever it was kept insisting that he was Hannah.

"How the fuck did you do that?" I demanded of Hannah/Granger. "Where's Granger, then?"

"I did nothing," Hannah/Granger wailed. "They did this to me."

"Who?" Deris demanded. "This is the work of a talented warlock. They have no warlocks."

"I don't know who did it." Now they-he-she was crying. It wasn't appropriate, watching a grown vampire cry like that. The real Granger wouldn't have.

"Then tell us what happened." Daris stood nearby, her arms crossed tightly over her chest, probably to cover up the fact that she had small breasts.

"I was with Charlene—ask her," Hannah/Granger sobbed. "And suddenly, I was in the desert with those—those thugs of yours. They thought I was Granger. How could they think that?"

"This is getting nowhere fast," Daris grumbled. "Deris, can you reverse the spell?"

"Not until I know more about it," he hedged.

He didn't know? He told me he was one of the most powerful warlocks of his race. "What's that supposed to mean?" I snapped. "I want Granger back here. Like ten minutes ago."

"We have to search for Granger, so you'll have to calm down," Deris turned toward me, his eyes narrowing. I didn't like his attitude and considered telling him so.

I didn't want to end up like Hannah, though.

"Let me know when you find Granger," I said and stalked toward the house. I didn't give a fuck about Hannah, or the fact that she now had a dick. Granger was an ally and I wanted him back.

Kordevik

Onion? She lay beside me, sound asleep. I'd found her there when I opened my eyes for the first time in who knew how long.

"Hmmm?" she stirred at my mental nudging.

"Baby, I'm going to touch you," I whispered before reaching out a hand and smoothing hair away from her face.

"Kory?" She huddled into a smaller ball.

"Come on," I ran a hand down her shoulder. "Wake up and talk to me."

"Noo." With eyes still shut, she moved to turn over.

"Come on." I scooted closer and pulled her against me.

"Cold."

"I can fix that."

"Mmmm. Love it." I'd turned up my heat just a little, so she'd be warmer.

"Love *you*," I whispered against her hair.

Lexsi was right—we needed to set a date and do this—the bite. I had a rock-hard erection and no relief in sight unless I left her shivering in my bed while I dealt with the problem myself.

At that moment, I wanted to shout at all gods responsible for the fucking bite in the first place. I didn't care if it was easier on the female now. It was still a load of falaca dung and I wanted to say so. I could be fried to a crisp for it, but it still needed to be said.

"Kory?"

"What baby?"

"I'm hungry."

~

Lexsi

Anita and Watson sat at the kitchen island, drinking coffee and deliberately not speaking to each other.

Strained relations? Kory asked as he steered me toward the coffee pot.

Looks that way. Will you help me make breakfast?

If it involves bacon, I'd even go to the store for you, he grinned.

I think we have bacon, but let me check. We may have to feed an army, I said. Kory lifted down two coffee cups from the cabinet while I brewed more coffee.

We'll need bacon, eggs and milk, I determined after studying the nearly-empty fridge for a moment.

While Kory and I held our silent conversation, no words were exchanged between Watson and Anita. In fact, the silence was distressing. Anita watched Kory and me weave past one another as we made coffee and mental grocery lists.

Watson frowned as he drank from his cup. I had no idea what the fight was about, but I wasn't looking forward to a protracted silence between those two.

"Here." Kory took Watson's nearly-empty cup from his hand so fast the werewolf didn't have time to blink, and thumped a fresh cup onto the island.

Watson jumped when Kory did that.

"What the fuck, man?" Watson snapped.

"I was about to ask you the same fucking question, man," Kory snarled at Watson. "You have a woman sitting beside you who wants your sorry ass, although for the life of me I can't figure out why. She could do a hundred times better than this." Kory flung out a hand.

I watched as Anita sat straighter in her chair, her interest piqued in this verbal exchange between Kory and Watson.

"I'll uh, skip to the store," I said, although I wanted to see how this turned out.

"I'll come with you," Anita slipped off her barstool. "I don't want to watch when Kory rips out werewolf fur."

"What?" Watson's attention turned to Anita, who wore a smug smile.

"I wouldn't care if Kory stomped you so far into the tile you wore the pattern when he peeled you off it," Anita snapped. "I'm going to the store with Lexsi. Go ahead, make your case with a High Demon," she gestured toward Kory. "I think he's frustrated enough to smack you senseless."

"What's that supposed to mean?" Watson huffed, rising from his barstool. Kory was blowing smoke, so it was probably just as well to put distance between them.

"Come on," Anita grabbed my arm as I blinked at Kory and Watson. "Let's go."

Without waiting for me to agree, she folded space to the supermarket.

~

Kordevik

"What the fuck is with you, man?" Watson backed away from me. My Thifilathi was so close, the heat of it would have melted the paint off the kitchen wall if I'd touched it.

"You," I pointed a finger at him, "Get to have sex any fucking time you want, with someone who loves you more than your sorry ass deserves," I growled. "I can't. Not unless I follow a stupid, archaic ritual and put my fangs in Lexsi's neck, first. She's terrified of that and I can't blame her. Now is the picture clearing up for you?"

"Not with all this smoke, it's not," Watson fanned the smoke I'd blown in his direction. "Damn, dude, you could have told me this before instead of wading into the middle of one of our fights."

"It's time you figured out what's important," I said. "If you can't tell her how you feel, or if you don't feel the same, at least back off and let someone else win her affections. This hot and cold business is bullshit."

"What?"

"Just what I said. If you don't care about her, other than having an easy lay because she loves you so much, then do the right thing and let her go."

"But," Watson began.

"But what?" I said.

"She's not werewolf," he hung his head. "I'm the last male of my line. I need," he stopped. I hoped it was because he realized how stupid that sounded.

"Your sister can continue the line," I pointed out. At least I'd stopped breathing smoke, and it had almost cleared out of the kitchen.

"But not with a vampire," he shouted.

"You are such a backward, backwoods, back-ended nitwit," I grumbled. "Find a werewolf who wouldn't mind providing sperm. I think Mason would make a top-notch dad."

"What?" Watson blinked at me for several seconds while the idea churned in his brain. "Who?" he demanded.

"I think Davis or Thomas would be excellent choices. We met another werewolf in D.C. who'd be a good choice, too. His name's Jorden Billings."

"Huh?"

"You heard me."

"No," he held up a hand. "You met Jorden?"

"He works for Opal."

"Damn. I haven't seen him since he moved back East. Had no idea what he was doing."

"You've had your head up your ass for a while, I take it?"

"Yeah. I guess so."

"Besides, there's no guarantee that you and Anita won't," I began.

"A werewolf who grows scales?"

At that comment, I was ready to throw him onto the floor and show him what somebody with scales could do to his furry ass.

"Wait, that was stupid," he amended. "She's as badass as they come. Can you imagine what a werewolf mixed with her race might do?"

"Plenty," I said. "So if it happens, be sure to raise him or her right, although I think Anita would have that covered anyway."

"Yeah. It's a cinch he wouldn't be bullied at school."

"Just make sure he isn't the bully."

"We'll make sure of that."

"Well, all right, then. What the hell was this fight about, anyway?"

"Moving in together," Watson mumbled.

"You didn't want to?" I couldn't believe what I was hearing.

"No, I asked her to, but I think she wanted something more."

"I think she's waiting to hear that you love her, you stupid prick. I figure she's worried that she's only a temporary thing in your life, until you establish yourself as the big, bad Packmaster and have werewolf women flung at your feet."

"That's not all," Watson sighed and turned his back to me.

"What, then?"

"She's, well, she's bigger and badder than I am."

"You're worried you won't be king in the castle?"

"Something like that."

"You are the biggest fucking difik I've ever met," I fumed.

"What's that supposed to mean?" He turned back to me, then.

"Difik means idiot. Make that slow idiot. A difik is somebody you have to hit with the brick wall, to show them what brick wall really means."

"You don't know how I feel, man." He turned away again.

"I don't know how you feel? Damn, you're worse than I thought. Lexsi is related to royalty on two sides, man. You think I have that in my background? Do you? She has talents I can't begin to duplicate. You don't see me whining, do you? She saved my ass twice. I'm not about to quibble over who's more of a badass. I think Lexsi and I work well together. That's that. I have no idea what's going on in that fucked up male brain of yours, but you need to allow somebody else to be strong. Strong enough to stand beside you when things turn to shit."

"Are you two arguing?" Kell walked in and headed for the coffeepot.

"I figure you could hear us from a mile away," I raked fingers through my hair.

"I heard you from my bedroom. If I disagreed with anything you said, I'd have shown up sooner." Kell's grin was slow and welcome.

"What the hell is going on?" Opal was three seconds behind Kell and still in her robe and pajamas. I blinked.

Well, it was bound to happen sometime. Opal looked happy, I knew that much.

"Kordevik is dispensing wisdom, dearest," Kell leaned in to kiss Opal. "Want coffee?"

"I'd love some." Opal took a seat at the island while Kell poured two cups.

"We're back. Is the fight over? Please say the fight's over," Lexsi announced as she and Anita appeared in the kitchen.

"Ah. Just in time. Shall I help you with the meal?" Kell asked. "I haven't cooked in a very, very long time."

"Thank the gods," Anita sighed and planted two bags of groceries on the island. Watson gave me the finger and went to help put food away.

Opal grinned at me behind Watson's back, and that made me laugh.

～

Lexsi

Opal, Anita and I had a private meeting after breakfast, while Kory, Kell and Watson went to the gym.

"I got mindspeech from Esme," Anita said, spreading her fingers across the cool granite of the kitchen island. Kory made Watson clean after the rest of us cooked breakfast, so there wasn't so much as a smudge on it anywhere. It was only fair that he do his part.

"What did Esme say?" Opal didn't sound surprised at all. More and more, I suspected that Opal had a place in the hierarchy of gods, I merely didn't know what her placement was. Being of that caste held certain drawbacks—at times their hands were tied because of noninterference rules.

"Just in time," Opal lifted her head as Zaria and Klancy walked into the kitchen. I blinked. The sun was shining, yet there Klancy stood, as if he were used to being awake during the day.

"It is a gift," Klancy smiled at me. "I do not question the miracle of it, only my deserving of it."

"Have a seat," Anita patted the chair next to hers. "I heard from Esme."

"What did Esme have to say?" Zaria sat on the chair Klancy pulled out for her.

171

"She says that the assholes in Peru have a hostage."

"Who?" Opal went still.

"Crown Princess Amalthea," Anita's shoulders sagged.

"Tell me," Opal said.

"Amalthea and a few others were out patrolling their area, when three Sirenali showed up," Anita began. "There was a skirmish. Two of Amalthea's guards were killed and Amalthea was folded out of the water. We figure she's at their compound in Peru, now. If she's smart, she won't turn back to human while they have her. She's a novelty for now, but that may not last."

"Who is Amalthea?" I asked.

"Phineas' daughter. Phineas, as you won't know who he is, either, is King of the Merfolk."

"She's a mermaid?" I blinked stupidly at Opal.

"Yes. Phineas is one of the old-school holdouts against organizing the shifters and forming a council. He says there's no need for it. I hope this changes his mind."

"There are mermaids." I turned my gaze on Zaria.

"I've never met one personally," she shrugged. "I do know about them. There are extensive files in the Larentii Archives."

"You know Nefrigar?" I whispered.

"I do."

"Small universe," I muttered, staring at my hands. For me, Nefrigar, Chief Archivist of the Larentii Archives, was *Uncle* Nefrigar. He was my mother's Larentii mate, although I seldom saw him.

"Not everybody has a Larentii in their family," Opal smiled.

"I'd like to be able to introduce a Larentii to Watson," Anita said. "Like, Watson, meet my really tall, really blue friend, and then watch Watson piss himself," she giggled.

"Still in the realm of possibilities," Zaria said. "You never know. Stranger things have probably happened."

"What can we do to help Amalthea?" I asked. "Is Esme all right?"

"Esme is fine for the moment, but she and a few others are contemplating a trek into Peru. I don't think that's a good idea," Anita said.

"I think it's a death trap," Zaria stated bluntly. "If they have any sense at all, they'll hold back until we can send help. A mister may be able to get across the border, but once across, you'd have to look for blank spots that aren't guarded by N'il Mo'erti or covered in spells before you became corporeal. If you hauled others in, same thing." She hunched her shoulders.

"N'il Mo'erti?"

"Death machines. Created on Tiralia."

Every Alliance schoolchild knew about Tiralia. How it had destroyed itself with dangerous chemicals and weapons. I was now learning what they'd called those weapons that had effectively killed an entire planet.

"It's what caused the hole in those vineyards east of here," Opal explained. "Just one of them, not operating at its full capacity."

"You didn't have anything to do with these, did you?" Opal turned to Zaria.

"No. Just the ones in the future."

"Huh?" Anita and I said at the same time.

"Nothing to worry about. It's just that Zaria has seen these things before. It's a long story and sort of irrelevant at the moment."

"If you say so." Opal's answer didn't satisfy me in the least, and I was determined to find out what the long story actually was.

"It involves a doubling back on the timeline. What happens the second time around that didn't happen the first time, and vice versa," Zaria explained.

"That doesn't make any sense," I countered.

"Ah. It doesn't make sense to you now, but it could have made sense before—or after."

"You're making my brain hurt," I complained.

"Sometimes, time looks like spaghetti," Zaria sighed.

"Cooked or uncooked?"

"All right, now we're getting somewhere," she smiled. "Cooked."

"In other words, I should stop worrying about it."

"Exactly," Opal and Zaria chorused.

"Okay. What can we do to help Esme and Amalthea?" I asked.

"A trip to Ecuador may be in our future," Opal said. "We just have to pack up our little army and move into suitable quarters down there. I warn you, they're completely patriarchal. We'll need the men to do the talking for us, so we'll fit in."

"I sort of hate that," Zaria blinked at Opal.

"Sort of?"

"Okay, I really hate it. If I set some pants on fire, you think they'll listen to me, then?"

"Kell and Klancy speak fluent Spanish," Opal ignored Zaria. "I think Kory speaks enough to get by. Tibby, if I can convince him to come, will be a big help."

"Farin won't let him leave without her," Anita pointed out.

"Then Farin will come. I hope she understands how important this is. Besides, he got paid for that fight, so he owes Kory and the rest of us for that."

"He still got paid?" Anita's eyes widened.

"In the contract. Lover Boy Landon didn't show. Tibby won by default."

"Wow," I breathed.

"We received a letter from State Senator Maria Riveras, pledging her help in our endeavors since we saved Tibby and Farin," Opal said. "I think a trip to Ecuador isn't too much to ask."

"Nice," Anita grinned.

"I think Diego and Tibby's cousins could help out too," I suggested.

"I'd think so," Opal agreed. "They're on standby. If Tibby goes, they can go. Just remember, we'll be right on top of the equator, so pack lighter clothing."

"Can animals go back and forth across Peru's boundary without getting dead?" Anita asked.

"Good question. Let's find out," Zaria laughed.

~

Kordevik

"I believe a trip to Ecuador is in our near future," Kell lifted the barbell from my hands and placed it on the floor. "I hope you speak Spanish."

"I have enough to get by," I said, lifting my towel from a nearby chair and wiping my face with it. "Languages have always been easy for me."

"Good. It will be required where we're going," he said.

"What's this?" Watson rolled off the weight bench and stretched. He'd worked out shirtless. As a result, two women and at least one man were staring.

At all of us.

"*Hablas Espanol?*" Kell asked.

"Not much," Watson rubbed the back of his neck. "Shower here or at home?"

"I suggest going home. The scent coming from the men's shower isn't pleasant. I detect fungus," Kell said.

"I'm anti-fungus. How about you?" I swatted Watson with my towel.

"All the way, dude. You providing transportation?"

"The minute we're out of sight."

"Good. Shall we?" Watson gestured toward the door.

"He does possess manners." Kell lifted an eyebrow at me.

"You have a cool accent, man," Watson pulled my towel away and swatted at Kell. "If I had an accent like that, I'd never shut up."

"And just as swiftly, the manners have departed," Kell moaned. "Shall we ever survive this dearth of civility?"

Watson snickered as we walked out of the gym.

Peru

Laurel Rome

"I don't like her." Granted, the swimming pool was a saltwater pool to start with, but now it held—*her*. "She's half naked, for Christ's sake," I gestured at the mermaid, who was glaring at me from beneath the surface.

"She's half fish. Leave her alone." Hannah, still looking like Granger, was half-dressed, too. At least she could avoid the tan lines from a bikini top, although the bottoms didn't hide much. I'd caught a flash of knob and balls at least once.

The whole thing was disgusting—she hadn't bothered to shave.

"You're just jealous because she has perfect breasts," Hannah went on. "If you're so offended, toss her a top."

"V'ili said we couldn't interfere," I snipped.

"Then shut up," Hannah retorted. "Some of us like peace and quiet while we're tanning. Just look at this body—as pale as a peeled potato."

"Granger's a vampire. The whole sun thing is a bit extreme," I hissed at her.

"He's not a vampire now—well, I'm not a vampire. I just look like a vampire. Him. Granger. Get out of the way, bitch, you're blocking my light."

"You little, two-faced trollop." I went after her.

"Stop now."

V'ili's voice halted me just as I was ready to jab my fingernails into Hannah's eyes. "Leave. I wish to enjoy my prize without your, ah, noisy discussion."

"She's a prize?" My voice betrayed the disgust I felt. "She's half of a fucking fish."

"And you, my dear, are half of a fucking moron. Leave. Now." Power invaded his words. "Do not wander far. My men will be convinced to shoot you if you do."

I wanted to gouge out his eyes. Peel off his toenails until he screamed. I couldn't. He smiled at me with the pointed teeth he often displayed. It let me know he wasn't happy with me at the moment.

I reminded myself that it was wiser to play his game. Someday, he wouldn't be looking.

Someday.

~

Lexsi

Wow, Anita's voice sounded in my head. With Kory in the lead, he, Kell and Watson traipsed through the kitchen, all of them half-dressed and sweaty from working out.

I'm surprised they weren't kidnapped by desperate women, Opal's voice sounded in our heads.

Or desperate men, Zaria added. *Just as well, I'd be forced to go looking for them, and I really don't have time for that.*

Anita snickered.

Watson stopped in his tracks, turned around, walked straight back to Anita and pulled her up for a kiss. It lasted a long time, too.

Damn.

I wanted a kiss like that.

Peru

Vic Malone

Loftin Qualls paced the floor of our shared bungalow like a caged tiger. The one called V'ili told us that from now on, we would only kill at his command. It chafed, but we found we had no choice but to bow to his wishes.

What did V'ili have that nobody else did?

He'd taken our phones, television and everything else away; we only had a tablet each with books and prerecorded movies on it.

Nothing from the outside world came to us. I may as well have been back in prison. Loftin, though, at times the crazy came through in his eyes. I worried about that. Crazy was something that maybe V'ili couldn't control.

I still didn't know what V'ili was, and he didn't understand the need I had—the need to see the blood flow. To witness the pain before death.

The pain shot through my head from just thinking about it.

V'ili had done this to us. If my head hurt, Loftin's had to hurt ten times as bad.

Fuck. I wanted to kill V'ili with my bare hands. The pain in my head was so bad after that thought, I believed I was going to die.

∼

Lexsi

"León and Diego will come with Tibby and me," Farin dumped fresh tomatoes onto the salad. "He says Ecuador is nice, and we'll be close to the beach."

"Farin," I caught her arm. "You know this is dangerous, don't you?"

"Yeah." She dropped her eyes to the salad bowl. The bowl was huge —we had many people to feed.

"Look who I found." Zaria walked into the kitchen, followed by a sheepish Jamie Rome.

"Where have you been?" I demanded, waving the wooden spoon I'd used to stir the broccoli-cheddar soup I was making.

"I ah, went to visit my mother and brother—with Zaria's help," he sighed.

I studied him for a moment. He looked better. Not nearly as thin. Somebody had bent time with him.

I refused to ask how long the visit was. Had to be a few weeks, at least.

"He feels better, now. I found him a shrink," Zaria said. "Need help?"

"It's almost ready," I said. "Table's set, drinks are made, all you have to do is sit down and enjoy."

"I'm sorry I made you worry," Jamie pulled me into a hug. "It won't happen again, I promise."

"Tell that to Anita," I said pulling away and going back to the soup.

"She's going to kick my ass," he said.

"I won't, but I'll think about it," Anita arrived and pulled him into a tight hug. "We missed you."

"Yeah," he said. I noticed his eyes were misty when he pulled away.

CHAPTER 12

*L*exsi

"We have Zaria to thank for this," Opal said beside me. She'd left her dark hair loose; it clouded about her face in the breeze off the ocean below us. I leaned my arms on the half-wall surrounding the patio of our borrowed housing, while Opal stood straight and tall beside me.

Our temporary home in Ecuador was in Punta Blanca, half an hour north of Salinas. The ocean view from our extensive compound was breathtaking, although the breeze off the water at this time of year called for a light sweater.

We had two vehicles in the garage if we needed them—since Punta Blanca was mostly residential with no markets or stores in easy walking distance, we needed a vehicle to get around. Or at least to keep up appearances.

"Anita says Esme will join us for dinner tonight," Opal went on. "She's made several trips to the Galapagos, trying to contact Phineas. He isn't answering."

"That doesn't sound good."

"I'm worried he'll attempt to get into Peru himself, and that could be fatal."

"I hear you."

The water near the shore turned a deep turquoise as clouds moved across it. Farther out, the sun glinted off the South Pacific so brightly I almost couldn't look at it. For me, it was difficult to imagine shapeshifters who spent most of their time in the water.

"Do they come out for, ah," I floundered.

"Yes. Sex is, by nature, safer and much more pleasurable when they're humanoid. It's standard practice among shifters. Before you ask," she said, folding her arms over her breasts and lowering her eyes for a moment, "I'm a rare breed. There are no others like me, now. I'm an overly tall, overly fast velociraptor. I was young when I watched Europeans crowd into these lands and take them by force, in many cases. My family of shifters was revered by our tribe. Most of them died protecting that tribe. I'm the only one left."

"I'm sorry about your family." I wanted to hug her but held back. Opal was such a private person, and I felt as if I were eavesdropping on a precious, painful memory.

"It was a long time ago," she said. "And so you know, I appreciate hugs just as much as anybody."

I did hug her, then. I couldn't begin to imagine what it was like, watching your family and friends die in front of you. It must have been horrible.

"Thanks," Opal wiped moisture from her cheeks when I stepped back. "I don't tell many that story."

"I'm glad you told me. It helps," I said, "to know what you're fighting for. Who you're fighting for."

Gran always said that everybody had a story. We needed to learn as many stories as we could, to add to our own. *It makes us better people,* she'd say, *because we know their pain. At times, it coincides with ours. At other times, we can only shake our heads at the strength it must have taken for them to endure the hardships and adversities of their lives.*

I knew Gran was one of those people. She'd fought hard for herself and those around her. I was only beginning to earn a place for myself in the universe.

"You do well enough," Opal smiled at me.

"Save that for when we get rid of the mess in Peru," I whispered.

"Agreed."

Kordevik

"I prefer tea," Klancy refused my offer of coffee.

"I think we can make a cup of tea," Anita said. She and I stood in the kitchen at the compound in Punta Blanca, digging through supplies for something to snack on for lunch.

The kitchen wasn't as nice as the one in San Rafael, but we could make do. Instead of an island, we had counter space and a large table set near a window for a view of the ocean. Klancy sat there, watching Anita and me as we prowled the new space.

"Esme's coming for dinner," Anita informed me as she sifted through a box to find tea bags. "Earl Grey?" Anita turned to ask Klancy.

"That should be fine. Thank you." Somehow, Klancy was less grave and serious, after—well, after he'd met Zaria, and she'd made it possible for him to walk in daylight and eat normal food.

I almost asked him where Zaria was, but held back. Maybe it was none of my business. "We get hot water the traditional way," Anita turned a stove burner on and filled the teakettle with water.

"Want me to do it?" I asked.

"You'll just melt the teakettle."

"Probably." I put coffee in the coffee maker. "I tried to fire ceramics, once. Broke everything. Too hot too fast," I explained.

"Seriously? That's funny."

"It's a part of army training on Kifirin," I said. "How to control your heat levels."

"Now, that I didn't expect," Anita handed me a coffee cup. "There I was, imagining that you'd taken time to explore your artistic side. I should have known better."

"Dude, you have an artistic side?" Watson shuffled in and began opening cabinet doors, no doubt searching for something to eat.

"Doubt it," I said, watching the coffeemaker do its work, steaming and sputtering as it filled the pot with dark liquid. "Although I might be able to shave an important message in your fur come the full moon."

"What message would that be?"

"I'm a difik?"

"Don't fall for it." Anita's whisper was loud enough for the neighbors to hear.

Klancy laughed.

I had to admit, I'd never heard him laugh until that moment. Even Watson grinned at the sound.

Lexsi

"Dinner will be better, I promise," I told Watson, who'd grumbled over ham sandwiches for lunch. "I need to find a local market, to buy fish or whatever is fresh."

"Thank you," he mouthed at me before grinning.

"I'll come with you, as protection," Anita offered.

"I'm coming," Kory insisted.

"Will the market hold all of us?" I asked.

"It'll be fine. Have money? Let's go," Zaria arrived with Klancy not far behind her. "Want to go to the market, honey?" she turned to ask him.

I learned Klancy had a dimple, then, because he smiled at Zaria.

"I will go wherever you go," he said.

The market was more than a mile away, so Klancy drove the SUV we found in the garage.

"Are you kidding?" Anita disagreed with Kory's choice of cookies. "That's all sugar."

"Are you saying I don't need sugar?"

Anita blinked at him for several seconds before grabbing a second bag and tossing it into our cart. Zaria snickered as she walked behind them. I realized they hadn't been talking about sugar.

Not exactly. I felt my face warm as I quickened my pace toward the meat section at the back of the market.

Anita and Zaria—did they realize how lucky they were? That they could kiss and make love whenever they wanted?

It just wasn't fair.

People don't die of sexual frustration, I reminded myself as Kory came to stand beside me. For a moment, I watched the smooth, bulging muscles in his arm flex beneath the short sleeves of his T-shirt, and wondered what it would be like to have those arms wrapped around me while—I forced myself away from that image.

"The tuna steaks look nice," Kory rumbled beside me.

Closing my eyes, I took a deep breath before opening them again and studying the fish behind the glass. "*Por favor, señor*," Kory called to the aproned man standing behind the counter, "*Esta fresco el pescado?*" He pointed at the tuna steaks.

"*Si*," the man nodded and moved forward. "*Cogido esta mañana.*"

"I want all he has," I looked up at Kory. Kory relayed my instructions. We watched, Kory's hand rubbing my back, as the man wrapped all the tuna steaks for us and handed them over.

"Tell him I want two kilograms of the large shrimp, too." They'd make a great appetizer.

The man grinned as Kory translated.

"We may need a bigger cart," Anita said dryly.

We have people to feed, I reminded her.

After getting several other things to make sauce for the fish and fresh vegetables to go with the meal, Klancy drove us back to the compound. Esme, Anita's cousin who looked enough like Anita to be her sister, waited there for us, and it looked like she'd brought a guest.

An unhappy guest.

I was introduced to Phineas, King of the Merpeople in South American Waters. If restless anger could kill, we'd all be dead within seconds.

~

Opal

"These people are allies," I snapped at Phineas. He was a grump at the best of times. With his daughter in the hands of the enemy, his foul mood had ramped up to impossible levels.

"You're having a party, while my daughter is in the hands of filth," he snapped back.

"It's not a party. It's dinner. We have to eat, and we have to plan. You have no idea what you're up against, and if I know you at all, you'll go marching in or swimming in, and that will get you fried and on a plate in thirty minutes."

At least he'd agreed to go to the garage before venting his anger. I had some of my own to toss back at him. The others had made an effort to make him comfortable—he'd been rude in each instance.

"I don't know whether she's alive, and neither do you," he accused, pointing a finger at me.

"Someone reliable says she probably is—she's a novelty to them."

"Put in a tank for humans to gawk at."

"Look, you can turn everybody against you now and die going in by yourself, or you can be civil, accept our help, play a part in this and hopefully come out with your life and your daughter's life intact."

"Who says she's alive?"

We were back to that.

"Zaria."

"The one who found me." His voice was flat.

"Yes. Zaria is quite talented. If anybody can help find your daughter, it will be her."

"I want to grind them between a rock and the seabed," he hissed, clenching his fists.

"I want that too, only I want it to be more painful than that."

I'd surprised him—his eyes widened for a moment at my words. "I've already seen the dead they left behind. The machines that kill on command," I hissed. "I've dealt with the creatures they've hired into this mess to kill anyone they don't like. Money, greed and power is at the root of this. Your daughter is a pawn to them. A fish in a tank, kept because she's pretty and a rarity. Don't give them a motive to harm her."

"You think they will?" Anguish filled his words for a moment. Say what you would about Phineas, he loved his daughter.

"I hope not. We really need to pinpoint their location. They're growing a plant, the seeds of which produce a terrible drug. That doesn't mean the bulk of them are somewhere amid the fields. If my guess is correct, they have taken something luxurious for themselves. That means we must systematically rule out those places we can, to get a better vision of where they may be."

"And then what?"

"We attack. I'm hoping for more recruits, but that's not something we can rely on. Regardless, we have a small army here. It may be enough."

"Faugh." He threw out a hand. "Three of theirs killed Amalthea's guards and captured her. What do we have to fight against that?"

"More than you know," I said.

~

Lexsi

"This is awesome. I mean, we have good cooks on Grey Planet, but this," Yoff pointed his fork at the last bite of tuna steak in sauce. "This transcends every spell I could ever make."

"Stop it," I grinned at him. He and Kell had been out all day; I had no idea where or for what reason, but I figured Kell was teaching Yoff what it meant to be a spy.

"What are you?" Phineas interrupted our happy food session. Whatever came out of that man's mouth sounded as if he were displeased with the universe. His question was pointed at Yoff, who studied Phineas for a moment.

"I am the son of a winged vampire, who is also the son of a winged vampire, and I have skills as a wizard." Yoff lifted a hand, causing Phineas' wineglass to lift from the table.

"So you can lift a glass off the table," Phineas snorted.

I watched Kory instead of Yoff; Kory sat closer to Phineas, and I was surprised he wasn't blowing smoke by this time.

"Oh, sure. I do party tricks," Yoff agreed, just before Phineas' plate turned into a vicious lion's head that snapped at him. Phineas' chair scraped across the tiled floor in a blink and Phineas almost toppled over it in his haste to get away.

"Yeah. I do party tricks." Yoff lifted the last bite of tuna steak to his mouth and chewed. It was just as Great-Uncle Erland said. High Demons had a strange knack of knowing when a spell wasn't threatening and allowing it to continue.

The phenomenon had been studied in my mother's time with the ASD—they'd first discovered that talent in her back then. It was natural, something that wasn't consciously done. Yoff's spell hadn't threatened me or most of the people about me—in fact, it had helped. Phineas was more than surprised, I knew that much.

Good one, cousin. I wanted to laugh. Phineas, on the other hand, looked from Yoff to Opal and then back to Yoff. Lifting his chair off the floor, he set it down at his place at the table with barely a thump. The lion's head disappeared, leaving Phineas' food untouched.

"The food is excellent," Phineas muttered.

"Thank you," I smiled at him.

"It's called the RDS effect," Kory grinned at Anita. "Actually, it's Lexsi's mother's initials—Reah Desh Silver. She's the one who first proved its existence when she was with the ASD."

Anita was puzzled as to why Yoff's spell hadn't been nullified. She was grateful, but mystified by the whole thing.

"That's interesting," Anita chewed her lip as she studied Kory. "Would it have been nullified if he'd aimed the spell at one of you?"

"Yes," Kory and I answered together. "If either of us were threatened, the spell would have been nullified for everyone within our protective perimeter. That's only about twenty feet, tops," Kory continued. "So it's wise not to wander too far."

"Here's my question, then," Anita sounded thoughtful. "If Yoff launches a spell against the enemy within your protective circle, what happens?"

"Uh," Kory looked at me and shook his head.

"I think," I said after considering it for a moment, "that the spell against the enemy may go unimpeded, if the enemy is threatening us. Mom would know for sure, but she's not here to ask."

"What is this race?" Phineas asked. "I fail to understand any of this."

"High Demon," Kory leveled a look at Phineas. "This," he tapped his chest, "is our least threatening form."

"Demon?" I could see he was used to the Earth tales of demons. We weren't those demons.

"They're not the demons you've read about in Earth tales," Opal pointed out quickly. "They're from light-years away and have nothing to do with what you know or think you know."

"How can I trust this?" He was back to being an asshole quickly.

"Because I trust it—and them," Zaria said.

Phineas turned to her, studying her face for several moments before nodding. I had no idea what she'd done to get him to trust her, but it had worked, whatever it was.

"Then I will reserve judgment," Phineas stated, his voice flat. That was probably the best we would get from him until he had more proof.

"We are allies here," Tibby spoke for the first time. "They have already saved my life more than once. If you wish to be suspicious of those who are ready to defend your life with theirs, then go ahead. Align with the enemy. They are suspicious of them, too. Suspicious enough to want them dead many times over. These, my friend," he pointed at Kory and me, "are the biggest threat to our enemy as the enemy perceives it. Treat them badly; you may be left on the outside when they rescue your daughter."

"Is that your intention?" Phineas turned a skeptical gaze in our direction.

"To rescue your daughter and eliminate the enemy?" Kory asked.

"Yes," I nodded at Kory's words. "Those are our intentions. If you want in, now's the time to say so."

"And be honest," Opal warned. "Lexsi will know if you speak the truth."

"She's a guli—a truthspeaker of her race," Zaria told Phineas. "She will know if you lie."

"I want to believe," Phineas admitted, rising from his seat and walking toward the window. "With this, I no longer know what to believe. It is my fear that I will never see my daughter again."

That was truth in anybody's mind.

"I promise this," Zaria spoke. "If it is within my power, you will have her back, unharmed."

Opal drew in a breath. She knew something about Zaria that I had yet to learn. I could almost hear my mother speaking in my mind. *Have patience*, her familiar voice said. I released a sigh and fought the urge to reveal my impatience by asking questions now.

"I never knew Merpeople were real," Farin broke the silence after Zaria's statement. "I dressed up as a mermaid for Halloween once, but I always thought they were a fairy tale."

"You see the truth of it before you now," Phineas sounded civil for the first time since I'd met him. "It is my wish that you keep our secret."

"I know what can happen if I don't," Farin ducked her head. I knew that under the table, she gripped Tibby's hand. She could ruin—if not kill outright—Tibby and his family, including Tibby's grandmother, who held an important position in the California legislature.

One of Tibby's cousins was already dead, because he'd helped save her life. She'd led the enemy back to Kory, too, and he'd been attacked in Las Vegas. Farin had learned a very important lesson about keeping secrets.

"Excuse me," Opal said when her cell phone rang. She walked toward the hall leading to the bedrooms before answering. Only the werewolf and the vampires at the table could hear the conversation past that, and they'd never reveal what they'd heard.

She was back in ten minutes. "I have information from Mason, Thomas and Davis," Opal said. "They and a few others working undercover for the Secretary of Defense have been watching the known locations for body dumps along the Peruvian border. The bodies of children and people from high, remote villages are now appearing at those locations. I don't know about everyone here, but that makes my blood boil."

I understood what she'd said and why she'd said it. Those people were native to Peru. As in the past, they were being systematically slaughtered by the invaders.

"I have images," Opal set a tablet on the table. "None of it's pretty." She'd seen this before, countless times, I realized.

"I have a question," I said as Phineas pulled the tablet to him to examine photographs.

"What's that?" Opal turned dark, troubled eyes in my direction.

"The enemy knows when somebody tries to get in. Do they know when those people who are already there try to get out?"

"I don't think they'd care, one way or the other," Esme observed.

"So they're only killing the people who won't cooperate with them —either to do their dirty work or to move from their homes to make way for drakus seed fields?" I asked.

"Lexsi, I doubt they want anyone to cross the border who might carry tales of what's really happening," Opal frowned. "That's why the President and the Secretary of State can conveniently keep their heads up their posteriors. No hard evidence."

"Except for the surveillance planes getting shot down," Klancy pointed out.

"Then how can we protect the indigenous population while we plan our attacks?" Kory asked. "It was part of my military training," he added, turning to Phineas. "Not only to engage the enemy, but to get as many innocents as we could out of the way beforehand. We learned that lesson when so many comesuli died in Veshtul."

"I may have a solution," Zaria said, her words tentative. "But we really need the cooperation of our High Demons and Secretary of Defense on this."

"Whatever it takes," Kory said, "I will do."

"I stand with Kory," I said. "No matter what."

"Want to have a short planning session before I contact Colonel Hunter?" Opal asked Zaria.

"Yeah." She hunched her shoulders. I could see there was something else there, but she'd spoken the truth. I didn't want to pry into personal affairs, and that's how it appeared to me. Zaria had her own demons to combat, and didn't need curious or idle questions bringing out what could prove painful for her.

I stood and began collecting empty plates while Zaria and Opal walked out of the dining room. Anita, Esme and Kory rose to help.

"I saw those photographs after Phineas was done." Watson lifted the heavy bowl from Anita's hands and placed it on the top shelf of a kitchen cabinet. "They didn't spare anybody, and it just looks—like genocide."

There was a tightness to Watson's mouth and a frown on his lips. I considered that if the carnage looked that bad to a werewolf, then it had to be terrible. I didn't want to see the photographs. The pictures in my mind made me queasy enough.

"It is genocide," Esme agreed. "Eventually, all of Peru may die, and Colombia may die soon after. Wherever that drug can grow isn't safe from the predations of this evil, if they are not stopped now."

"You know what concerns me?" Kory asked. I turned to look at him; he wore a thoughtful expression and I could see the worry in his dark eyes.

"What's that, bro?" Watson asked.

"That we could see this drug used as a bigger weapon than what they have already—not just here, but elsewhere."

"Let's hope that doesn't happen," Esme whispered, although I could see the idea of it taking hold in her head.

"How will they do that?" I asked. "In Vegas, they had targets. Who else would they target? Their main goal is to take us down. For the moment, I hope they don't know where we are."

"Baby," Kory pulled me against him, "they have rogue High Demons. They can skip anywhere. They also have rogue warlocks and witches, who can send that stuff anywhere with power. I'm concerned that anybody who opposes or speaks out against them could be targeted."

"You're scaring me," I mumbled against his broad chest. "I don't know how to fight this."

You don't have to fight it by yourself, onion, he whispered into my mind. *We'll figure this out.*

~

Opal

"I agree with Opal; something needs to be done," Secretary of Defense August Hunter stated flatly. He and I had a meeting with the Secretary of State and the President at breakfast the morning after my team sent the photographs of the Peruvian killings.

"We'll strongly condemn these actions, since you so unwisely sent these photographs to the UN," Secretary of State Hinson snapped.

"We have an obligation, and you promised them intel," I snapped back at him. "It was on your orders that I sent them."

"When I promised that information to the Secretary General, I had no idea how sensitive the information would be," he hissed. "I expected the deaths of a few dissidents in Peru. Not this," he swept a hand over the hard copies of images I'd provided.

The photographs were scattered across the breakfast table in the private dining room chosen for the meeting. So far, the President hadn't said anything, allowing Wilbur Hinson to carry the bulk of the conversation.

"We'll condemn this publicly," the President's voice was terse. He wasn't about to send troops to the Peruvian border. I knew mortal troops wouldn't have any defense against what had taken over the country, but didn't say it. The President knew about the paranormal employees working under different department heads, but preferred not to talk about them.

Yes, he was prejudiced in that way. He expected the Department heads to utilize those employees; he merely didn't want to hear about it. If I attempted to explain what had invaded Peru and was responsible for the damage and deaths in California and Nevada, he'd likely cover his ears while singing the National Anthem.

I worried about all those things, plus several others. A few prisons were still on my to-do list—prisons that held probable innocents instead of the original criminals. I was concerned about exposing Kory and Lexsi that way. The enemy was desperately attempting to eliminate both; they'd gone so far as to recruit Ra'Ak and rogue High Demons to do it. Who knew what they'd try if Kory and Lexsi showed up anywhere near one of their duplicate prisoners?

I knew the UN was preparing a statement on the genocide occurring in Peru; it would be released in twenty-four hours. A meeting would be called by the Security Council, of which the US was a member. I could hear our representative now, spouting off whatever the President told him to say.

The whole thing sickened me. Already we'd been attacked on American soil. I wondered how many deaths it would take before the President stood up for what was right. The citizens needed warnings instead of reassurances that the events in California and Nevada were isolated incidents.

The other thing that nagged at my mind was that the enemy could still be taking convicts from prisons. I hadn't gotten intel on that for more than a week and worried that the enemy was getting better with their replacements, and better at controlling wardens and guards.

"I'm concerned that those in Peru may align themselves with our other enemies," I said before I could stop myself.

"Which enemies? That's preposterous," Wilbur said.

"Which enemies would like to do us the most harm?" I countered.

"This is ridiculous and I have a meeting in fifteen minutes," the President shoved photographs in my direction. "Either bring me hard proof that our enemies are collaborating with these idiots in Peru or don't mention this to me again. Peru is in South America, for fuck's sake. Not our problem."

"Until it becomes our problem," Colonel Hunter rose from his seat. I understood he was seething; I was, too. Wilbur Hinson had become the poster child for those whose heads were buried in their asses.

"Thank you for meeting with us, Mr. President," I nodded and refused to meet his eyes. When this blew up in his face as it surely would, he'd be looking for someone to blame. He and Hinson would be happy to place that blame on Colonel Hunter and me. After all, we were the thorns in his side, leftovers from the previous administration. The Directors FBI and CIA were his appointees and his ass had their lip prints all over it.

"That was just as useless as I thought it would be," Colonel Hunter sighed as we walked along a marble-floored hall together.

"Yes, but it had to be done," I responded.

"I recorded the whole thing," he added.

"Good. So did I."

Vic Malone

"Kids and old people," Loftin mumbled as he paced. "Not like."

He wanted women to kill. Pretty women, in their prime. V'ili told us to kill Peruvian natives. Loftin didn't get off as well with those. His crazy had ramped up to new levels as a result, until I watched my own back with him.

"Shut up," Charlene snapped, causing Loftin's head to twist in her direction. He drooled while looking at her; it was disgusting. He wanted to kill her so bad he had a hard on.

V'ili said no killing of the women in the compound. Loftin held his head in his hands—he'd gotten pain from his desire to torture Charlene before she died.

I wanted to kill her, too—because she was a bitch and deserved it. Pain lanced through my brain at the thought.

"Both of you, to your cabin," Daris ordered. V'ili made sure we did as Deris and Daris commanded. Not Morgett, though. Morgett had his own way of making us suffer. I grabbed Loftin's arm and dragged him toward our quarters. No need to tempt fate, in case Daris decided to contact her uncle and tell him what bad boys we'd been.

"Kill them all." Spittle flew from Loftin's mouth as he spoke.

I wished at that moment it were possible.

CHAPTER 13

*P*eru
Laurel Rome

"They want in so badly, they're willing to pay us instead of the other way around," Morgett paced inside the compound's library. The books were gathering dust; nobody was interested in them, so they weren't cleaned.

"As long as they don't come near me," I insisted. Terrorists made me shiver. Not only could they do hit-and-run bombings whenever and wherever, they wanted to kill anybody not aligned with their particular organization or their version of religion. That included other terrorist groups. "I don't understand them or their language."

"My dear, we will supplant them, do not concern yourself," Morgett's grin revealed rows of sharp teeth at first. I blinked before my vision cleared and I saw they looked normal. I was so worried about the terrorists that I was seeing things.

"You mean we'll be terrorists?" I asked.

"We already are," he laughed.

❀

195

Lexsi

"Mason, Davis and Thomas will be coming in tonight," Opal said as she joined us for lunch. "Had a meeting with POTUS and SecState this morning—It didn't go well. I expect all this to blow up in our faces as a result."

"Politicians," Jamie snorted and crunched into a taco.

"Meanwhile, people are dying and we can't do anything about it." A curl of smoke escaped Kory's nostrils.

"We could try, but that would be playing our hand prematurely, and likely get us killed," Opal pointed out. "They have a spell set around the border. Anybody who crosses it gets fried. If you show up unannounced wherever they are, you get blasted to bits and fried. Either way, you're dead and they're still armed to the teeth. Phineas wanted to go in underwater. Davis and Thomas tried that last night with a droid in a river. The robot was destroyed in the middle of the night, almost the second it passed the border."

"What about shifters?" Watson asked.

"I'm terrified to try it," Opal admitted. "We could lose an ally, in the name of dangerous experimentation."

"Birds as camera carriers?" I asked.

Opal's mouth tightened.

"You're worried about retaliation, aren't you?" I asked.

"Not only that, but there are reverse spells they can implement, to track any creature or device to its origins."

That came from Zaria, who walked into the dining room with Klancy and Kell. Kell went straight to Opal and leaned down to kiss her. A short, private conversation occurred between the two before Kell took the chair next to Opal's, sat and pulled the plate of warm taco shells toward him.

"I have another concern, too," Zaria said as Klancy pulled a chair out for her.

"What's that?" Opal asked.

"I'm beginning to be concerned that they have someone with them who can read power signatures."

Opal, who'd been helping Kell put tacos together, stilled.

"Just what we need," she said after considering Zaria's words. "One more unholy alliance."

I had no idea what she was talking about, but the fear in her voice terrified me.

"We can't risk anyone going in as mist," Opal said. I'd approached her on the patio after lunch; she and I stood at the half-wall again to have our conversation. "Look at it this way, if I were going to allow anyone to go in as mist, I'd send Mason. He's vampire and can be—well, somewhat less affected by what he may see there. I'm concerned that if you materialized—either of you—it may be exactly what they're waiting for. I'm not risking your life for this. You're too important."

"Those people who are dying; they're important, too," I pointed out.

"I know." Opal hung her head. "There's only one of you, young one. We have to send you and Kory into the fight when it will do the most good."

"What if there's another way?" I asked.

"What way?"

"I don't know," I floundered. "But there has to be one." I couldn't help thinking that my mother would have found a way around this already. I felt inadequate, still, because people were dying and I wasn't doing anything to help.

"If you come up with any ideas, I'll be willing to listen." Opal turned away from the wall and walked toward the house. I stayed behind, my eyes unfocused on the Pacific to the west.

Kordevik

"Do you think they have every inch of the border controlled?" I asked Kell. He, Klancy, Jamie, Watson and I were in the media room, a European football game on television but muted, so we could talk.

"So far, it appears that way. It's mind-boggling that they may be able to do this, but those machines they've set to guard the perimeter will mean death to anyone they target. We cannot risk anyone, including your misting mate."

"There has to be a way," I fumed. Like Lexsi, the thought of innocents dying made my blood boil. For a High Demon, that statement was literal and not figurative only.

"They will have to transport that filth somewhere, when it is harvested," Klancy observed. "Will we know when that happens? Do we have anyone with the talent to know when it leaves this world, bound for another?"

"May we join you?" Zaria and Opal opened the door and peeked in. A smile lit Klancy's features and Kell grinned at Opal. "We'll take that as a yes," Opal said. Once the women were inside (Zaria sat beside Klancy and Kell patted the sofa next to him, inviting Opal to sit with him), we resumed our conversation.

"I'd need a sample of the seed they're shipping, hon," Zaria answered Klancy's question. "That way, I could set a spell with that particular vibration, so I can capture a signal when other seed matching it left the planet. It's a complicated spell. Not many can do it."

"You're saying it has to be seed from the same harvest?" Kell asked.

"Yes. It has to have the exact soil, growing conditions, amounts of water—you understand? That means seed from the same fields may be mixed with other seed from fields with different conditions, but the spell will lock on the seed it's meant to detect, even when hidden with other seed."

"That takes talent," Opal said.

"It's a difficult spell and takes time to do, but it can be done. The problem, of course, is getting the sample to begin with."

"And we can't get across the border to do that. Even if we did, the infiltrator could be attacked or killed at any time. Those seed fields are probably guarded more closely than Fort Knox." Kell grimaced as he considered the problem before us.

"I may have an answer," Lexsi burst through the door, holding a tablet in her hand.

"What?" Opal and Zaria spoke at the same time.

"The oil pipeline," Lexsi breathed, setting the tablet in Opal's outstretched hands. "The environmental groups have been complaining for years about it, saying it endangers the indigenous people living in the Pastaza Basin. That's on the border between Peru and Ecuador. If we send cameras through, maybe we can find something out before they're discovered. If the enemy destroys the pipeline to get rid of our spying equipment, their source of energy fuel dries up, too. They've been bringing oil in for the past ten years, because the country uses more than they can produce. That's why the second pipeline was built next to the old, original one pumping domestic crude out of the country for refinement. If we do this it may endanger the indigenous peoples, but the way I see it, they're endangered more by what's taking over their lands."

"This," Opal tapped the tablet with a finger, "has possibilities. Let me look into this to see how well guarded the pipeline is on the Ecuadorian side. It makes me happy that they haven't upgraded to another fuel source."

"If you need our help," Yoff and Esme walked into the room, "We'll do whatever we can."

"Zaria and I will consider all our assets," Opal said.

"So stay tuned," Zaria wrinkled her nose at Yoff.

"What does stay tuned mean?" Yoff asked. I giggled. The phrase was an old Earth term and one he'd never heard before.

"Want a history lesson on the television and radio industries on Earth?" I asked.

"Not really," Yoff shook his head and grinned at me.

"Can you miniaturize small cameras?" Opal asked Yoff.

"Sure can," he answered, turning back to her. "Why? Won't they recognize the work of a wizard the second it crosses the border?"

"That's exactly what I'm hoping for," Opal replied. "If we release your miniaturized cameras hundreds of miles away from the pipeline, we may be able to get the real project done while they're distracted."

"Nice," Kory acknowledged. "When can we hear the full plan?"

"When Mason and the others get here," Opal replied.

"I need to go back to the market," I said. With so many people in the house, food disappeared quickly.

"We may need three or four carts this time," Anita said. "The two we filled two days ago just vanished."

Anita, Esme, Watson and Kory volunteered to go with me to the market. It wasn't difficult to see that Opal, Zaria, Kell and Klancy wanted to have a private discussion while we were gone. It didn't concern me; they'd tell us what we needed to know afterward.

The market was more crowded than I expected when we arrived, and the puzzling thing was there were few vehicles parked around it.

Where did these people come from? Anita sent mindspeech as we took three carts from the dwindling supply outside the door.

No idea, I responded.

Looks like a mixed gender version of the Stepford Wives, Esme said. I didn't understand her reference, but Kory did. He grabbed my arm and pulled me to his side immediately.

Baby, act normal, he sent. *We'll get our stuff and go.*

What is it? I did my best to look natural as we surveyed the fresh fruit and vegetables on tables. I wanted to make artichoke hearts in sauce and studied what was offered as I waited for Kory to reply.

Look at the wrists, Kory responded.

I wouldn't have noticed if he hadn't pointed it out.

Nearly two-thirds of the adults inside the store wore silver wristbands. The realization caused the hair on my arms to rise and every cell in my body to prickle.

We need one of those cuffs, Anita broke in.

Are you thinking what I'm thinking? I returned. Gentry Mullins had a plain silver wristband, and somebody thought it was important enough to steal after his death.

Yeah. Those cuffs get them across the border into Peru safely. Why the hell are they here, though, shopping for groceries?

I have a theory, Kory interrupted. *Get your stuff, baby, and we'll work on the rest later.*

We methodically went through the shopping list, only getting what was on it and nothing else. Before and behind us, when we stood in line to pay, were wristband wearers.

Yes, I wanted to ask Kory what he'd come up with, but forced the question back. How did these arrive? How were they planning to leave?

We found out, the moment we left the store. A huge passenger bus was parked close by; I assumed it had gone to get fuel somewhere while its passengers were shopping for supplies.

So many theories and options ran through my mind while I glanced at the people loading onto the bus with their bagged items.

This meant they had a drive ahead of them to reach the border of Peru—in any direction.

Unless—someone with power could meet them outside Punta Blanca and transport the entire bus back to their headquarters. All the wristband wearers looked to be servants to me. None were dressed as tourists or carried anything that looked like personal items, such as a tourist would have—items such as cell phones and purses. All paid in cash before leaving the store and loading onto the bus.

Zaria, I sent mindspeech in a mental whisper. *Can you see this through my eyes?*

I'm seeing it now, she replied. *We really need one of those cuffs.*

How? I queried.

I know this is dangerous, she replied, *but can you mist onto that bus and cause the driver to have an accident after they drive away?*

I can try, I began.

Take Kory with you, Zaria said. *In your mist. He'll have a conniption if you don't.*

I will have a conniption if you don't, Kory confirmed. Zaria had included him in her mindspeech.

What are we supposed to do after that? I asked.

Skip to the house. Opal and I will handle things from there.

Don't worry, Opal chimed in. *I think we're about to start a riot, and you don't need to be anywhere near it.*

We'll get in the car and drive away, Kory said. *Anita, Watson and Esme can take the groceries home while Lexsi and I take care of business.*

We were unloading our carts into the SUV by that time, and Kory quickly informed the others about the plans. I could see Anita and Esme wanted in on it, too, while Watson was doing his best not to growl as he shoved bags into the back of our vehicle.

He wanted a piece of those people, but they weren't the ones causing problems. "Baby, they're all obsessed," Anita informed Watson softly as she leaned next to him to hand him the last bag. "They're not the enemy. The ones controlling them are."

We climbed into the vehicle then, allowing Watson to take the wheel and drive us away. When we'd gone about a quarter mile, I told the others that Kory and I were going and turned both of us to mist.

❧

Opal

That girl is better than she imagines herself to be, I sent to Zaria the moment the large bus veered off the road and into a power pole. The power pole fell with a crash and a billow of sparks, ensuring that the surrounding neighborhood was now without electricity.

Just as I'd wanted, people began pouring out of their houses to see what the trouble was. That's when Phineas' merpeople arrived, pouring in from between houses as if they belonged there. Phineas himself started the argument with the bus driver—the downed pole meant the neighborhood was without power until someone arrived to repair it. In this area, it could take days.

Showtime, Zaria sent, heading straight for the obsessed woman who stood farthest away from the bus.

In moments, a replica of the woman stood beside our target, while Zaria employed her talent to whisk the real one—and us—back to the house.

Kory, Lexsi and the others waited there for us, while the hapless woman, who was so obsessed she didn't know how to react, merely blinked at her change of venue.

"Lexsi," Zaria said immediately, "Turn her to mist for thirty seconds and then release her. I want to prove our theory by reproducing the results of the last experiment."

I understood what Zaria meant. Lexsi had inadvertently released one victim from an obsession after he'd taken a known criminal's place in prison, by turning him to mist. If Zaria's suggestion bore fruit, then Lexsi could become the enemy's worst nightmare.

If they found out about her.

~

Lexsi

"Somebody time it," I said. The woman, completely oblivious, stood waiting for someone to tell her what to do.

The same person who'd placed the obsession, I imagined. "Go, baby," Kory jerked his head at me. He would count off seconds in his head. Probably another trick learned in the military on Kifirin.

I didn't waste time, going to mist quickly and gathering the unsuspecting woman up to hold her inside my mist. All of her particles, for a brief period, anyway, would be enveloped by mine.

"Time," Kory announced after what felt like an eternity instead of half a minute. I released the woman and became corporeal beside her. Nobody had to ask if the experiment had worked. The woman screamed in terror, then began to weep.

~

Kordevik

"What about the substitute?" I asked, once the screaming woman had been calmed and placed (by Zaria) in a healing sleep.

"Disappeared, once she was on her seat at the back of the bus,"

Zaria shrugged. "Women disappear in this country frequently—there's a thriving sex slave trade, or didn't you know that?"

"So her captors will think she was kidnapped?"

"I certainly hope so. We don't need them searching this city, looking for us," Zaria sounded weary, now. "At least we know Lexsi's misting talent, combined with her High Demon nature, can nullify an obsession. That will come as welcome news to many. I warn you, however, that the information cannot leave this group. For obvious reasons."

"She's in enough danger as it is," I agreed.

"You both are." Zaria hugged herself and stared out the library window.

"Dearest, do not upset yourself." I jumped when a very tall Larentii appeared beside Zaria.

Zaria had a Larentii mate. That in itself was a rarity. I was beginning to think Zaria was quite rare, indeed. As rare as my Lexsi was, if not more so.

"I can duplicate the wristband, but there are codes inside it," Zaria shivered before the Larentii had time to speak. "They'll probably deactivate the code inside the one we have the moment they learn the woman is missing."

"It is my guess that these wristbands keep the N'il Mo'erti from firing at the wearer if they happen to cross the border," the Larentii *Pulled* the wristband into his hand to examine it.

This Larentii was unlike most I'd seen. He was ten feet tall, blue-skinned as they all were, but had red, shoulder-length hair, whereas most had some shade of blond hair, cut short.

"Kory, this is Kalenegar, Head of the Larentii Council," Zaria introduced us while Kalenegar continued to examine the wristband.

"I've heard of you," I said.

"And I have heard of you," He lifted his head and nodded at me. "Nefrigar thinks very highly of you. And of Lexsi, of course. You may not know this, but Nefrigar, our Chief Archivist, is mated to Lexsi's mother."

"I'm sorry, I have trouble keeping track of Reah's mates," I hung my head.

"Understandable—there are many," Kalenegar smiled. "You would be most familiar with Torevik, as he is High Demon like yourself, and Lexsi's biological father."

"I've met him—and her mother. He's the one who gave me photographs," I admitted. "He said she was beautiful. I wanted to see for myself, so I was given photographs when she was eighteen and twenty."

"What did you think?" Zaria asked. "When you saw photographs, knowing she knew nothing about you?"

"I feel guilty about it now, but I won't ever forget the rush that went through me when I saw her image the first time. It's as if I'd never seen a woman before."

"That's how M'Fiyahs work," Kalenegar smiled. "If Lexsi had seen you before, she may have shown up for her wedding."

"I want to marry her. I think she wants to marry me. She's terrified of the claiming."

"Ah. The barbaric High Demon tradition of marking one's mate," Kalenegar agreed. "Did you know it was originally intended to ensure that the female only reproduced with the one placing the claiming marks? In recent history, that has proven untrue—with two others. I suspect it is only because of those two females' heritage and the innate power they possess."

"Lexsi's mother being one of those. I know Lexsi has six full sisters and two half-brothers."

"Lexsi's grandmother, Queen Lissa, is the other one," Zaria pointed out.

"Which doesn't sound good for me, does it?" Smoke clouded my vision for a moment. I'd forgotten my manners in my concern that Lexsi could find other mates besides me.

"I think Lexsi may surprise you in how traditional she can be," Zaria smiled. "Once you get past the claiming, that is."

"Yeah. There's the problem," I grimaced. "I don't want to hurt her or scare her, and she's afraid of both those things."

"Then you will make a good mate," Kalenegar's smile widened. "Now, may my mate and I have some privacy? I wish to—as those from Earth might say—catch up?"

"Sure." I rose from my seat and walked out of the room. I think the Larentii had a shield up before the door latched shut.

Zaria

"Are you planning to tell them that the drug may not be the sole reason that a powerful witch and warlock are interested in Earth?" Kal's eyebrows were as red as his hair. The left eyebrow rose after he posed his question.

"It's Deris and Daris' excuse for being here—and working for that wealthy, evil bastard they found. I suspect that a long-lost relative of theirs may be the impetus for choosing Earth as the planting fields so Dervil San Gerxon can ply his drug trade. When Dervil promised his Earth investors that he wouldn't sell that filth here—that was just a lie to convince them the planet would remain intact and much as it is. I believe V'ili knows about Deris and Daris' true intentions, but Dervil doesn't. How's that for a conundrum?"

"The drug is bad enough on its own," Kal raked fingers through his hair. "What is reportedly hidden here was never meant to be found. It could prove most dangerous if these acquire it."

"Then we need to make sure it stays hidden, is removed, or, as a last resort, is destroyed," I said.

"That, beloved, could prove more difficult than you know."

Lexsi

Opal brought Mason, Sandra, Davis and Thomas in shortly after nightfall. Kory and Watson were helping Anita, Esme and me in the kitchen, although they were eating and tasting as we went along.

I guess I hadn't thought about Sandra being with them, but it made sense once I thought about it. Neither she nor Mason were willing to let the other out of their sight.

"Dinner's almost ready," I informed the three werewolves while slapping Watson's hand—he was lifting another shrimp from the appetizer tray.

"Thank you," Sandra smiled. "We're starved. Mason's had dinner," she added.

"Yeah, okay," I said. "Have a seat. I'll find something for you to drink."

"Have any bourbon?" Opal took a seat beside Sandra. Kell sat next to her and blinked expectantly—he wanted a stiff drink, too.

"I have some," I said, turning toward the liquor cabinet.

"After Phineas dropped his argument with the bus driver this afternoon, we found out the bus drove south before it disappeared. Either somebody met them at that point who could transport them, or there was already a spell in place that would take the bus back to its origin." Opal's expression was grim, with a touch of frustration.

Kell rubbed her back while I poured two generous portions of bourbon in glasses and added ice and club soda.

"Thank you," Kell spoke for both when I set glasses in front of them. Something was definitely bothering Opal; that was easy to see. She wasn't saying what it was, though.

"Phineas didn't wish to drop his argument, even with my Opal telling him that the one he shouted at had no control over his actions."

"Trust him to take things to extremes," Opal mumbled and lifted her drink. She emptied half the glass before setting it down again.

"He's used to being in charge and getting his way," I said. "It's something I studied at school on Wyyld—*the psychology of power*," I said, pushing a plate of broiled shrimp appetizers toward Opal and Kell.

"Too bad Phineas has let it go to his head," Kell observed, his voice dry.

"His head?" Opal huffed and emptied her glass. "It's all over him, head to ass. Probably his thighs and fins, too."

"Vampires," Zaria shouted, while appearing in the kitchen. My skin itched so badly it was on fire seconds later. Dinner was forgotten as someone—either Opal or Zaria, folded all of us to the neighborhood with the downed power pole. That section of Punta Blanca burned, vampires killed innocent residents and others ran away screaming.

The enemy in Peru was expressing his displeasure at the accosting of his slaves, and the subsequent kidnapping of one of them.

Those he'd sent vampires after had nothing to do with either of those things.

Baby, turn with me, Kory said and became his smaller Thifilathi. I followed his lead, my slightly smaller, silver-scaled Thifilatha wading into the fray behind his black-scaled one.

Opal and the werewolves turned while Kell, Klancy and Mason attacked the first vampires they found, claws out and deadly as they fought. When Mason punched one, sending him flying, Kory plucked the unlucky vampire from the air and burned him with half a thought.

I ran toward a small knot of other vampires, who were herding a family into a tight circle. They wanted these alive, children too, I think.

I misted toward them in a blink and had two vampires decapitated by squeezing their necks until the heads popped off.

Yes, it turned my stomach, but I wanted their friends to know I wasn't fooling around and intended to kill them, too. Sure, somebody may have intended to use their witch or warlock's power to abduct people, but those spells were useless wherever I was.

The three remaining vampires turned their attention to me, then, while the family ran toward the street. The noise of fire, other battles and screaming people was all around me as the vampires studied me. Yes, they were likely intending to attack me at once in an effort to bring me down.

After all, I wasn't on fire like Kory was.

Maybe I ought to be. I just wasn't sure how. The last time I'd been on fire, I'd pulled the fire—wait.

Houses were on fire all around me.

Sure, I made myself a target when I became my larger self and stood straight, held out my arms and closed my eyes. I felt vampire claws digging into my scales as they climbed my body.

It didn't last long.

The moment I pulled every bit of fire from all the burning houses, leaving them dark and smoldering about me, three vampires had already turned to ash. That night, I became the High Demon version of a bug zapper that could skip from one battle to another. Any enemy vamp that still lived was fried against the heat and fire clinging to and permeating my Thifilatha.

I roared a challenge when the enemy vamps were all gone; somewhere, a country away, I hoped the enemy was listening.

CHAPTER 14

*K*ordevik

It took some time to get Lexsi back to normal. Zaria and Opal finally suggested that I take her to a high peak so she could discharge the fire she'd gathered. It hadn't taken much of it to destroy vampires, who were on the heat sensitive side of things anyway.

I wasn't damaged when she released her fire atop the mountain I'd skipped her to, but anybody else might have been.

Unless they were extremely powerful.

Once the fire and energy left her, she became humanoid and dropped at my feet, naked and only half-conscious. I lifted her in my arms and cradled her against me; once the fire was gone, she shivered in the high mountain air.

Warming her with my heat, I skipped her to the house in Punta Blanca. Zaria and the others were picking at dinner, waiting for me to arrive with Lexsi.

"The enemy knows where we are," Opal frowned. "We have to move or they'll be back to kill more locals."

"How many died?" Lexsi turned in my arms to look at Opal.

"At least eighty people," Opal didn't sound happy. "Most of those before we got there to help."

"Dude, you gonna walk around naked all night?" Watson asked.

"Kory," Lexsi made herself smaller in my embrace.

"We'll get dressed, then we'll eat, and you'll tell us where we can go from here," I blew a cloud of smoke in Watson's direction. He was only dressed in jeans and didn't normally give a damn about nudity.

I skipped Lexsi into her bedroom, so I could get her covered first. She was cold.

~

Lexsi

I dressed in a long-sleeved T and a sweater; I was chilled completely after coming back to myself on top of a peak in the Andes. Kory was still warm enough—he'd banked his fire. I'd forced all of mine away from me.

"That's some talent you have, onion," Kory said as he shrugged into a T and jeans. "I'm concerned that the enemy will figure it out after tonight," he added.

"Fuck them. They killed innocent people," I muttered. "If they want some of my fire, I'll be happy to give it to them."

"That's not what I meant. You're now a target too, unless I miss my guess. Come on, baby. Let's eat and listen to what Opal and Zaria have to say about relocating."

"We need to punch Phineas in the mouth," I said as I trailed Kory. He strode determinedly toward the kitchen. I hoped Watson left some shrimp for us; I was starved.

~

"Opal got a phone call," Anita whispered as I took a seat next to Kory at the dining table. "She and Zaria are in Opal's suite, talking to somebody."

"Somebody knows already?" I asked as Farin set plates of food in

211

front of Kory and me. She was the only one left at the house while the rest of us had gone to battle vamps.

"I don't think that's it," Anita grimaced. "I think this is something different and maybe just as bad."

"That doesn't sound good," I dipped a shrimp in sauce and bit into it. "You think it's global, national or local?" I asked after chewing and swallowing.

"No idea. Eat while you can. We may be traveling in a bit."

"I believe the enemy suspected we were here," Kell said. "There's no need to send more than a hundred vampires to terrify a small portion of the village—four or five would have worked well enough against humans."

"Eat and pack up, we have to go to D.C. tonight," Opal walked in. She looked gray in my estimation, and it wasn't because we'd fought off more than a hundred vampires earlier.

"What happened?" Anita asked.

Zaria appeared beside Opal. "New York was hit by terrorists tonight," she said. "Early estimates say that at least fifty thousand are dead across the city. I went to check for myself just now. It's worse than they think."

I never expected to meet the Secretary of Defense in person. Yes, I would have liked to interview him—if I were still a reporter and under much better circumstances.

"We found one of the terrorists involved. He's in interrogation now," Secretary of Defense August Hunter said. Opal insisted that Kory, Anita, Zaria and I be allowed in the meeting she was holding with Colonel Hunter.

"May I have one of mine watch the interrogation?" Opal asked.

"Why?" Colonel Hunter's dark eyes settled on Opal.

"Because she will know if he's telling the truth," Opal replied.

"Are you sure?" I could tell he wanted to believe Opal. *Very much.*

"I have others who may be able to command the truth," Opal added. "Provided he hasn't been obsessed already."

"This troubles me—that obsession as you've explained to me can happen at all," Colonel Hunter observed. He was in his late fifties and short, dark hair was going gray at the temples.

"This is tied to Peru—I'd bet my life on it," Opal said.

"Unless we have solid proof, we can't take that to the President," Colonel Hunter smacked a fist on the polished wood meeting table where we sat.

"We were attempting to get something when the village around us was attacked earlier," Opal said. "The plan still may work, but we'll have to set up a base elsewhere. They knew where we were when they sent their vampires in."

"Where are they now—these vampires?"

"Dead. We have some injuries, but no losses."

"I wish I could say the same thing about New York," Colonel Hunter said. "The situation there is only going to get worse, as damage and lives lost is taken into account. The subway system is destroyed. City blocks are nothing but rubble, and they hit where populations were heaviest. I have difficulty understanding how the bombs were brought in without anyone knowing."

"It's because those bombs were transported in only seconds before they exploded," Zaria spoke for the first time.

"How? Do I know you? You look familiar," Colonel Hunter studied Zaria.

"Maybe we knew each other in another life," Zaria sighed. "The truth is this, Colonel Hunter. Our enemy in Peru has unusual assets. Some of those assets are power wielders from other worlds. Getting a bomb into a subway or a building is child's play to them. It's my assumption that the terrorists have paid for these services."

"They're not allied?"

"The ones in Peru are only interested in wealth, power and destruction. The terrorists will learn soon enough that their lives are no more important than anyone else's."

"Won't the terrorists target them, then?"

"You understand that nothing can get across the border into Peru?" Zaria pointed out. "Let the terrorists try. They'll die, like anyone else. What's in Peru is a cancer on the Earth. If we don't cut it out soon, the entire planet will be destroyed."

"I'll get you a front row seat to the interrogation," he said. "I'd appreciate any information you can give me. My hands are tied until I can provide the link between these murderers and what's going on in Peru."

"We'll do what we can," Opal rose from her seat.

"Good. I'll have transportation here in five."

He's young, angry and disillusioned, Zaria sent the moment we saw Mahmoud through the one-way glass. *No, it doesn't excuse his part in any of this,* she held up a hand. *When will people learn that what they do comes back to them? That they own their mistakes?*

My favorite is two wrongs never make anything right, Kory said. *You don't kill your sister because your brother stole from you.*

They're big on displacement, Opal agreed. *Let's listen.*

Not much was coming from eighteen-year-old Mahmoud, including where he lived or who his parents were.

"We need names. Tell us who orchestrated this attack," the interrogator asked.

"Sheik Al-Harub," Mahmoud replied.

"Lie," I said.

"Jeff, that's a lie," Colonel Hunter spoke into a microphone. Jeff had an earpiece in and could hear Colonel Hunter clearly.

"That's a lie, try again," Jeff snapped at Mahmoud.

The boy rattled off several other names. "All lies," I said.

"Send me in, I don't think he's obsessed," Anita said.

"What good will that do?" Colonel Hunter covered the mic before he spoke.

"You'll see," Opal jerked her head sharply, telling Anita to go.

"All right, but if this doesn't work," Colonel Hunter began.

"It'll work, Auggie," Zaria said. "Trust me."

Anita

At least I wore a nice blouse over my jeans when I walked into the interrogation room at NSA Headquarters. Mahmoud barely looked at me; I was a woman and an infidel, in his eyes.

"Mahmoud," I walked toward him. "You're going to look into my eyes and tell me every damn thing you know about this attack."

Lexsi

Everything came tumbling out of Mahmoud's mouth that he knew. It wasn't everything we needed and certainly didn't name those at the top, but he knew enough for Homeland Security and the NSA to begin their investigations.

He confirmed what Zaria said, though. His terrorist organization had paid for services rendered; he merely didn't know how much and in what currency it was paid. What worried me was that the enemy in Peru could use this as a form of blackmail; that they'd give further assistance to terrorist groups if we didn't back off and leave Peru alone.

That infuriated me. They were killing Peru's indigenous people off by the hundreds and we were powerless to do anything about it.

"Now tell me what you know about your allies in Peru," Anita asked a final question.

"They say they were sent by the one god," Mahmoud claimed. "I think they may be something else." Well, he'd been born and educated in the US. At least he knew enough to be skeptical when somebody claimed to be sent by a god.

"Did you see any of them?"

"I saw the one named Deris."

"Ah. Would it interest you to know he's from the devil instead of a god?"

"What if you're lying? You all lie," he insisted. He spoke a personal truth—as he'd been taught it.

"There are billions of people on this planet," Anita pointed out. "Not everybody lies to further their personal goals—or their religions. I'm done, here." Anita turned and walked out of the interrogation room.

"My people are exhausted, Colonel," Opal declined Colonel Hunter's offer of food and drinks. At least D.C. was still in operation. New York was shut down, along with all neighboring cities. I was glad nobody suggested we go to New York right now; I didn't want to see the tragedy that night. We'd already seen enough to do us for a few hours.

"I'll have guards posted at your hotel," he said. "I know you have your own people on the job, but it will make me feel better if there's a military presence, too."

"We'll discuss this tomorrow morning, I trust?" Opal asked after accepting Colonel Hunter's guards.

"Yes. And your presence may be requested in a meeting with the President."

"I'll be happy to," Opal confirmed. "Anytime."

Baby, I want to hold you tonight, Kory sent as we were checked into the same hotel in Silver Spring that we'd used before. I could see that this place was used to diplomats and dignitaries staying with them; the night manager didn't even blink when our crowd of security guards stood in the lobby, waiting to escort us to our rooms.

I was glad Kory asked; I didn't want to spend this night by myself in a strange place. Not while every news station everywhere reported on the New York bombings while showing images of smoking rubble and emergency workers desperately searching for the lost and wounded.

We have every werewolf and vampire in our employ working those sites, Opal sent mindspeech. *They can scent the people trapped under rubble. We don't have nearly enough dogs on the scene to help with that.*

"Give us one room," I half whispered and gripped Kory's arm when my turn came to check in. His arms wrapped around me; I discovered I was shivering. The question that kept hitting me, much like a vehicle repeatedly racing into a solid wall, was—*why?*

I didn't—and couldn't—understand.

What I did understand was this; without the help of Deris and Daris Arden, those bombs wouldn't have been planted so easily. Earth had no answers for a powerful witch and warlock, whose endgame I couldn't guess at any longer.

They had Peru locked up for whomever they worked for, and Sirenali to hide important facts and players from us. It could take days or weeks, even, to get a final total—in lives and destruction, caused by their interference.

If they'd stood before me at that moment, I would hurt them before they died. Yes, I knew that was wrong. I'd once heard Great-Uncle Gavin say that a swift death for our enemies separated us from them.

These took pleasure in the pain of others. That understanding was coming to me. *There are two kinds of people,* Gran said once after coming from a long Council meeting on Le-Ath Veronis. I'd watched as she'd removed the jeweled coronet from her head and set it on her dressing table.

"What kinds are those?" I'd asked. I was twelve and visiting her at the time.

"People who want to hurt and people who want to help," she said simply. "Sometimes the ones who hurt don't really intend to, it's just that they think they're protecting themselves in some way. The end result speaks otherwise."

She wouldn't tell me what had transpired in the Council meeting. I still didn't know. I hadn't forgotten her words, however. Deris and Daris—they wanted to hurt. I had no idea why.

~

Kordevik

We only had two changes of clothing and a few necessities with us; Zaria had transported our other belongings back to the house in San Rafael. The compound in Punta Blanca was now empty. I worried that the residents could be attacked again.

It was late and I sat on the bed, waiting for Lexsi to come out of the bathroom. The violence was difficult for her to accept—that someone would willingly attack and kill those they didn't know and hadn't harmed them personally.

I'd seen too much of the same during my lifetime.

I watched her walk out of the bathroom, showered and dressed in pajama bottoms and a stretchy, sleeveless shirt. This Lexsi looked lost. I understood it was overwhelming her now, whereas she'd acted professionally in Peru.

The New York bombings were a different story. We'd been there for Peru. Nobody had been there for New York.

"Come here, baby," I held out my hands. She came to me—slowly. Tentatively. I wrapped her against me the moment she was close enough. A part of me felt just as helpless as she did.

"We'll get them," I whispered against her hair. "I promise we'll get them."

~

Opal

Kell, Klancy, Zaria and I were in the hotel coffee shop. We didn't need bodyguards for what we were about to do.

After I'd suggested something of the sort, Zaria offered her services, on the condition that we not kill unless forced to do so. I'd already asked Colonel Hunter to arrange for holding cells. We had terrorists to hunt. A few thought they were beyond our reach; they'd flown out of the country before the bombs went off. They were about to be surprised.

Currently, all airports were closed and on lockdown because of the extensive bombings. Yes, Zaria was violating her non-interference status, because I'd asked her to. In this case, I just wanted a cage full of murderers—*all* the murderers involved in this attack.

They didn't have Sirenali to hide them. Hadn't known they might need them, after all. They were used to hiding beneath baseboards and in cracks and crannies, blending in with their surroundings.

I wondered how they were going to take being caught, no matter where they were.

"Ready?" I took one last sip of my coffee. It could be a long night, followed by an early morning meeting with the President.

"Yes." Zaria took a deep breath and allowed Klancy to take her hand and help her from our booth.

Kell's hand was beneath my elbow as he helped me rise. These two would die for us; there was no question. I also understood that Zaria and I would protect them with our lives, if necessary.

"Let's go collect terrorist ass," I breathed.

~

Lexsi

After a restless night, during which Kory was always there with a warm embrace, shushing me when I woke, shaking and terrified, we watched the morning news together.

Yes, I understood that some that we knew had been busy through the night. Face after face, name after name, appeared across our television screen, while journalists explained that these—the ones involved in the bombings—had been captured after authorities interrogated one captured suspect the night before.

They thought all those names had been given to them by Mahmoud. I knew differently—he'd only known a few of those names. The rest were likely supplied by someone else.

I had suspicions as to whom that could be, but didn't want to voice them aloud. Kory's arms, warm and strong, were about me as we watched the news together from our bed. As expected, the death toll in New York had risen dramatically. One hundred thousand lives was now the estimate.

"I saw Zaria's Larentii mate," Kory confessed. "The other day. He just showed up unannounced."

"Who?" I asked.

"Kalenegar," he breathed, his mouth next to my ear.

I went still. "He's the Head of the Larentii Council," I whispered. "Why would he be here?"

"Because he's mated to Zaria?"

"Oh. He may not be the only one, then," I said.

"Only what?"

"Only Larentii. Sometimes, people get more than one Larentii mate. Gran has two," I pointed out. "What did he say?"

"Not much—they discussed the wristband and the likelihood that it was worthless, or would be whenever the enemy discovered it was missing. Kalenegar wanted to see Zaria in private after that, so I left them alone."

"I wish I knew who she really is," I sighed. "She's important, I know that much. I don't think she'd be here, otherwise. And the fact that she's mated to the most powerful Larentii? You can't discount that for a minute." I moved to slide away from Kory.

"I have a raging erection," he murmured while pulling me back.

"You're the one who said no sex before kissing, and we haven't set a kissing date, remember?" I looked up at him. His eyes were dark while a wicked smile tugged at one corner of his mouth.

"Too bad we can't bend time, then. We could show up for our own wedding," he teased as he let me go. "Would you kiss me then—when your father handed you to me? I'd catch you when you fell and take such good care of you afterward."

"Kory," I pushed myself off the bed and stood, still gazing at him. "I'd marry you *and* kiss you. Without qualms. But we sort of have this in front of us now," I swept a hand toward the television, where more journalists were speculating on whether other terrorists were involved or if we'd collected all of them.

"Then will you wear this? It was what I had for you, when you married me." He leaned over and pulled a small box from his shirt pocket. He'd left his clothes on the small chest beside the bed.

"What's that?" I blinked at the box, dwarfed in his large hand.

"The ring I picked out for you. When I ordered it, I didn't know how much I'd love you," he lifted the lid. "I know how much you mean to me now."

My breath caught. The gem was Tiralian crystal, there was no doubt, and not a small one, either. "Kory, I," I didn't know what to say. The ring had to cost a fortune. I told him that, too.

"I was given a discount," he said, "By somebody who regularly trades Tiralian crystal. Through a third party—your great-aunt Glindarok."

"But it's still so much," I breathed, my eyes going from the ring to his face and then back again.

"You're worth everything to me," he said simply. "This ring couldn't come close to what I think your worth is. I want to marry you, Lexsi Silver."

"Will it fit?" I whispered.

"Want to find out?" He lifted the ring from its bed of velvet and held it out to me. "Give me your hand, baby, if you want to marry me."

My left hand trembled, but I held it out to him. With gentle fingers, he set the ring on the proper finger. It fit perfectly. Someone had given him my size. Perhaps my father had told him.

It didn't matter. The man I loved and wanted to marry had put a ring on my finger and asked me to marry him. He'd promised to catch me when I fell after he kissed me. He promised to be gentle when placing the claiming marks.

I believed him.

I wanted to marry him right then and there. So many things had to be done, first and it made me want to weep. I had happiness while so many others grieved from terrible tragedy. Was all of life destined to be such a confusing paradox?

"Come here." Kory pulled me against him and kissed the hand that wore his ring. "We belong together. To each other. That's what matters right now. We'll deal with the other stuff where and when we can. Get dressed, onion. We have bad guys to fight."

~

Kordevik

We had breakfast in a hotel cafe while Opal met with the President, Colonel Hunter and every other bigwig who had anything to do with the US Government. I was pleased to see that our werewolf friend, Jorden Billings, had arrived to help guard us and drive us if necessary.

"I was hoping we'd see you," Lexsi gave him a quick hug. He grinned and shook my hand after Lexsi moved away.

"I was hoping I'd get to work with you again," he said. "I'd have asked if the boss hadn't told me to come."

"What's on tap, then?" Watson joined us. He grinned and punched Jorden on the shoulder. They knew one another; Watson had already told me that much.

"Last time I saw you," Jorden said after clapping Watson on the back, "I was in the Navy and stationed in San Diego, while you were serving drinks in San Francisco. Now I'm with the D.C. Pack and working for Director Tadewi."

"I'm the new Packmaster for the rebuilding San Francisco Pack," Watson sighed.

"Heard about that," Jorden jerked his head in a quick nod. "Never did like Claudia. Scent was off, in my estimation."

"I hear that."

I'm surprised there was no butt sniffing, I sent to Lexsi, who turned her head so the wolves wouldn't see her smile.

Jorden's cell phone buzzed. He excused himself and walked away to answer the call. He was back after a minute or two had passed. "We'll transport you in—the boss has asked for a meeting with your crew."

222

We were herded into dark, bulletproof vans a short time later, and our convoy headed toward a building not far from the Capitol. Jorden hadn't told us where we were going; he drove while another guard sat on the passenger seat up front. Yoff, Anita and Watson rode with us; Zaria, Klancy, Kell, and Tibby rode in another van. Mason, Davis, Thomas and Sandra were in the last van, while Farin and Jamie were left behind at the hotel under heavy guard.

They weren't happy about being left behind, but I hoped they'd understand eventually. If it weren't for Opal and Tibby wanting them where they were, I'd have asked that Farin be sent home to be with her parents, while Jamie stayed at the San Rafael house with hidden guards close by.

I'm sure they could allow Farin's brother to stay there, too, and merely move his guards to his parents' home so they could watch both.

It occurred to me then that I could remove the obsession from Rick; he'd be back to himself the moment I released him from my mist. I made a mental note to ask Opal about it when we had a private moment together.

Jorden parked our van in an underground parking area and waited for the other two vans to pull up beside ours before stepping out of our vehicle and searching the area to ensure it was safe.

We unloaded after that and headed for a nearby elevator. Jorden used his badge to convince the elevator doors to open; we crowded inside while Jorden pressed the button for the fourth floor. Half of us were taken on the first trip, the rest waited until the elevator deposited us in an empty foyer, then returned for the others in our group.

When we were all gathered in the foyer, Jorden led the way to a locked door in the center of the foyer. Swiping his badge got us past that door and into a hallway. At the end of that hallway was another locked door. It opened for us before Jorden could swipe his badge again.

Opal, Colonel Hunter and several others, including the President, waited inside for us.

~

Lexsi

I had no idea I'd be hearing what we did; Kory's hand gripped mine beneath the table while the President spoke of a declaration of war and Opal attempted to talk him out of it.

I understood Opal's reasoning; declaring war against Peru because they were a stationary target could be the worst mistake of his career. It wasn't Peru he had a problem with; it was what had taken over Peru that was our difficulty.

Opal had attempted to warn him at the beginning of this mess; he and the Secretary of State hadn't listened. After seeing the recorded version of Mahmoud's confession, naming those in Peru as the facilitators in the New York bombings, they'd swung from one end of the pendulum to the other.

Already, Congress was called to convene and declaring war would be on the agenda. The fact that the Secretary of State's multiple calls to the puppet government in Peru had gone unanswered had convinced him and the President that we were now engaged in a conflict with that South American nation.

If troops were sent to Peru's border, the moment they attempted to cross, they'd be fried by the death machines that waited. The president shouted about being betrayed by supposed allies, while the Secretary of State nodded his agreement.

Opal and Colonel Hunter weren't able to interrupt and attempt to convince him to listen to reason.

In the President's opinion, Peru had just joined the terrorists and would pay for their involvement.

It wasn't that simple. Colonel Hunter pointed out that Peru was engaged in killing their own. We didn't need to add our help to what amounted to genocide in that country by attempting indiscriminate bombings.

In essence, those who held Peru would likely hold the innocent population hostage if we attempted to cross the border. They were already killing enough as it was. What the President suggested could destroy millions.

"We have a plan, Mr. President," Opal sounded weary as she spoke during a lull in the President's tirade. "We're trying to avoid senseless loss of life, sir."

"Then you have two days. I'll have Congress convinced to declare war by that time. I'm ready to go," he jerked his head toward several Secret Service agents who stood at the back of the room.

In other words, this entire meeting had been off the record. He and the Secretary of State had barely looked at any of us after our arrival. He'd been pleased enough to unload on Opal and Colonel Hunter while ignoring the rest of us. It made me wonder how we'd been allowed into the meeting to begin with.

We were forced to wait until the President had vacated the building before we were given permission to leave.

Opal blew out a breath while Kell hovered. She and Zaria looked as if they were ready to drop, Kell and Klancy likewise. "You need rest," I said before I could stop myself.

"We have two days, young one," Opal said. "There's little time to rest for us." All of us followed her and Kell from the building. We had sketchy plans at best, and all of it could explode in our faces.

～

Peru

Laurel Rome

Charlene knew something. She'd been spying on Deris, Daris and Morgett whenever he was here. Why she included me in her current shenanigans, I didn't understand.

"They keep talking about a treasure," she hissed as we walked through the back garden toward the pool. "I want to ask the fish bitch if she knows anything about it."

"Treasure? You're an idiot," I whispered at her back as she ducked through closely-planted banana trees on her convoluted trip to the pool. "We're growing the treasure. Dervil says so."

"Dervil doesn't know about this," she turned and snarled at me. Shoving banana leaves out of her way, she stalked ahead of me.

"Why are we hiding?" I spit a mouthful of green banana leaf out of my mouth; she'd let the long, broad leaf slap me in the face while I had my mouth open.

"Because we don't want V'ili to see us. He knows about this, too. In it up to his neck, actually. He's working with Morgett, or didn't you know that? He's only pretending to take orders from Dervil."

"That's insane. You're insane."

"No, but you're blind if you haven't figured out there's something else going on, here."

"Well, well," V'ili's voice was unexpected as we cleared the long stretch of banana trees. He stood, hands on hips, on the flagstones surrounding the pool while Loftin Qualls drooled behind him.

"Kill Charlene," V'ili shrugged at Loftin. "We'll let Laurel live. This time."

I shrieked and shrank backward as Loftin grabbed Charlene by the throat. Producing a sharp knife, he began to cut into her skin while she screamed.

CHAPTER 15

*L*exsi

Yoff spent the afternoon in a nearby lab, casting spells to miniaturize spy cameras that were already minuscule in size. The rest of us listened while Opal and Colonel Hunter went over the plan to smuggle someone or something through the petroleum pipeline on the Peruvian/Ecuadorian border.

Tibby spent time on the phone with his cousins, who'd been transported back to California when the rest of us came to D.C. He'd already offered his services through the pipeline. Opal wasn't willing to risk his life.

"Let's send something else through first," she turned his and his cousins' offers aside. "Small drones roughly the size of a pellet from a pellet gun," she added.

"But you need someone who can speak at least one language those mountain people speak," he countered. "They speak enough Spanish that I can make them understand."

"We don't have a solution, Tiburon," Opal said, patting his arm. "No gathering place is safe for them, yet. We have to have good news before we send someone through."

I saw her glance at Zaria, then. Something passed between them, but I had no idea what it was or what it meant.

There was an alternate plan, perhaps, but it was a plan of last resort.

I wondered briefly what it could be.

Kordevik

We had two days to solve the problem in Peru before US and Coalition forces moved toward Peru's border. Several allied nations had pledged to stand with the US after the attack on New York.

Mangled bodies, few of which were whole, were pulled from entire city blocks leveled by blasts. US citizens couldn't understand or even speculate how bombs of sufficient size could be set without anyone noticing. They had no idea that the skills of a talented witch or warlock could achieve that very thing.

Yoff continued miniaturizing cameras. How easy would it be to for the enemy to place tiny explosives that had timing spells set upon them? They could become normal size just before their detonation.

I was beginning to detest anyone with Karathian blood. Yes, I knew that was wrong—the vast majority worked within the laws set by their planet and their alliance. Those who operated outside the law could cause terrible harm.

"When will Yoff be finished with his project?" I asked when Opal walked in after another meeting with Colonel Hunter and the Joint Chiefs. I understood that the President and Secretary of State were calling in every favor from every politician in D.C. so their proposal for a declaration of war would go smoothly in two days.

"He's almost ready," Opal sighed. "I want you and Lexsi with us when we send our drones through the pipeline at the same time."

"Sure," I agreed. "Whatever you need."

"Do you think there are spells on the pipeline?" Lexsi handed Opal a cup of coffee in a paper cup. It was all we had available at the hotel.

"There could be," Opal said, taking the cup and nodding her

thanks. "We want to cover every possibility when we send those drones through."

"Phineas is missing—again." Zaria folded in. Nearly all of us had gathered in Lexsi's and my suite—it was large enough for everyone.

"What the hell is he doing now?" Opal muttered. I could see she was angry.

"I hope he isn't attempting to swim his way into Peru," Zaria replied. I could tell she was just as upset as Opal by this development.

"How long has he been missing?" Opal asked.

"Since last night. That means he hasn't gotten to the border, yet, unless he decided to drive as far as he could before turning."

"He can fuck everything up. Can't he?" I asked.

"He's susceptible to obsession, like most people," Opal grimaced as she emptied the coffee cup. Lexsi had done her best with the coffee, but hotel room coffee was never what I'd call decent. It was enough caffeine to get you up, dressed and looking for better-tasting caffeine.

"Get everybody together—we'll launch our offensive from San Rafael," Opal announced. I strode toward the door. Tibby, Farin and a few others were in his suite. If necessary, I could get them to California.

~

Lexsi

I was grateful to be back in San Rafael, but there was very little food in the house. Gran was right—an army does travel on its stomach.

"Let someone else do the grocery shopping," Opal placed an arm about my shoulders as I studied the empty fridge. "I need you, Kory and Anita with me at the pipeline. Zaria is taking Yoff, Kell and Klancy farther south to release the miniature spy cameras."

"Man, I hope this works," Kory said, pulling me away from Opal and the fridge and folding me in an embrace. "If we could find some weak spots to sneak in," he added.

"I want the locations of those fucking N'il Mo'erti," Opal said. "We really need to take those things out, first. Without those, we can get troops safely across the borders. With them still in place and operative, the invasion forces are all dead."

"Won't it take time to move tanks and equipment to the border?" Lexsi asked.

"Not as long as you think. We have military bases all over Colombia—we've had an agreement with their government for years. While it looks as if the part of Colombia that borders Peru is in league with the enemy, it doesn't appear as if they're protected on that side by the N'il Mo'erti. Colonel Hunter told me that forces are already moving through Colombia to set up a temporary base on their side of the border."

"What does the Colombian Government have to say?" Kory asked.

"They don't care. They know our guys are toast if they try to cross the border."

"Not good," I said. "Let me change clothes and I'll be ready to go with you."

"Dress warmly; we'll be in the higher elevations where we're going."

Opal left Davis, Thomas and Jorden in charge at the house while she and Zaria transported those of us going to Peru. They knew where they were going; I didn't. Not exactly, anyway. All I'd seen was a tiny dot on a map when I'd offered the pipeline as a possible way to get into Peru.

We were about to see whether that was actually possible.

The pipes were larger than I'd thought when we arrived; the older one was smaller and narrower next to the large, new one installed in the past decade. The new pipe was big enough for an adult male to slide through—provided he could hold his breath long enough.

"You'll have to mist these inside," Opal held up a clear, plexi box with a hinged door. Inside, tiny spy drones hovered. They had their programmed orders; I hoped they wouldn't be destroyed before sending information back to our side. "Just form hands long enough to allow them to get out; they're built to survive in gas or liquid."

"How will they get out?" Kory asked.

"Good question. One of those little things will go ahead of the others. It's spelled by Zaria to become larger and drill a hole in the top of the pipe to let the others out."

"So we nullify enemy spells—if there are any at the point I mist inside, then they travel across the border through the pipe, where one will become larger and drill a hole big enough to let the others out?" Kory asked.

"That's the idea. I hope those idiot death machines know not to blast the pipeline—we could see a huge explosion, otherwise."

Opal was counting on that—that the enemy knew not to destroy their fuel source. If I were the enemy, I'd have been working to place solar energy panels everywhere. I hoped the enemy hadn't prepared for such an event—that their fuel source could be destroyed.

We were doing this without the knowledge of the Ecuadorian Government, too, and wondered how they'd feel if part of their income were shut off; they had a deal with Peru to allow the pipeline to be placed on Ecuadorian lands.

In the long term, it probably wouldn't matter—those in Peru would kill any who opposed them, and they were about to be opposed.

Opal handed me the plexi box, bringing me back from the paths my mind had wandered. I nodded, gripped the box tightly and turned to mist. All I had to do was mist inside the pipeline and release the contents of the box. I wasn't prepared for how dark it would be, or that my hands might fumble for seconds to release the tiny drones.

Zaria

Yoff had done excellent work; the spy drones were so tiny they couldn't be seen by a normal human. Some shapeshifters might see them, but we weren't dealing with that sort of shifter in Peru.

No, we had worse things to worry about. I imagined that what Dervil San Gerxon's power-wielding allies wanted would never be communicated to him. If they found their treasure, they'd leave him in an instant to wreak havoc and revenge against those who'd—in their minds—wronged them.

Most of what they wanted would never cooperate and would be useless to them. They'd have to search in that treasure for what they truly desired. I hoped if they managed to get their hands on it, it would take long enough that we'd be prepared to stand against them when they did.

Dervil and his drug fields were only a decoy for them and their true intentions.

"Are you ready?" I turned to Yoff, who held a small, plexi box in his hands. Farther north, Opal had a larger one that she'd just sent through the pipeline. Those tiny drones had almost reached the border.

Ours had to coincide with those.

"Yes," Yoff placed his hand on the tiny latch.

"Release them," I said.

Yoff opened the door and dozens of microscopic spy drones flew across Peru's border.

~

Lexsi

"So far, so good," Opal said after we'd landed at the house in San Rafael. I saw that Tibby, Farin and Jorden had gone shopping for groceries. They'd brought a fair amount of food back from the supermarket—enough that I could make lunch and dinner for everyone.

"We'll know if any of the spy drones are destroyed—we have a military team in Colombia recording information from the drones. As soon as I log in on my computer, I'll have the images, too."

"You still need sleep—all of you," I pointed toward Opal, Kell, Zaria and Klancy.

"Maybe a couple of hours," Opal yawned and nodded. "It may take that long before the drones pick up any useful information."

"I'll have food ready when you wake," I said.

"Thank you." Opal took a step toward me and hugged me tight for several seconds.

"No problem," I said when she pulled away. "Let's hope those drones get what we need before they're found."

Opal and Zaria slept for four hours. It wasn't until after they woke that the images—and sound—came through.

There wasn't supposed to be any sound.

Somehow, our enemy had arranged it. Whether by spell or science, it didn't matter. Kory and I were allowed to see it with the others after Opal was on the phone with the President for nearly an hour.

Kory wrapped his arms around me after we sat down to view the video sent by our enemy in Peru.

"Hello," the man said. Only his image was visible against a black background. "I am Dervil San Gerxon," he went on. "This planet is mine. If you don't believe me, send your army across the border. I intend to kill all who oppose me." The screen went dark.

"All our drones stopped working at the same time, shortly after that message came through," Opal said. "I don't know yet what they used to detect both sets of drones, but whatever it was, it was effective. We have nothing useful from any of them."

"At least he named himself," Kory pointed out.

"Sure. Name yourself when you believe yourself invincible," Anita grumbled. "Dervil San Gerxon, asshat extraordinaire."

"We have less than a day and a half to do anything else before our forces line up at the border. Nobody can get across alive in either direction. I have information from the station where Davis and Thomas were. Native Peruvians are lined up just across the border in the mountains. They're stuck there, because of the piles of bodies scattered across that part of the border. Bodies of those who'd attempted to cross before the next wave got there."

"They'll be marked for death, just for attempting to escape," Zaria said.

"What can we do?" I asked.

"I need some time to make a decision," Opal said. "Zaria, will you and Klancy come with Kell and me? I need to work this out before we send any of ours into danger."

"If they blitz part of the border with rockets and remotely fired missiles," Davis offered.

We were having our own meeting, where ideas were being kicked around like a soccer ball.

"The N'il Mo'erti will just shoot them down—they're too advanced for even the best Earth has to defend itself," Kory pointed out.

"How do you know all this?" I turned to him to ask.

"Onion, they were using these things when—uh, where we came from. You probably didn't hear about it on Avendor."

Yes, I understood most of my life had been sheltered, but this— surely I would have heard about *this*. I hadn't and Kory had, somehow. That would teach me to pay better attention in the future.

Kordevik

I wouldn't have known, had Li'Neruh Rath not told me about the N'il Mo'erti three nights earlier—when he handed me the ring I'd bought for Lexsi. Somehow, he'd also known I'd need the ring and the information, so he told me what I needed to know.

He explained that more High Demons waited in Peru, should we manage to get across the border. He said Lexsi had a set of blades in her bedroom, just as I did. We might need them with us if we went to Peru.

When I asked him if there were a way into Peru that we didn't know about, he frowned. "Zaria knows," he answered. I racked my brain, wondering what Zaria knew that the rest of us didn't.

Whatever it was, it must be dangerous, because she hadn't said anything about it, yet. Time was passing, too, and there was little of it left. Every news program was running updates on whether war would be declared.

At least we had inside information on that particular subject. The President was determined to send troops to Peru, and several other countries were aligned with him. Even the UN wanted to send their forces, after attempting to get the President's attention for months about the goings-on in Peru.

No matter what, people were going to die. Whether in Peru or outside it, people would die. How many had yet to be determined. I'd heard an updated count on the death toll in New York; estimates now said more than half a million. I hoped the news station was padding those numbers to garner ratings.

We were down to one day—one day before coalition forces would attempt to invade Peru. Visions of fighter jets shot down, tanks obliterated and missiles detonated before they reached their targets filled my imagination.

We needed another option and soon.

"Kory?" Lexsi scooted onto the sofa next to me. I'd chosen a seat in the family room and watched television with the sound off. I didn't need to hear the bluster—the crawler at the bottom of the screen told me everything I wanted to know.

"Onion." I pulled her against my side and wrapped her in a snug embrace. She was worried and had been for days. I'd promised her that we'd get the bad guys. I had no idea where to start.

Yes, feeling helpless was aggravating. I hated it, yet that's exactly where we were. Lexsi felt the same; I could see it in her eyes. Sure, I wanted to be a hero to her, but I was just as worried and scared as she was.

"Baby, we'll do what we can," I breathed against her hair. "I don't know what that is, yet, but whatever it is, we'll be ready."

"Kory?" She looked up at me.

"What, baby?" I wanted to kiss her so badly by that time it had become a physical pain.

"I'm glad you're here with me. Even if I could call someone else, you're the one I'd choose."

My heart skipped to a stop for a moment, then reawakened and thumped rapidly to make up for its brief cessation. We were going to stand together in this, no matter what happened.

"It could kill us, onion," I admitted, my voice soft. "I believe they have more High Demons waiting there for us."

"Then we'll go together," she said and wrapped her arms around my waist.

~

Lexsi

The latest development, when there was barely twelve hours left before the President and Congress acted, was that somehow, every terrorist who'd dealt with the enemy was found dead in his cell.

Opal looked gray when she heard the news from Colonel Hunter. In each video, because the recorders had been left on and unimpeded, a man appeared in each cell. The terrorist began silently gasping for breath while the man disappeared.

"An asphyxiation bubble, tight around their heads," Zaria explained, her tone grim. In each case, the victim fell to the floor, clawing at his face while struggling to breathe. They may have deserved death, but it aggravated me that this was the method dealt by those who'd allied with them in the first place.

Opal exchanged glances with Zaria and both left the kitchen while the rest of us considered what we'd heard.

Were our enemies in Peru afraid the terrorists would tell what they knew? That we didn't already know who most of the players were by this time? Perhaps they'd decided to make enemies of all instead of most, as it was before.

Either way, the terrorists were dead and I worried that more people could die just as easily on the whims of the enemy.

"We have terrorists posting their jihads against Peru online," Thomas interrupted us as we sat around the kitchen island, watching the small television in the kitchen.

"Of course they are," Anita sighed. "Because all of Peru is responsible for what a few people did to them." Her sarcasm was unmistakable as she frowned at Thomas.

"Just the messenger," Thomas held up his hands. "I think the boss will have information for us in a few."

Here it comes, Kory gripped my hand. *The plan of last resort*, he added.

There are volcanoes in Peru and Ecuador. Some dormant, some not. I'd read about them when I researched the pipeline between Ecuador and Peru. At the time, I didn't think they were important.

I was learning otherwise.

"A system of caves connects Ecuador and Peru," Zaria said. "But there's a problem. Sure, a few have gotten in and out. Told fantastic stories afterward, but then never found the caves again. Most people paid no attention to the stories, because those people couldn't prove anything."

"What are you talking about?" Watson demanded. "If they got in once, they should be able to get in again."

"Under normal circumstances," Zaria's smile was tight. "Those people talk about finding treasure, but they haven't produced any of it for anyone else to see. There's a reason for that."

"You're not making sense," Watson folded arms over his chest.

We sat in the media room, taking up all the chairs, sofas and part of the floor to listen to Opal and Zaria's plans. So far, we were in the preliminary stage and I waited for their objective to be revealed before making comments.

"What she's trying to say," Opal leveled a quelling gaze on Watson, "Is that what's in those caves has power—and talent—of its own."

"I think I saw that in a movie, once," Watson wasn't convinced.

"Shut up or I swear I'll punch you," Anita hissed at him. He turned toward her and blinked several times. "You'd really do that? Punch me?"

"I will if you don't keep your mouth closed until they're done."

"Okay. I reserve the right to be skeptical," he said and turned back to Zaria and Opal.

"Some people call it the metal library. There's a crystal library attached to it. It's online, feel free to look it up," Zaria jerked her head at Watson.

"If they found it, why haven't we seen any of it?"

"Shut. Up." Anita smacked Watson's arm.

"Mortals can't take anything from it," Zaria said. "The caves move. I realize that sounds crazy, but it's true. Not only do the caves move, but the library moves, too, from place to place. It contains false libraries to detract from the real one. That's part of how it protects itself. There is evidence that mortals created their own versions of some of the artifacts after a brief glimpse of the false libraries—those reproductions can also be found online. The real metal library protects itself."

"That makes it sound as if it's not native to this planet," Kory said.

"Bingo," Zaria tapped her nose.

"What is it, then? Really? And why is it here?" Anita asked.

"Now that's the real question," Zaria said. "What is it and why is it here? Let's just say that things as they are wouldn't exist without it. I know that's not a very good answer, but it's all I can give you for now. It's important. Extremely important. This is our last option—the very last one—to deal with the problem in Peru. If it weren't our final option, I'd never have brought it up."

"How will this help us with the enemy in Peru?" I asked. "If the caves move, how will we get through them in the first place?"

"I'm glad you brought that up," Zaria said. "There's one way to keep the caves from moving and the library stationary so we can get through it and into Peru—underground."

"How's that?" Watson said.

"By walking through Tungurahua," Zaria replied.

Tungurahua.

An active volcano. Kory and I could walk through it—Zaria said we had to walk through molten lava to find the cave entrance that would ensure all the connecting caves didn't move. She said our Thifilatha and Thifilathi could carry the others and keep them safe.

Yes, High Demons could protect others from heat if they chose to do so. I worried that we'd be carrying so many. Zaria said not to worry, that she and Opal were working on a plan to make that happen.

Moving caves. A library so important it protected itself.

What the hell were we dealing with?

"I'm not the one making the others smaller," Yoff explained as he sipped tea and ate a slice of strawberry cake. I'd worried about what Zaria told us, so I'd dealt with it by baking.

"This is awesome," Watson mumbled around a mouthful of cake.

"You say that about anything edible," I pointed a finger at him.

"But it's true," he said. "Everything you make is awesome."

"It wasn't awesome the first time I made it," I said. "Uncle Fes grimaced when he tasted it."

"How old were you?" Kory flashed a welcome grin at me.

"Seven. And I forgot the sugar."

"Did you know your uncle Fes is married to your aunt Bree?" Zaria appeared at Kory's elbow and silently asked for a slice of cake.

I went still. I knew Bree was Gran's sister, but I didn't know she and Uncle Fes were together.

"Um, no," I said. "Why didn't I know that?"

"Your aunt is very careful. It's her way of protecting your uncle," Zaria replied.

"She's protecting Uncle Fes?" I cut a generous portion of cake for Zaria.

"Fes could become a target if certain people found out he's connected to her like that. Only a few people know, since he insists on living in Targis."

"You know about her—what other people won't say, don't you?"

"Yes. But it's not my story to tell. You should ask her yourself, the next time you see her. I think she'll tell you."

"May the Three be merciful," Kory sighed.

"Exactly," Zaria grinned at him and dipped into her cake.

∼

Opal

"You know we're going to war in those caves?" I said.

"I know," Zaria agreed and handed me a saucer with a slice of strawberry cake on it. "This is probably what they've waited for. They have no idea where the door is, but they knew enough information to explore the tales that have been spread in the past about the library."

"So they've set us up and we're going to lead them right to it," I said, cutting into the cake with a fork Zaria produced and handed to me.

"I hope the library will act to protect itself, if it becomes necessary," Zaria sighed.

"That means we're all dead," I pointed out. "It won't discriminate if it perceives itself under attack."

"Yeah. I know. We're all dead anyway, if they get their hands on the dark books. It'll take a little longer, but we'll all die."

"Fuckers," I cut another piece of cake. "Damn, this is really good."

∼

Kordevik

"Your blades—they'll withstand the heat?" Kell asked. I had them on my bed, checking everything about them.

"As I understand it, yes," I said.

"They will," Li'Neruh Rath appeared. "I have placed my blessing upon them. Upon Lexsi's weapons, too."

"Why don't you come with us?" I joked.

Li'Neruh frowned and blew a cloud of smoke in reply. "Okay, I get that this isn't your thing," I held up a hand.

"This is your assignment," Li'Neruh replied. I glanced at Kell; he studied the god of Kifirin in fascination, although he hadn't spoken. Most people, if they knew anything at all, wouldn't speak to Li'Neruh Rath. It could draw his ire.

I'd spoken to him after he'd sent me to Earth, mostly because I didn't care at first what happened to me after the wedding fiasco.

"Will Lexsi be safe?" I dropped my eyes and stared at the ten-foot, black blades that lay across my bed, with only the center portion of each blade resting on the cover.

"I can't answer that question. All I know is that it will take both of you, if you are successful in this."

"She's only twenty-three," I whispered.

"I know." Li'Neruh disappeared before I could ask more questions.

Questions.

I had many.

We were walking into this nearly blind; Zaria had more information on the caves and the library they housed, she just wasn't telling us. I'd dealt with this sort of thing in the army—go where you're told and do what you're told. Oh, and don't ask questions, because you don't need to know.

Fuck.

Lexsi could be in terrible danger, and I had no idea whether I could protect her or not. Li'Neruh's comment—that it would take both of us to be successful—held the unspoken fact that we could fail in this.

If we failed, I had the idea we'd die. I couldn't say where that feeling came from, but it was there, nonetheless.

Who do you pray to if the god of your planet has come and gone, without saying so much as *good luck, asshole?*

Snorting a smoky breath, I nodded to Kell and lifted a blade to sheath it. They were in perfect condition; I'd known it before I'd unsheathed them. Kell was impressed, I could tell, that the blades looked deadly enough and that Kifirin's god had placed his blessing upon them.

I hoped they'd save us all, but in the end, they were no better than the High Demon wielding them.

~

Lexsi

My blades lay across my bed, but they'd changed. They were now nine feet long, with an envelope lying atop them on my bed.

I understood who the note was from—Aunt Bree.

She'd left me a note when they'd first appeared on my bed. Now, they were changed, so my Thifilathi could use them. She'd made that happen, I had no doubt.

Lexsi, the note began. *The mystery is nearly unraveled. You and Kordevik are charged with keeping its secret. Remember that when the time comes.*

B.

I crumpled the note in a shaking hand. "*Da'quon, the'lat vic nacca,*" I whispered.

First, kill your fear.

CHAPTER 16

$\mathcal{P}$eru

Laurel Rome

V'ili told me I couldn't say anything to anyone about what I'd heard from Charlene. Sure, I could scream from the rooftop that Charlene was dead. Dervil didn't care. Hadn't cared from the moment her dismembered body was found on the patio not far from the pool.

Just Loftin having a bit of fun, he'd joked and went back to planning shipments with Berke to this planet or that.

Berke. He'd been ignoring me lately. I wanted to taunt him. Wore bikinis often to tempt him. He still chose to ignore me.

The bitch in the pool had gotten out of the water to vomit after Charlene's death, then jumped back in before Loftin could go after her.

At least V'ili called him off her; I doubted he'd do the same for me. Hannah was no help whatsoever; she'd begun to explore her male urges—she still had Granger's body, if not his suaveness, and was having sex with any woman she could overpower.

No, I'd never pictured her as a rapist, but it appeared she was making up for lost time. After all, she was practically guaranteed an orgasm as a man.

Since I couldn't tell Dervil what little I knew, Morgett had begun taunting me with the knowledge, and speaking openly in my presence of a Prince he served, and that the treasure would be taken to him.

I had no idea who the Prince was, but he didn't sound like a nice person. As for the treasure, they never said where it was or how they intended to find it. They merely spoke of the stupidity of those who'd attempted to destroy us, and that they'd lead us straight to the treasure.

We were far too powerful for them. I understood that. The bombs and planes and warships that they were gathering? They'd be destroyed in a blink. Nothing on Earth was prepared for what we could hurl against them.

Nothing.

~

Lexsi

As it turns out, we didn't have two full days. Congress approved an air and ground strike against Peru before the declaration of war was hammered out.

Opal paced and cursed while news of bombers being shot down was broadcast everywhere. The missiles shot from miles away were destroyed before getting close to their targets.

Dervil San Gerxon released another video—this time holding the head of the former Peruvian President by the hair and laughing at what we'd sent against him so far.

The video was three solid minutes of him laughing and then telling us we would be destroyed, down to the last child.

I felt sick. He *was* sick. I wanted to crush him and then vomit in a toilet, somewhere. The others who'd watched the video with me were grim and silent when the television was shut off.

"It's time to go," Opal announced. "Zaria and I will give you information as it's needed. Both cages are in the garage. Kory, you'll carry me, Kell, Tibby, Mason, Sandra, Davis and Thomas. Lexsi, you'll carry Zaria, Anita, Yoff, Watson and Klancy. All of you will be made smaller by Zaria to allow our High Demon friends to carry us easier. They'll be wading through waist-high—for them, anyway—lava to get us to the cave entrance. Esme has been notified and is working an assignment off the coast of Peru. Anybody who wants to back out now, speak up."

Farin, Jamie and Tibby's cousin, Diego, watched the rest of us as Opal spoke. Diego would stay to guard Jamie and Farin; they were human and couldn't make the trip. Opal already told them they'd die if they went.

Neither wanted that to happen.

At least Aunt Bree's house would serve as protection for them, too.

Opal had allowed Tibby to inform his grandmother of what we were about to do, although most of the particulars had been left out of that conversation. She only knew that we were attempting to reach Peru through caves.

She'd wished us luck and told Tibby to come back to her. She'd already lost one grandson. I understood that she didn't want to lose anyone else.

In seconds, Farin gasped. Those going, including Zaria and Opal, were now half their size. Zaria had also taken our blades and made them tiny, so she and Opal could hold them for us. Kory's arms slid around me. *I love you,* he sent mindspeech.

I understood his words and their timing as well as he did.

We might not come back.

I love you, too, I returned. *More than anything.*

Kordevik

The cages Opal and Zaria supplied were clear and glass-like, although I imagined they'd be unbreakable. I hoped she'd allowed for enough fresh air for the cages' inhabitants—we were about to walk through an area where the air itself was unbreathable and would sear any normal person's lungs.

Each group settled inside their cage while Zaria employed power to seal them shut. Zaria would supply directions for us; Lexsi and I were merely transportation.

～

Washington, D.C.
 The Capitol Building
 Notes—Colonel Hunter
I stood in a hallway, drinking a cup of coffee and contemplating what was going on in the joint congressional meeting feet away in the House Chamber. Opal told me in a phone call that she and her crew were attempting what could prove to be impossible. She'd also told me that should they fail, everything could be destroyed.

It would be destroyed anyway; this was merely a faster destruction than what those in Peru had planned.

I hadn't bothered to tell my wife—or anyone else. Why? What good would it do to tell them they had perhaps a few hours to live?

Opal said the Earth could be blasted to bits if things went wrong.

Things were already going wrong.

We were losing troops, aircraft and weapons at an alarming rate. Anything we threw at Peru was destroyed.

Decisively.

We had nothing to combat this new form of terrorism. Even the terrorists we'd dealt with in the past had no way to fight or infiltrate this.

It sounded comical and I might have laughed if it weren't so deadly serious.

"Sir, they're about to take the vote," my assistant appeared at my elbow to inform me of the action we were about to take.

"I'm coming," I said. Straightening my tie, I followed him toward the door.

～

Kordevik

I skipped us to the top of Tungurahua; Zaria would direct us in mindspeech after that.

You look amazing against the snow, Lexsi informed me as we teetered on the volcano's lip.

My black scales against a backdrop of deep snow ensured I'd stand out. Lexsi's silver scales, on the other hand, glittered and almost blended with the snow she stood upon.

Like Yin and Yang, I whispered to her. *Two parts of a whole.*

I know, she acknowledged. *I wish—well, you know.*

Yeah.

So many things lay between us. I hoped this wasn't the end for us.

Fly into the crater until I say, Zaria instructed.

Gripping the cage tighter in my arms, I leapt into the abyss.

Lexsi

Kory's dive was swift and elegant. He held his wings tight against his back until he was a hundred yards down before snapping them open to glide. I hurled my Thifilatha off the snow at that point, hoping my dive would be half as assured as his was.

I didn't wait as long to snap my wings open to glide downward; all I could see was the fiery depths of the volcano speeding toward me at a terrifying rate.

See, there on the right—a ledge, Zaria instructed when we'd almost reached the bright orange lava near the center of Tungurahua.

The ledge was narrow—to an eighteen-foot Thifilathi or a fifteen-foot Thifilatha. *We'll have to land carefully and walk sideways or we'll never get over it carrying the cages*, Kory informed me.

You won't be walking on the ledge, Zaria said. *That's just a place to land before dropping into the lava.*

Great, Kory responded. *Out of the frying pan and all that.*

You go first, I begged him. I wanted—needed to see how he'd land on such a narrow ledge.

Kory furled his wings and dove toward the ledge, before snapping his wings open again and flapping twice, turning neatly in mid-air and landing like a ballet dancer on the ledge.

The claws on his black-scaled feet hung over the edge, while I flew in circles over hot lava. *Don't mess this up,* I warned myself. I'd never had flying lessons. I'd only had a Thifilatha for a few months, and had only brought it out a few times.

Kory had years—if not centuries—of experience with his.

Baby, you can do this, Kory said. *If you find yourself falling, push off and start flying again. Nobody will think worse of you if it takes a try or two.*

I already think worse of me. I gulped a breath—at least the hot, corrosive air near the bottom wasn't damaging my Thifilatha. We—Kory and I—had been made to survive this as long as our Thifilathi and Thifilatha were engaged.

Mark your spot, Zaria instructed. *Don't get too close to Kory—you could cause both of you to fall. If a cage drops into the lava,* she didn't finish.

Can't you or Yoff do something if a cage falls? I asked.

No power can be used near the cave entrance, young one, Opal broke in. *You and Kory are using natural talent. The fact that you and he are holding our cages keeps the door warden from engaging.*

There's a door warden? If I'd spoken aloud, my voice would have risen an octave.

Don't worry, we're okay for now, Zaria soothed. *Take one more turn, fold your wings and dive toward the ledge.*

I took one more turn, but it wasn't enough. I took two turns. Then three.

Onion, you can do this, Kory said. *Take one more turn. When I say, fold your wings and head for the ledge. When I tell you, open your wings and turn your body in mid-air. One good flap or two will settle you onto the ledge with your back to the wall. Fold your wings quick after that and drop onto the ledge.*

All right.

Keep your speed steady, now, he said as I made one more turn. *Fold baby,* he said. I gulped as I folded my wings and dived toward the ledge.

Open, he shouted into my head.

My wings snapped open as I turned my body in mid-air. I flapped once—twice, just as he said and dropped onto the ledge.

My wings! I forgot to fold them fast enough. I teetered on the ledge and almost dropped my cage.

Nooo! I shouted at myself and clutched the glass-like cube close against my chest. With all the strength I could muster, I dug clawed toes into the ledge, while rock crumbled and huge chunks of the wall fell into the waiting mouth filled with lava. I slid down the rock wall as the ledge disintegrated beneath my feet.

Gripping the cage with one arm, I flung a hand backward to grasp at the wall. The claws on my fingers forced more rubble from the inner walls of Tungurahua and into its maw. My slide downward was barely affected by my desperate efforts; the fiery lava hissed and chuckled as it waited for me to fall in, too.

Hold on, baby! Kory shouted mindspeech at me. With the ledge completely gone and the sloping wall crumbling around me, I struggled to do just that. Inside the cage I held, I could hear Anita shrieking as I slid farther down. With an effort, I gripped it as best I could. Gritting my teeth, I dug claws on hands and feet deeper into the rock.

Keep it up, it's working! I finally heard what Anita shouted at me. I did. With claws on both feet buried in the sloping wall of rock and one hand doing the same behind me, we eventually slid to a stop.

Kory still stood on the ledge, nearly fifteen feet above my head. At first, I couldn't move to loosen my claws on hand or feet.

Everyone waited patiently until that happened. Gulping in breaths of poisonous air as if it were lifesaving oxygen, I struggled to steady my nerves and calm my heart. *I'll bet you wish you'd gone with Kory,* I sent shaky mindspeech to Anita.

Too boring, Anita said with a smile in her mental sending.

Yeah? I'd settle for boring, I retorted.

Take a few minutes, Zaria said. *We're in good shape as far as finding the lava path,* she added. *We're fifteen feet closer to it than Kory is.*

Right. Kory would leap like a prima ballerina and land exactly where he was supposed to, while I scared all my passengers to death for a second time in less than ten minutes.

Kory, are you ready? I'll be instructing Lexsi to land right behind you, so be careful where you set your feet, all right? Zaria said. *The lava path is almost as narrow as that ledge.*

I'm ready, Kory confirmed.

Good. Below the ledge where you're standing, and four feet from the edge of the lava, is the lava path. It's four feet wide. There, the lava is only eight feet deep. The path is wide enough for you to walk it, as long as you don't stray from the path. If you land on it properly, you'll see the cave entrance across the lake of lava. Wait for Lexsi to catch up to you before going through the cave entrance.

Don't worry. I want her as close behind me as she can get, he said.

What he wasn't saying was that I'd just scared the hell out of him. I'd scared the hell out of myself and my passengers, too. He knew not to yell.

I was grateful.

Do you have the spot targeted? Zaria asked him.

I do.

Then go—and be careful.

Kory let several seconds pass as he made sure of his grip on the cage he held. My breath caught as he leapt from his narrow perch and landed in the lava below.

He teetered on one leg for two seconds before setting both feet firmly on the path beneath the bubbling lava.

I'm good, he announced. *I have room on both sides.*

Lexsi, set down right behind him, Zaria breathed into my mind. *Push away from the wall, open your wings and glide towards his back. Don't knock into him, just set down gently.*

All right. I gazed down at the cage I now held in both arms—for a while, it had hung precariously as I gripped it in the crook of my right arm while clawing into the rock wall at my back with my left hand.

Crouching down as well as I could, I leapt away from the wall and snapped my wings open before gliding toward Kory. At the last moment, I flapped upward and circled, before coming in above and behind, then folding my wings and dropping into place behind Kory's broad back.

I didn't even teeter when I did it.

You're getting the hang of this, Kory said. *Come on, onion. We have a cave entrance to find.*

Several minutes passed as Kory and I, holding our cages higher so as not to expose them to the lava bubbling about us, walked across an invisible bridge beneath our feet. It took those minutes for our eyes to adjust to the brightness and find a darker darkness above melted rock —the cave entrance.

I wanted to ask Zaria about the door wardens. Instead, I shifted my grip on the cage in my arms, refused to look at Anita and the others inside and followed in Kory's wake.

Peru

Laurel Rome

"We've destroyed a warship off the coast of Colombia," Berke crowed as he took the chaise next to mine at the pool.

That's when the woman in the pool pulled her head above the water right in front of us. She settled her arms on the flagstones at the edge and glared at us. If V'ili hadn't told me to leave her alone, I'd have thrown my chair at her.

"I hope you all rot in hell," she snapped and dived into the water, her tail thrashing angrily as she swam from one end of the huge pool to the other.

"I didn't realize those machines could hit something so far away," I said, ignoring the mermaid.

"It took three acting together to do enough damage to sink it. What's funny is that the ship didn't have a target to return fire. Dervil is still laughing."

"What about V'ili and the others? Where are they?" I asked. "They should be celebrating with Dervil on this."

"Morgett arrived and said they had an errand to run. Didn't say what it was, but I heard Deris say that they'd spotted the enemy somewhere, and that they'd played right into our hands."

"The enemy isn't hard to spot," I snorted. "They're lined up across the border."

"I got the idea this wasn't about the military," Berke said, reaching out to take my hand. He lifted it to his lips and kissed my palm. "My dearest, when this is over, we'll own the entire planet. I shall enjoy giving you whatever you want from its wealth."

My breath caught.

Morgett. The treasure he wanted. I couldn't say it, but I knew that's what he and Deris meant about the enemy playing into their hands.

They'd gone to collect it.

I wanted it. Why should they have it all? Surely it was enough to share. I opened my mouth to tell Berke what I wanted. No words came. Silently I cursed V'ili for perhaps the hundredth time.

~

Lexsi

I had no idea what Zaria meant by a door warden. When we passed through the cave entrance, I saw nothing except rock walls. An icy blast hit us as we stepped through, shocking me immediately. It was contrary to what should have been—we'd just waded through a quarter mile of molten lava. The severe cold at the cave's entrance was a weapon in itself.

Keep going—just a little farther, Zaria instructed. *Then you can put the cages down.*

Kory jumped when light illuminated the cave a hundred yards in. I stifled a scream at the same time and almost dropped my passengers.

Set the cages down here, Zaria said. *We're past the door warden's eyes.*

~

Ecuador

Tungurahua

V'ili

Morgett's information proved true—every step of the way. He said we'd need to ally with High Demons. He'd managed to corrupt many.

High Demons in Full Thifilathi flew us toward the center of the volcano, where lava boiled and bubbled.

The one carrying me was stupid and beneath me, but I didn't voice my opinion aloud. *It will require them to carry us past the cave entrance,* Morgett had warned us. *Any use of power, for even the most mundane of reasons, will result in our deaths.*

It wasn't difficult to see where the enemy had traveled—their wake was marked by a brighter, more molten path in the lava.

The cave lies at the end of this path, Morgett sent mindspeech. Deris and Daris, nephew and niece to Morgett, worshipped him and what he'd been able to do for them. They'd supplied the plans for the N'il Mo'erti; he'd arranged everything else, including our alliance with Dervil to hide our tracks and true purpose.

"All will be ours, not just the Earth," Morgett had promised. "If we can collect this treasure."

I understood the treasure held power. If we held that power, we held everything. My High Demon conveyance grunted as he settled onto the path. He stood waist-high in burning lava while the stench assailed my nostrils.

Hurry, Morgett snapped at the High Demons in mindspeech. *We cannot hold our breaths for long.*

Four High Demons quickened their pace while Morgett, Deris, Daris and I rested in their arms. Behind us, eight more High Demons, carrying only themselves, waded through molten rock as if it were water on a sunny day.

~

Lexsi

However Zaria and Yoff had designed the cages and spells to make them smaller, they melted away of their own accord and all our passengers stretched to their full height.

No use of power and silence is a must, Zaria warned as she came to stand beside me. *Lexsi, you have to take the lead, now.*

She directed me forward, but after a while, the cave branched into four choices. *Take the one on the left,* Zaria said when I hesitated.

I think I read this in a book, once, Kory joked.

Kory, please save it for later, I begged. Every step I took was filled with dread. I felt as if the cave were watching us. Judging us. Waiting to strike against us.

We're with you, onion, Kory soothed. *Keep moving. That's all we can do for now.*

I turned my head to glance back at him. He was at the rear of our party, with all but Zaria between us.

I could see they were uncomfortable, too. Watson looked as if he wanted to turn to wolf and run. Thomas, Jorden and Davis kept a close watch on him, probably for that very reason. Kell and Klancy kept an eye on Anita, Tibby and Mason.

That's when the cave shook around us, and rock and dust dropped from the roughly-hewn ceiling overhead.

Somebody activated the door warden, Zaria's mindspeech was a bare whisper. *They're here.*

CHAPTER 17

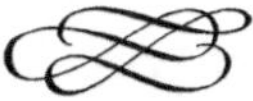

$\mathcal{L}$*exsi*

Who? I asked.

The ones who want us dead, Zaria replied. This has been their objective all along. We have to draw them in. I need to see their faces.

Why? I didn't understand at all.

They know where the N'il Mo'erti are positioned. I need that information to destroy them—after we face off against what's following us.

Wh-what's following us?

Don't worry about that now—keep going. They're far enough behind us that we'll reach our destination before they do.

I felt as if I'd been drawn into a trap of someone else's construction. Zaria—I'd trusted her. Was she intending to get us killed?

Yes, Kory and I knew that much—that we could die in this. I just didn't want someone else deliberately planning my death in a situation from which there was no escape.

Lexsi, if there is any way, Zaria began.

She knew what I was thinking.

Save it, I snapped. We live or die—together.

255

∾

Tungurahua

  V'ili

Two High Demons who thought to growl in surprise as they passed the cave's icy entrance were introduced to—I couldn't explain it.

The cave's walls moved. Living rock peeled away from the entrance; between the two terrifying creatures that manifested, two High Demons were crushed to death as if they were nothing. They didn't have time to attempt to skip away, the attack was so sudden.

Keep moving, Morgett's voice growled in my mind. He didn't voice my concern; that we were down two soldiers in our small army.

∾

Lexsi

We began to pass pools of water; my Thifilatha could smell it. The springs smelled fresh. Natural. I wanted a drink.

No, Zaria warned. *Don't even touch the water.*

An image of another unsettling inside the cave was sent to me—and then of people dying.

The waters are full of bones, Zaria informed us. *Of those who succumbed to their thirst.*

Good to know, Kory sent back.

Keep moving, Opal instructed. *Your thirst may pass after we clear this section of the caves.*

How much farther? Anita asked.

Perhaps a mile—maybe more. It depends on the mood of the library, Zaria replied.

Great. The library has moods, Kory grumped inside my head.

Kory, I'm scared, I said. *Nobody told us about any of this before we started. I'm not sure we're going to Peru any longer.*

I know. Just keep moving, onion. We'll either get out or we won't.

Another mile to go—if we were lucky. If we weren't, how much farther than that would it be?

This library—what did it hold that was so important the enemy wanted it? Why were they willing to kill to get a clear path to it?

Surely it wasn't to sell—I couldn't imagine going to all this trouble for printed pages of gold or information embedded in crystal.

Information.

I chewed my lower lip. The library held information so important it could make lives of no consequence to obtain it.

But—what information could that be?

I had no idea.

The next test the cave tossed at us I was completely unprepared for.

Tungurahua

V'ili

Don't touch the water—I don't care how thirsty you are, Morgett ordered. *It will kill you.*

At least three High Demons blew smoke in Morgett's direction, but after the attack at the cave's entrance, they were more willing to listen.

Like I said—stupid. All of them.

I considered the levels of their stupidity until it hit me.

The waters sang a song to me—to change and swim in their depths. They sang of untold wonders if I sank into their bliss and allowed them to caress my body.

Focus! Morgett barked at me.

Tearing myself away from the visions the waters offered, I plodded behind Morgett and the High Demon he'd placed at the head of our small army.

Lexsi

I blinked and refused to walk any farther. Ahead, I saw it—the strangest sight anyone could expect inside a cave.

As if it had been planted there, waiting for Kory and me to pass.

Yes, our humanoid companions could get through it with no trouble. The sharp, crystal spikes lined the cave ahead of us, placed in such a way that the razor-like tips would scrape into our scales if we attempted to walk through them.

Can we change? Kory asked. He wanted to be smaller, just as I did, so we could pass this section intact.

No, Zaria sighed mentally. *You have to allow the spikes to take your blood.*

~

Washington, D.C.

Notes—Colonel Hunter

"Baby, we're officially at war with Peru," I sighed into my cell phone. Laci, my wife, had called to ask what our status was.

"But they're showing planes being shot down on every news network," Laci said. She was close to tears; I could hear it in her voice.

"I know," I said. "This wasn't my choice, but they weren't willing to listen to anything I had to say. Want me to come get you and take you to your sister's place? That way you won't be by yourself when you watch those blasted reports."

"Would you? I want to go, but I didn't want to drive. I'm too shaky," she admitted.

"I'll come get you," I said. "Right now. They're all warmongering at the moment and won't miss me if I'm gone for a couple of hours."

"I love you," Laci said, her voice cracking. "I'm just so scared about all this."

"Yeah. Me, too, baby."

~

Kordevik

Not only was Zaria saying we had to walk through that land mine of sharp, pointed crystals shaped like giant elephant tusks, but that Lexsi had to walk through it first.

Those spikes, unless I missed my guess, would pierce a High Demon's scales easily. They were spaced too far apart to touch anything humanoid, but a High Demon would be scraped in several places when they passed through it.

Why didn't you fucking tell us? I sent to Zaria. *Why won't you let me go through first?*

It has to be Lexsi going through first, Zaria snapped at me.

Why?

Because of the rules. The most innocent among us has to pass through— and offer blood, she replied.

Is this where that fucking myth of tossing virgins into volcanoes originated? I demanded.

As a matter of fact, yes, Zaria turned toward me and shrugged.

Fucking bloody hell, I sent. Ahead, Lexsi stood, gazing at the spikes before her with shivering uncertainty. I didn't blame her.

What happens to the rest of us? I thought to ask.

If Lexsi passes the test, the rest of us are allowed through.

Fucking. Bloody. Hell.

Lexsi

Make your way through the best you can. Don't worry if some of the spikes scrape your scales, Zaria said. *We'll be right behind you.*

The sharp points glittered on the spikes that emanated from the ceiling and walls of the cave, then curved this way and that for thirty feet or more.

Don't worry if some of them scrape your scales, she'd said. As if she expected them to scrape my scales.

Well, it was a given. To get my Thifilatha through, some of them *would* pierce my scales.

I hoped they weren't sharp enough to draw blood. I didn't want to be bleeding all over the place after walking through that piece of torturous ground.

Go on, Zaria urged.

I'd forgotten that we had unwelcome followers. She didn't say it, but we needed to hurry. Drawing a breath and letting it out slowly, I took a step toward the spikes. *You can do this. You can do this,* I kept reminding myself.

~

Kordevik

When the first spike pierced Lexsi's scaled left arm, I held my breath. She hesitated for barely a second before taking another step while the spike ripped into her scaled skin and left a bloody slice behind.

She didn't see it; her eyes were pointed ahead as another spike pierced her right upper arm.

The first spike retracted silently behind her. Once she was past the second spike, it did the same.

The third spike touched her left leg; the fourth, her right thigh. Lexsi was bloodied in four places already when one hanging low from the ceiling touched her head.

I wanted to kill something—or someone—when dark-red blood stained her snow-white hair. *Keep going, you're doing fine,* Zaria sent to her.

It took two minutes, perhaps, for Lexsi to walk through this section. Once she was through, all spikes withdrew into the walls and ceiling to allow the rest of us to pass. Zaria let out a heavy sigh and motioned for the rest of us to move forward.

We were nearing the one-mile mark when a light appeared ahead.

Last test, Zaria informed us.

~

Tungurahua

V'ili

The young High Demon that Morgett insisted we bring with us was brought to the fore. He quailed at the sight of crystal spikes extending from a long portion of the cave. His Thifilathi was bound to touch several as he passed through.

Don't be a coward, Morgett hissed mentally at him. *It'll draw some blood. I doubt it will be fatal. Now get going. We have to catch up.*

This was another test—like the rest of it. I considered asking Morgett why a younger High Demon was necessary. I didn't. Morgett watched intently, his eyes never leaving the High Demon as he made his way through the spikes. He stopped still the moment the first spike drew blood.

Keep moving, Morgett insisted. *Don't stop again or you'll be sorry.*

~

Lexsi

The light ahead beckoned; I focused on that instead of the pain on my scalp, arms and legs.

Was there more of the same? The cave was testing us; I would swear to it. The light was perhaps a quarter mile away, maybe less. I lengthened my stride to keep the image of bloody hair from my mind.

Uncle Sal always said scalp wounds bled profusely, even when they were less than serious. I assumed that's what my wound was—bleeding and not serious in nature.

Zaria had to trot to catch up to me. I slowed down, once I noticed her struggle to keep up. Behind her, Opal was now walking, with the others still between Kory and me.

I hoped the light meant the end of our journey. Fear and stress had taken its toll and I felt weary. I wanted nothing more than to rush back to Kory and let him hold me.

As if cued by a movie director, the image in my head was splashed across the cave's dark walls. There I was, buried in Kory's arms while he stroked my hair. Then, he lifted my chin and kissed me.

I dropped to my knees and wept silent tears.

~

Kordevik

When Lexsi's thoughts were splattered all over the cave wall for everyone to see, I wanted to burst into flame and melt the walls.

No, my brother, Tibby's voice—a mental voice—came from far away.

Someone had given him mindspeech.

We have made it this far, he went on. *We know your pain, and Lexsi's, too. Let us stand with you. There is very little time. I hear heavy footsteps behind us,* he added.

Lexsi, baby, I sent while my eyes misted over. *Get up, hala avilepha. We must move on. They're coming up behind us.*

~

Lexsi

He'd spoken the High Demon words for *my heart's love.* It stopped my tears for a moment as I realized he'd never said those words before.

They meant one thing—that a High Demon was confessing his love to the one he'd pledged his life to.

My legs were far from steady as I rose to my feet. Wiping my tears away, I gazed one last time at the images playing across the cave walls. Those images were my dreams. My desires—that the cave had pulled from me.

Now everybody knew.

There was no time to deal with tears or embarrassment. The light still shone ahead of us. I began to walk toward it, hoping there were no more tests.

~

Tungurahua
   V'ili

Morgett was now in the lead. Ahead, a light could be seen. I squinted. Amidst that light, I could see shadows of the ones we hunted. I wanted to shout at Morgett to increase the pace. This treasure—he'd promised to share it with me and those of my kind that I chose.

It will rebuild your world, Morgett promised. *You will rule as you were meant to rule. Only the dark worlds will exist, if this treasure comes to us.*

It was my desire—to not only rebuild Sirena as it had been, but to rid the universes of that filth who called themselves Larentii.

When the images splashed across the caves, I paid them no mind at first. But then Morgett's image appeared, and his appearance changed as the image morphed him into another creature.

A creature I hated almost as much as the Larentii.

Morgett wasn't just a Karathian warlock as he'd claimed.

He was also Ra'Ak.

Lexsi

The shit's hit the fan behind us, Opal shouted into our minds. I already knew that; the cave was shaking again and rock, rock dust and boulders were dropping around us.

Run, Zaria sent. *As fast as you can.*

I broke into a run; a huge rock glanced off my Thifilatha's shoulder as I raced toward the light.

I think I realized then that the crevice surrounding that light was closing.

He's coming, Anita's mental shout came.

I didn't want to find out who *he* was. I forced my weary body to run faster. Light blasted my eyes shut as the crevice was suddenly before me. I didn't have a choice whether I wished to go through it; the crevice had moved, appearing behind the others and me.

It's not closing fast enough, Anita shouted again. I turned to see her standing at the edge of the crevice, which slowly attempted to shut itself against more intruders.

Past the crevice and into the cave, I saw at least three rushing toward us.

Move forward, Lexsi, Zaria said. *Quickly. We're almost there.*

I turned and ran again, toward a brighter light that I couldn't see through. After tears formed at the brightness of it all, I shut my eyes and ran blindly forward.

~

Kordevik

If he'd turned before he reached the crevice, the cave would probably have killed him. My Thifilathi recognized him however, the moment he and his niece and nephew slipped through the crevice. It closed completely behind them, then, with a loud rumble of thunder.

Ra'Ak.

This one—Morgett Blackmantle—was Ra'Ak.

I wondered briefly how I'd known his name but discarded the thought. With smoke pouring from my Thifilathi's nostrils, I strode toward him. I intended to end his life, right there.

Until I heard Lexsi's shriek.

Turning swiftly, I blinked at the brightness ahead. Lexsi shrieked again. I began to run. Morgett could wait—Lexsi was in pain.

~

Lexsi

With my eyes shut, I'd run directly into a wall of books.

Not ordinary books, no.

These—were made of metal. I smacked into them with all the force my running Thifilatha could muster.

No, I hadn't expected a wall of books so close. I'd only run for a second or two. What happen after the breath was knocked out of me?

Pain.

Searing, indescribable pain. I couldn't move away from it either—

it's as if the metal books were pulling me into them instead of allowing me to push myself away.

The moment I could draw breath again, I screamed.

Voices sounded in my head, but I was in so much pain I couldn't tell one from another, or one word from another. I screamed again as the books rolled me across their surfaces—I felt as if they were burning into my scales and skin. I wanted to shout for help.

All I could do was scream again as the pain increased.

~

South Pacific Ocean
Tanker Vessel Nautilus 17
One mile West of the Peruvian Coastline
Esme

"We'll go when I get the signal," I pointed the weapon at Phineas. Behind Phineas was an army of Merpeople. He and I, and by extension, they—were having a standoff on the wide deck of the supertanker. Opal had lent me the pistol and said it would bring a helicopter down from half a mile away.

I didn't doubt her word. Phineas, on the other hand, was being an asshole.

And a jerk.

"Then what the hell is happening?" Phineas demanded.

"As well-mannered as always," I leveled the weapon at his heart. "I'm waiting to hear from my sister," I added. "Until that happens, we're staying right where we are."

"Sister?"

"The one who introduced herself as my cousin. Anita. That's my sister. Now shut up and stop fidgeting. She'll send mindspeech when she knows where to send us."

Phineas cursed but stayed where he was. If he wanted a ride to get to his daughter, then I was that ride.

If he chose to dive overboard, then his fate was in his hands, not mine.

~

Kordevik

"What's happening to her?" I shouted at Zaria.

"I don't know," she shouted back.

Lexsi was rolling back and forth against a wall of metal books that held her captive and wouldn't let go.

"We have company," Opal shouted behind me.

We did. Morgett and the evil twins were coming toward us. None of them looked friendly. Tibby and four werewolves moved together to form a barrier between them and the rest of us.

"No," Opal screamed as Morgett began to change.

Lexsi's scream behind me was louder, this time.

I couldn't say how I knew, but if Morgett expended the power to become Ra'Ak, the library could protect itself by killing all of us.

Meanwhile, Lexsi was already suffering.

It was a snafu. A conundrum. A no-win scenario. With barely a second's hesitation, I turned back and launched myself at Lexsi's contorting Thifilatha. If the library intended to kill her first, it would have to kill both of us.

The moment my body covered hers, and before I could attempt to pry her away from what held her, it burned into my body, too. My scream joined Lexsi's as the metal library taught us that it wasn't to be trifled with.

~

Opal

"Don't change, you idiot," I shouted at Morgett Blackmantle, who was phasing from humanoid to Ra'Ak as the library continued to rain rock and debris onto all of us. I doubted a Ra'Ak had ever gotten this far into the library without being killed.

Trust the Blackmantle line to fuck everything up at the worst possible moment, however.

He completed the change, his Ra'Ak serpent nearly sixty feet long, his head crowned with deadly, poisoned spikes.

"It's coming down," Zaria yelled.

She was right—the library was bringing the cave down around us. I barely had time to notice that the library itself was disappearing, too, amid falling rock and debris.

If it moved, we would have a very difficult time locating it again.

Morgett, ignoring the falling rocks, some of them bouncing off his serpent's scales and crashing toward us, moved back to strike at the five who stood in his way.

"No," I whimpered to myself as Kell and Klancy, their claws extended, moved in to slice into Morgett's serpent.

Changing into my velociraptor, I raced toward Morgett. Perhaps if he were attacked from several directions at once, we could confuse him enough to get in a killing blow.

Otherwise, we were all dead anyway.

~

Anita

Opal was a velociraptor. I blinked as she raced toward the Ra'Ak. Morgett Blackmantle was a Ra'Ak. An old one, judging by his length.

V'ili, almost in slow motion, appeared beside Morgett's serpent. I shouted at him while my clothing ripped and my scales stood on end. The cave shook so violently it almost knocked me down.

V'ili's eyes turned toward me. He recognized me.

"I killed you," I watched his lips form the words as I ran toward him, claws forming on my hands. He'd spoken aloud, but the cave was roaring its anger around us and nothing else could be heard.

Yes. V'ili, my brother, had brought my death long ago. But the gods had other ideas, bringing my sisters and me back to fight this battle against him.

The library continued to disintegrate around us, while Tungurahua woke and blasted fumes and lava into the sky.

Far above, a small patch of blue sky could be seen, as rock and rubble defied gravity and flew toward the sun.

~

Zaria

I'd never read a Ra'Ak before. I was reading one now. Anita—I didn't have time to convey a message to her; she was intent on killing V'ili.

Esme, I sent mindspeech. *They're east of Pucusana.* I sent mental images to her, so she'd know the spot to target.

Yes, I'd seen Amalthea in Morgett's mind, trapped in a swimming pool at the hacienda Dervil San Gerxon claimed for himself.

Be careful, I sent. Armed men are everywhere.

Any you want left alive? Esme's voice was calm as she replied.

None except Amalthea, I replied.

~

Opal

My velociraptor screeched when Morgett, V'ili and the twins disappeared in a swirl of dust and debris, swept up in the rush created by the disappearing library. Tungurahua roared and expelled a massive blast from its crater.

We had little time. I screeched again in frustration; I'd been willing to take on Morgett and his evil twins myself. Somehow, they'd gotten lucky and were taken away before I could reach them.

Lexsi, Zaria snapped at me. *We have to see to her and Kory.*

She was right. I could screech at the sky all day long and it wouldn't bring our enemy back—who knew where the library had sent them, or whether they were still alive? I came back to myself, sloughing away my velociraptor guise.

"Opal, this is not good," Tibby now stood beside me and took my hand to lead me forward.

Lexsi and Kory lay in a single, crumpled heap where the library wall had been, bare minutes earlier.

"I'll deal with this," Zaria spoke beside me. "Take Anita and the others to Pucusana. Esme needs your help."

ucusana, Peru

Anita

Esme, Phineas and an army of humanoid mermen and women, all armed, marched through Dervil San Gerxon's compound. The hacienda was huge, as was the amount of land about it.

A part of me wept for Lexsi and Kory—I had no idea whether they were dead or alive when Opal brought the others and me here. Somehow, the N'il Mo'erti had been deactivated, although the coalition forces had yet to discover that fact.

I was grateful for that much, at least—the US wasn't shooting at us as we combed the grounds and house for those we sought.

V'ili had been within my reach, just before he'd disappeared. I wanted to curse. That had to wait; other things had to be done, first. The prospect of mourning my friends—that would have to wait as well.

Yes, I wanted Dervil San Gerxon's death. I wanted one other just as much. If I found the bitch, so much the worse for her.

Almost as if she were called, she stepped from between banana trees and onto the flagstones in front of me.

Somewhere behind me, Phineas held a tearful reunion with his daughter.

While Laurel Rome gaped at me, Granger, or rather Hannah Tilton, looking like Granger, stepped out of the garden and onto the path behind Laurel.

"What are you going to do, bitch?" Hannah spoke with Granger's voice.

I shot her first.

Opal

With Thomas, Jorden and Davis behind me and Kell and Klancy on either side, I went looking for Dervil inside the house.

I didn't find him; those around me sniffed him out.

He hid inside a safe room, behind a hidden doorway. Kell and Klancy didn't bother looking for the release to open the door; they tore into the wall until they found the metal wall behind the original.

A vampire's claws can cut through steel, if it's less than three inches thick.

Dervil should have protected himself better.

We found him cowering with the prick who'd taken Jamie Rome's place. Both shrank back at the sight of Kell and Klancy's claws.

"Should we kill them?" Kell turned to ask.

"Let's take them with us. We have to have a scapegoat or two, don't you think?"

Zaria

I was forced to change to my other self. My taller, bluer self. Lexsi and Kory, both barely breathing, were unconscious. It hadn't been the library's intention to kill either of them.

What it had intended frightened me.

In all the Larentii Archives, nothing was said or hinted at regarding this.

Meanwhile, the library had disappeared. Relocated to who knew where, and sending Morgett, Deris, Daris and V'ili who knew where.

Perhaps it was because at least three of those four had roles to play in the future. I hoped their roles had ended on Earth in the past, but I worried that wasn't the case.

"I can't take the memory of the pain away," I said, touching Lexsi's head, first. "All I can do is heal the pain troubling you now."

～

Opal

"You didn't kill her?" I stared at Anita; she held Laurel Rome at gunpoint at the designated gathering spot around the pool.

Loftin Qualls' body, savaged by Watson and Jorden's wolves and then dragged to the pool area, lay in a spot by itself. Vic Malone, covered in bites and standing nearby under guard, couldn't take his eyes off Loftin's body or Jorden and Watson's huge wolves.

Thanks for taking out the N'il Mo'erti, I sent to Zaria.

I didn't, she said. *The library did.*

"Holy shit," I mumbled to myself. "No wonder she didn't say anything until now." *Any idea where the evil twins and V'ili are?* I asked.

None. I think the library sent them elsewhere. I have a theory, but can't prove anything. I'm worried they'll be back to trouble us again.

That makes two of us, I replied. *They have parts to play years from now, but Morgett? How does he figure into all this?*

No idea. You taking prisoners to Washington first?

Yeah.

Meet me at the San Rafael house when you're done.

Will do.

～

It took two days to convince the President and Congress that the threat in Peru was over. Fields of deadly drakus seed were burned, the smoke covering miles upon miles of the country. I worried about stores of seed and smaller fields we hadn't found yet, but that was a concern for another day.

Dervil couldn't prove his existence on Earth; he only had faked identification. He, Laurel and Berke were taking the brunt of the blame, while all three refused to speak to anyone, including their lawyers.

I visited Laurel at the federal prison where all three were held; extra guards were posted—not because they might get out, but because people were calling for their deaths.

Laurel didn't look good in orange or beige.

She even offered to bribe me to get her out, or, failing that, to get her a more comfortable cell.

"Jamie sends his regards," I said, then smiled at the shocked and sour face she made. "You're lucky to still be alive, you know."

"Come back here, bitch," she shouted at me as I rose and walked away.

I laughed for the first time in days.

It was time to go to California; time to assess the damage done to our High Demons. I was terrified that they'd sicken and die, after their experience in the library. As far as I knew, something like that had never happened before. With a worried sigh, I found a suitable place and folded space to the San Rafael house.

"They're sleeping," Zaria informed me when I appeared in the kitchen. "Come with me; there's something I have to tell you."

I followed her down the hall toward Lexsi's bedroom, puzzled as to what she needed to say that couldn't be expressed in the kitchen.

Zaria didn't speak again until we were inside the bedroom and the door closed behind us. Lexsi and Kory lay on the bed, unmoving, except for the slow breaths they drew as they slept.

"The library didn't intend to cause them pain, but it did when it marked them," Zaria's voice was soft.

"What?" I jerked my head toward Zaria, who frowned at the sleeping figures on the bed. At least they were back to humanoid. The last time I'd seen them, they were still Thifilatha and Thifilathi, crumpled together in a sad and terrifyingly unmoving heap on the cave floor.

The cave had disintegrated around us while the library relocated itself.

I still hadn't forgiven it for allowing Morgett to go free.

"You can't see it now. Only the powerful will see it when they change in the future, but it's there," Zaria whispered.

"What is there?" I demanded.

"The books. It's printed all over them—what the library holds is now embedded in those two High Demons. I wish I knew what that means."

"May the Three be merciful," I breathed.

Kordevik

I woke first this time. Lexsi, curled against me, slept peacefully with me in her bed. Someone had placed us together when they'd brought us back.

I couldn't recall being brought back to the house in San Rafael. I barely recalled when the pain had stopped. A black pit yawned between that horrible, painful experience and waking in Lexsi's bed.

Days, weeks or months could have passed and I'd not known of it.

"Eight days," Anita said and yawned. She sat on a chair on my side of the bed. I'd awakened with my back to her and hadn't known she was there until she spoke.

"Kory?" Lexsi stirred and whimpered.

"I'm here, baby," I soothed, pulling her against me.

"Hungry," she snuggled her head beneath my chin.

"Me, too," I whispered against her hair.

"I'll bring a tray," Anita said. I heard the door open and close behind her.

"What happened?" Lexsi pulled away to look at my face, her sky-blue eyes examining me for injury.

"I don't know," I said. "How do you feel? Does anything hurt?"

"I don't think so," she said, although I watched a shadow pass over her features. She remembered just as vividly as I the pain the library caused.

"I'd like a warm shower," she said. "I don't know whether I can get off the bed on my own, though."

"I'll help," I offered. "Maybe we can prop each other up and skip in."

"I have a better idea," someone spoke from the foot of our bed.

Lexsi sat bolt upright, then scrambled to pull covers against bared breasts.

"Stop worrying about that," the dark-haired woman said. "I just think it's time you two got married."

"Huh?" Lexsi blinked in confusion.

"Look, I can get you to your wedding, then bring you back here. How does that sound?"

"Aunt Bree, I am so, so sorry," Lexsi began.

"Honey, stop worrying. I hear that's the man you want to marry?" Bree pointed in my direction. I pulled Lexsi against me. I admit; a curl of smoke escaped my nostrils before I could stop it.

"Yeah." Lexsi hung her head while her cheeks flushed with embarrassment.

"Then what's the trouble? There's a wedding waiting in the future. What do you say? We can show up, you do your thing and I bring you back here last night so you can wake up this morning."

"I want to," I said. "Lexsi?" I tipped her chin up so her eyes met mine. "Remember my promise?"

"I remember," she breathed.

"Then come on," Lexsi's Aunt gestured. "Get up and let's go."

~

High Demon Palace
   Kifirin
   Kellik of Abenott

"I thought you told me the wedding wouldn't take place," I frowned at Rigo.

"The odds were certainly against it," Rigo said. "Come on, there will be cake. You know you love cake."

"I do. I detest weddings, however," I said.

"You need to see this one," Rigo placed a hand on my shoulder and grinned.

Lexsi

I'd almost finished the plate of food brought to me before I had to dress in the gown my parents bought for me.

My mother fussed with the fabric of the dress as it hung on the wardrobe door of a suite in King Jayd and Queen Glinda's castle.

Veshtul was filled with crowds of people while the town itself was decorated for my wedding to Kory.

No, I wasn't supposed to know him, when and where I was.

I wanted to tell my mother to stop fretting. She thought she'd done a terrible thing, agreeing to this marriage.

For a moment, my mind wandered back to Earth—we'd be going back, according to Aunt Bree. That meant one thing to me—our mission wasn't over. Something remained for us to do.

I had so many questions I wanted to ask Zaria and Opal—questions about Morgett, Deris, Daris and V'ili. This wasn't the time to worry about those things. Kory said he'd take care of me.

I believed him.

He'd been the one who'd thrown himself at the library wall in an attempt to pull me away. Instead, he'd suffered the pain I was suffering.

"Lexsi, you don't have to go through with this," Mom turned to me with a sigh.

"Mom, I want to do this," I said. "Trust me, all right?"

"Then let's get you into this dress," she said.

~

Kordevik

We'd settled for a wedding that was untraditional, as far as High Demons went. Queen Lissa, Lexsi's grandmother, had made arrangements. As she was originally from Earth, there were plenty of Earth references to this ceremony, including an expensive dress and other finery.

None of it mattered when I stood at an altar of sorts, waiting for Lexsi to appear. Music began. Lexsi, escorted by Torevik Rath, her father, appeared in the doorway to the palace arboretum, where the ceremony would take place.

I could see the tight grip Lexsi had on her father's arm as they stepped forward.

Baby, are you all right? I sent.

I'm okay, just a little nervous, she replied.

Don't be scared. I'll take care of you.

I know.

Slowly they walked toward me.

I waited at the altar, alone.

"I give her to you, Kordevik Weth," Torevik said, once they'd reached me. I held out my hand to Lexsi, who let go of her father and reached out to me.

Gently, I pulled her forward. Her eyes reflected my face as she gazed at me.

Trusting me.

"*Hala avilepha,*" I said, "*m'seidra camethei refieoru.*" My mouth came down on hers. With a sigh, she went limp in my arms. She didn't fall; I lifted her body to cradle it in my arms.

How sweet the kiss was, as brief as it had been. Afterward, the wedding guests would think I'd skipped away with her.

Only I felt the rush of power as Bree sent us back to Earth.

EPILOGUE

MORGETT BLACKMANTLE

"Y ou're telling me the library saved your life?" I stood before the Prince, who'd allowed me inside his private study. Outside, V'ili, Deris and Daris waited. Their lives were safe, for the moment.

"Yes, my Prince," I bowed my head. "It could have killed all of us easily. Instead, it flung us away from the enemy, who was prepared to attack."

"Where is the library now?"

"I have some information on its possible whereabouts. In my opinion, it is now studying the situation, and may allow me to approach it again, when there are no others there. Perhaps it will approve of my mission, or will hand the dark books to me."

"Why do you believe this?" The Prince handled a gold statue on his desk—a priceless artifact that meant nothing to him. It was merely a reminder of a world he and the others of my kind had devoured long ago.

"I stand before you. It knew my hopes and dreams—I outlined that in the report on the temptations it set before me."

"Yes, it did understand, didn't it?"

"Yes, my Prince. That is why I wish to pursue it a second time. It beckons to us. To our race. We could rule all, with you upon the throne."

"And you believe it is still on Earth, somewhere?"

"From what I have heard, it has always been there. It merely moves from one location to another, whenever it is threatened or discovered."

"Then go. I will allow you to search for it again, as it has left you alive to seek it a second time."

"Thank you, my Prince. You have my loyalty in all things."

I bowed and backed away.

Yes, he had my loyalty—until I found the library and then found a way to unseat him. Once, he'd been a mortal, without power.

I, on the other hand, had been born powerful and nearly immortal. We would see who would rule all—with the library's power behind him.

The End